MY FOREVER

TIFFANY PATTERSON

TMP PUBLISHING LLC

PROLOGUE

en

Ace

I sighed as I pulled into the parking lot of the jewelry store. I'd worked the overnight shift stacking shelves at my local retail job, and exhaustion weighed down my entire body. Yet I hustled my ass to the jeweler to pick up the ring I hadn't seen in months.

My steps felt heavy as I walked toward the back entrance. It was early morning, but the owner was the uncle of my coworker and had promised to come in an hour before the store opened to meet with me.

"I hope this works," I mumbled to myself right before I knocked on the back door of the shop.

"Ace," Ricardo, a man at least thirty years my senior, called as he pulled open the door. Even though the massive grin on his face was in complete opposition to my mood, I smiled back.

I couldn't remember the last time I'd given anyone a genuine smile. It'd been months. Not since…

I shook my head, forcing myself not to think about all that. Right then, I was doing something I hoped would bring a smile to the face of the one person whose pain I felt deeper than my own.

"Let's see here," Ricardo said while I walked behind him into the central part of the store. "Here she is." He handed me the refurbished ring.

The silver band shone. At the center sat a new stone—a one-carat cubic zirconia. My stomach plummeted. Savannah deserved better than this ring, which was only worth a couple hundred dollars.

But when I'd proposed, Savannah had looked at the ring like it was the most precious gem on Earth. She'd treasured it.

Months ago, when the damn stone had fallen out while we'd danced in the kitchen, she'd merely laughed.

I'd promised I would buy her the type of ring she deserved when we could afford it. Savannah had wrapped her arms around my neck and told me she didn't care about the ring. She'd placed my hand against her belly and said, "This right here is all I need."

Then we'd danced in our tiny kitchen while gazing into each other's eyes as our son had kicked in her womb.

My vision blurred, with the ring still in my hand.

"Son, are you okay?" Ricardo asked.

I cringed at the concern in his voice. It pulled me out of that memory.

"Fine. How much?" I pulled out my wallet.

Ricardo's lips pinched, and his bushy eyebrows lowered, causing the wrinkle in his already weathered forehead to deepen.

"For the ring. How much do I owe you?" I demanded, my voice growing impatient. I didn't need anyone's sympathy. I barely knew this guy, and he wasn't about to get a sob story out of me. I didn't care how much of a discount he'd given me to fix this ring.

"Fifty bucks."

It wasn't much money, but with all the medical bills we'd received in the mail over the past few weeks, fifty bucks was more than I should've been willing to spend.

She's worth it.

My inner voice reminded me why I would fork over the money. I would beg, borrow, or steal a hell of a lot more if it would bring even a hint of a smile to Savannah's face.

"Thank you," I told Ricardo as I completed the purchase.

Across the street from the jeweler's, I noticed a floral shop. An employee was opening the store for the day. Without a second thought, I jogged across the street to pick up a bouquet.

An array of pots with multicolored flowers lined the front of the stop. Flowers ranging from bright pink to red, blue, lilac, and more sat there waiting to be plucked and arranged into a bouquet. A bell chimed overhead as I entered the store.

A woman glanced up from behind the wooden counter and greeted me with a warm smile. The one I gave her was stiff, but at least I'd returned it.

"Good morning," she said.

"Morning. Do you have any sunflowers?" I asked.

She perked up even more. "We just received a new shipment this morning. They're gorgeous."

I followed her over to one of the refrigerators, where there were dozens of sunflowers.

"Aren't they darling?" she asked as she gazed at the bright yellow blooms.

"How much would a bouquet cost?"

"You're in luck. Because they're in season, we're running a special. A small bouquet is only seventy-five dollars."

I ran my free hand through my hair, grumbling.

The woman must've spotted the hesitation on my face. "If that's not in the budget right now, I might be able to do something. Hang on." She pivoted and headed toward the back of the shop.

I stared at the flowers, mentally berating myself for not being able to afford a simple bouquet for my wife. But the dough I'd just spent to fix her engagement ring was about all the extra funds I had until I got paid the following week. We had a little money in our account, but I couldn't touch that.

"Here we go."

I turned to see the woman enter the main area of the store with a bouquet of sunflowers.

"These are a couple days old, but they're still beautiful, aren't they?"

I nodded. "How much?"

"I can let this beauty go for twenty dollars."

"I'll take it." I didn't hesitate. I would add on a few more double shifts like I'd been doing for weeks now.

"Thanks." I gathered the bouquet and headed back to my Jeep to make the twenty-minute drive across town to get home to Savannah.

All the way home, I hoped the newly fixed ring and flowers would at least help bring Savannah some happiness.

For the past two months, the pain in her eyes had ripped at my very soul. It'd been eight and a half weeks since I'd had to witness my wife cradle our stillborn son in her arms and apologize over and over again.

I could probably count the number of sentences she'd spoken to me ever since. Most of the time, she told me repeatedly how sorry she was even after I'd assured her, just as much, that it wasn't her fault.

These things just happen sometimes.

You're young.

You can try again.

The doctor had spoken in a tone that lacked empathy of any sort. If I hadn't had my wife to think about, I would've slammed my fist into the prick's face for his lack of bedside manner.

I pushed those thoughts to the back of my mind as I pulled into the parking lot of our apartment complex.

I took one final look at the new ring and imagined it, once again, on Savannah's hand. After the engagement ring had broken, she'd only worn her wedding band, but the gold-plated metal had left her ring finger discolored, so she'd gone without it for months.

"She'll love it," I said, more to convince myself than anything, as I got out of the car. I took the stairs to our third-floor apartment, two at a time.

"Babe," I called out as I entered before kicking the door closed behind me. When I didn't get a reply, I paused to listen for the television, but it wasn't on.

Savannah had taken to keeping on the TV in our bedroom at all hours of the day. Even when she would lie down in bed, staring at nothing but the wall, she'd insist I keep the television on.

"Babe," I called again. I knew there was no way she hadn't heard me call out to her. Our apartment was just over four hundred square feet. Neither of us could make a move without the other one hearing it.

I placed the flowers on the coffee table in the middle of our living room and pushed open the door to our bedroom. "Savannah?" Our bed sat neatly made and empty.

My heart pounded in my chest.

Savannah hadn't gone out by herself in weeks. When she'd tried to return to work two weeks earlier, she'd had a panic attack, and I'd had to pick her up. She wouldn't have left the house without me, and certainly not without letting me know she was going somewhere.

"Sava—" I stopped when I noticed a single key sitting on top of one of the pillows. The pillows on my side of the bed, closest to the door.

I froze, unable to take another step forward. A ringing sound started in my ears. My mind tried to process what my eyes were taking in, but I couldn't fully grasp it all.

The key belonged to Savannah. It was her key to our apartment. The apartment we'd lived in, danced in, and even cried in together for the past year. It was small, but we didn't care. I knew we would eventually move out to something more fitting.

We had plans to move all over the world together, wherever the Air Force would send me.

That was supposed to be our course of action. Together. Every change and twist our life took was to be done side by side.

Somehow, I managed to lift one foot and then the other to stagger over to the bed. My knees gave out, and I slumped onto the bed.

I knew what her lone key on the bed meant.

Savannah abandoned me.

This couldn't be right. Savannah would never leave me. She'd promised me on the day we married. She was my forever, and I was hers. That was the vow we made to one another.

Nothing would ever tear that apart.

Not my plan to go to the Air Force Academy or hers to go to medical school. Not busy careers. Or parents who continually complained that eighteen was too young to know what we felt.

Refusal washed through my veins as I lifted the key from the pillow and tossed it across the room.

I picked up my phone and dialed Savannah's cell. A mechanical voice recording informed me the number was no longer in service.

"Fuck that," I cursed as I refused to accept this reality.

Instead, I raced back into the living room and grabbed my keys. I had every intention of getting my wife back.

* * *

A FEW WEEKS *later*

"What?" I barked at whoever knocked on my door.

"Open the door," Micah, my older brother, shouted through the door.

"Fuck off," I yelled back. Instead of going to the door, I picked up the half-empty beer bottle in front of me and chugged it.

I pushed a Styrofoam take-out box onto the carpet, next to an empty pizza box, and kicked my legs up on the couch to settle in for my second nap of the day.

"Open the damn door, or I'll break this bitch down," Micah warned.

I belched and griped as I stood up. "What part of 'fuck off' don't you get?" I yelled into Micah's face after yanking the door open.

"None of it." He pushed me out of the way, none too gently, and entered my apartment.

Reluctantly, I closed the door behind him and turned. He stood in the center of my dirty apartment, looking around. The expression on his face said it all.

I stared at the blanket hanging on the couch, which had an Ace-sized dip in the middle. Take-out boxes and beer bottles littered the floor and coffee table. The worst part was the bouquet of sunflowers that remained at the center of it all, on the table.

The dried and wilted petals lay on the table with the stems hanging over the vase, begging to be put out of their misery.

Unfortunately, I couldn't bring myself to throw them away.

I twisted my head, turning away from those fucking things. They brought back memories of our wedding day, when Savannah had worn a stunning yellow crown made of sunflowers.

The lump in my throat threatened to strangle my airway.

"What the hell do you want?" I heard the strain in my voice but chose to ignore it and let my anger fuel this showdown with my brother.

"Ace, you've got to snap out of this shit." Micah spun around to face me.

"Don't you have a case to solve or a criminal to track or whatever the fuck it is you do?"

I pushed past him and forged back into the messy abyss of my living room, planting my ass on the couch again.

"Did you even see there was an eviction notice on your door?"

Micah held up a folded piece of paper in his hand.

With a shrug, I said, "I get paid next week. I'll pay back rent then."

"Right." Miah shook his head. "You were supposed to get paid this week, remember?"

"What the hell do you care?" I lay back and started to cover myself with the blanket.

"I care," Micah said, yanking the blanket from my hand. "Because I'll be damned if I see my brother homeless."

The look he gave me was so full of sympathy I wanted to shove my fist down his throat.

"Listen, I know losing Savannah couldn't have been easy."

"Losing her?" I yelled, standing up but tripping over my own feet. I was drunker than I thought, but I didn't give a shit. I poked Micah's chest. "When you take a puppy outside, and it runs away, that's fucking lost. You misplace your keys. That's lost. I didn't lose my wife."

I stopped and looked him in the eye. "She fucking walked away."

I'd gone to Savannah's grandmother's trailer, hoping she would be there and that I could talk some reason into her. Her grandmother hadn't even known that she had left. None of Savannah's friends from high school had heard from her. She'd just up and disappeared.

I thought about asking Joel to track her down, but my father was vehemently against our relationship since we had gotten married a year earlier. Micah had refused to use his resources with the Texas Department of Public Safety.

"Fuck you," I growled

Micah pushed my hand away. "You're still pissed I won't help you find her."

"You think?" I roared.

He sighed. "Look, if Savannah wanted to be found, she'd let you know where she is. It's time you got your shit together and your head back on your shoulders."

"Fuck, you sound like Joel," I told him.

"He makes sense sometimes."

"Whatever," I replied. "I'm fucking fine."

"You're not fine. You've let your school admission expire. You're going to have to reapply if you're going to make it as part of the incoming class for the fall semester."

I waved Micah off and brushed past him to head to the kitchen. I yanked open the fridge and grabbed another beer. But before I could open it and bring it to my lips, Micah snatched the bottle out of my hand.

"I could arrest you right here and now for this," he warned. "You're not even twenty yet. How did you get a whole case of beer?"

"I bought it." I refused to tell my brother, the Texas State Trooper and Texas Ranger wannabe, that my next-door neighbor had purchased alcohol for me."

"Bullshit, Ace."

I rolled my eyes and moved past him again, exiting the kitchen.

"You're hurting. I get it."

"Get it?" I laughed because the thought that my brother could possibly understand what I felt was comical. "You get what?" I looked him square in the eye. "You understand what it's like to hold your dead son while your wife sobs her eyes out?"

My voice came out shrill and three octaves louder than usual, but all of my emotion from the past few months bubbled to the surface.

"You get what it's like to declare your love and life to one person and then have them walk out the fucking door, leaving nothing but memories and heartbreak?" I shook my head and pointed at Micah.

"No, you don't understand shit. Not Mr. I Won't Ever Fall in Love."

Micah flinched. A slight feeling of triumph coursed through me. I knew I stuck him where it hurt. He'd made his declaration after our mother died, and Joel went to pieces with grief.

Micah surveyed my apartment again. "Looks like my decision saved me more pain than it is you right now."

My top lip curled. In a flash of anger, I was in Micah's face, gripping his shirt in my hands.

"Go ahead," he goaded while keeping his arms at his sides.

He gave me ample opportunity to knock him on his ass. At six-three, my brother was only an inch taller than me, but he had more muscle on his frame, given our almost seven-year age gap.

I wanted to hit him. Not because I was angry at him, but because I was mad at the whole fucking world.

Life was cruel.

In the past few years, it'd given my mother a cancer diagnosis, followed by a horrible fight to stay alive, and in the end, she'd lost the battle. The only person who'd kept me sane during that time was Savannah.

When she and I married, I knew that was it for me. Months later, when we found out she was pregnant, nothing could've made me happier. Terrified, for sure, but I was ecstatic to be a father with the woman I loved. Then our son died, followed by Savannah's abandonment.

So yeah, I wanted to hit my brother but not because of anything he did.

I released his shirt and pushed him away from me while I stumbled over to the couch and collapsed into it.

"She's gone," I mumbled.

Micah didn't say anything as he moved closer and took a seat next to me on the couch.

I buried my hands into my hair and stared down at the floor between my feet. "She fucking left me." It was as if I had started to realize this truth for the first time.

"Savannah's gone," I choked out on a sob.

First my mother, then our son, and now my wife.

How much loss could one person take?

"Ace."

"Don't touch me." I pushed Micah's hand away and stood, fists clenched at my sides. I didn't want his sympathy or his comfort.

I stared at my brother. "Maybe you have the right idea," I said, rethinking this whole love bullshit.

His forehead wrinkled.

"If someone can get up and leave without so much as a fuck you, then you're probably right."

For weeks, I'd sat around pining over Savannah. Hoping beyond reason that she'd come to realize that she made a mistake. I dreamt that I would wake up the following day, open the door, and she'd be standing there with tears in her eyes. She would beg my forgiveness and say that leaving me was the worst mistake of her life.

But each passing day, that dream became less likely.

I peered down at my brother with renewed eyes. Slowly, it came to me. I'd been looking at the world through bullshit-colored glasses.

"She's not coming back." My knees weakened as I said the phrase out loud. It almost broke me to say it, but I remained standing.

"So, fuck her." I clenched my fists tighter, nearly drawing blood. With a shake of my head, I made my decision. Everything I had planned for my life was still in play.

I'd go to college, join the Air Force and fly fighter planes, just like I planned. I'd become the best damned fighter pilot I could be. And I'd do it without a thought of Savannah or any other woman.

"Fuck her," I repeated through clenched teeth. I pivoted on my heels to head to the bathroom to take my first shower in days.

It was time to get my life back.

CHAPTER 1

P resent

Savannah

My hands tightened around the steering wheel of my rental. A long, drawn-out breath spilled from my lips. Of course, I would get a flat tire at almost eleven o'clock at night.

With my nine-year-old son asleep in the backseat.

Luckily, I spotted a bar on my side of the road and was able to pull into the parking lot. We were only fifteen minutes from our hotel, but there was no way we would make it with this flat.

"Aiden, sweetie. Wake up." I shook him by the shoulder, though I hated to wake him from his deep sleep. But I couldn't leave him alone in the car.

"Hmm," he moaned and turned his head, nestling his body into a tighter ball, curling his arms around his tablet.

I ran my fingers through the dark brown curls at the top of his head. The poor thing was exhausted. As he should be. It was approaching midnight. We had a long travel day, accompanied by the fact that our second flight, which was supposed to land in San Antonio, had gotten diverted to Houston due to heavy thunderstorms.

Once we made it to Houston, the airline decided to cancel our flight for the evening and book us out in the morning. That solution didn't work for me, however, considering I had a crucial early-morning meeting with my grandmother's estate attorney.

I settled on renting a car and making the more than three-and-a-half hour drive. As I sat in the front seat and looked down at my sleeping son, I wondered if I'd made the right call.

"I swear if I didn't have bad luck, I'd have no luck at all," I murmured.

In the past month, the hospital where I worked as an emergency room physician assistant had been closed down, leaving me without a job.

Not even two weeks after that, I opened my door to a man holding a gun and threatening to take my son away from me. Which was why I had made the trip back to Harlington in hopes of getting enough money to pay the bastard off.

I pushed out a harsh breath. "Not now, Savannah." I couldn't fall apart. I was back in Texas to get the solution to my financial troubles and save my son.

I peered at Aiden's sleeping body, and despite how tired I was, I let out a faint smile.

I would have to eat my words about lousy luck. Aiden was the best thing in my world.

"Come on, sweetie. Mama can't leave you alone in here." I shook him again.

His eyes opened to tiny slits. "I don't wanna go, Mama," he whined.

"I know, but I can't leave you outside by yourself."

I glanced out of the passenger side window. It was pitch black outside, save for the overhead lights in the parking lot and streaming from inside the bar. I made out the name of the building: The Rustic.

The restaurant on the far side of the bar appeared to be closed. There were a few other cars in the parking lot, which helped me feel not as alone.

We weren't in a completely isolated part of town, which was good. But I still needed to contact AAA to have someone come and change my tire. And I'd drained my cell phone battery down to nothing to use the navigation system to get me back to Harlington.

The damn charger I bought not long ago wasn't working. Again, I wanted to curse my luck, but I didn't have time to fall into self-pity. All I wanted was to contact AAA, get my tire changed, and make it to the hotel where I'd made reservations.

"We'll be quick. I promise," I said, pulling him to sit up.

He yawned. "Can I bring my tablet?"

He was attached at the hip to that damn thing.

"Yes."

He sighed. "Okay," he conceded as if he had a choice.

I made sure to double-check our surroundings before getting out of the car. I grabbed Aiden's hand and pulled him in close to me. He was so tuckered out that he didn't even protest as I held onto his hand.

Instead, he laid his head against my hip, falling in line behind me a little.

I nearly had to drag him across the parking lot toward the bar. Also, I had to push thoughts aside of what a terrible mother I looked like pulling a young child inside a bar.

It wasn't like I had another option.

Harlington was the last place I wanted to be. It took sixteen years to get me back there, and as soon as I passed the sign that read *Welcome to Harlington,* my heart rate doubled. I wanted to slam on the brakes and turn right back around and make a beeline for the airport.

But I couldn't do that. I came back for Aiden. Because I needed to save my son, I wouldn't let my fear of my past stop me. His needs were more important than my fears.

Besides, I planned to be in Harlington for only a few days. A week tops.

The chances of me running into anyone I knew was slim to none.

"You can do this, Savannah," I whispered to myself.

I paused in reaching for the door, hearing the music coming from the other side. I just needed to use the phone in the bar, or at least find an outlet where I could charge my phone to call for help with my rental car.

The volume of the music doubled as I stepped inside, along with peals of laughter. I gulped and pushed myself forward but came to a stop when I caught sight of a familiar face.

I recognized Gabriel Townsend immediately. His eyes widened and then narrowed as his expression went from surprise to a hard mask.

Right then, the only sound I could make out was my heartbeat. It drowned out all background noise. Time stood still.

Gabriel Townsend, my brother-in-law. He was just a boy the last time we were this close.

It suddenly felt as if the entire room stopped to turn and look in my direction.

Slowly, I let my gaze travel over the rest of the room. That was when I realized this wasn't any ordinary night out at the bar. The streamers and signs congratulating Lena Clarkson on her album's success hung in the distance.

I blinked, and Lena Clarkson herself stood before me. I knew her music well and was a big fan. Under any ordinary circumstance, I would've been elated to meet her.

This wasn't an ordinary situation.

I could feel Gabriel's eyes on me, but even his glare wasn't what had my heart pounding and my blood pressure rising.

I could feel his brother nearby. Ace was somewhere in the room. The way the hairs on my arms and neck stood up and the zap of electricity in my stomach were my indications.

It astounded me that, even after all of these years, I could still feel him whenever we were in the same room.

I wouldn't allow myself to look around to search for him. No matter how much I wanted to see his face.

I kept my gaze on Lena.

"Oh, I'm sorry, I didn't realize this was a party." I paused, forcing myself to remember why I was standing there in the first place.

Aiden. My subconscious whispered to me, reminding me. I blinked. "I-I just need some help." I didn't know why I phrased it that way. I meant to ask for a phone.

But before I could correct myself, Lena moved closer, her face taking on a concerned expression. "Hi, it's not a problem. Are you from around here?" she asked. "What's your name?"

I opened my mouth to answer but got interrupted.

"Savannah." Ace's voice pierced through the crowd and music. He pushed past his younger brother and Lena, barreling down on me. "She's my wife."

My breathing halted altogether. The edge in his tone was so cold it could've iced over a Texas summer. He looked down at me with daggers shooting from his eyes.

I wanted to wilt underneath the weight of his ire.

My breathing shallowed, and it felt as if all the oxygen had been sucked out of the room. My eyelids drifted shut, but even that didn't stop me from feeling the intensity of Ace's glare.

I heard the faint sound of Lena's laughter, followed by her asking something, followed by Gabriel's voice. She seemed to have asked a question, and Gabriel answered it. Yet all I could concentrate on was my husband, standing before me for the first time in sixteen years.

My husband, because we never officially signed divorce papers.

"What the fuck are you doing here?" he barked. Venom coiled around every harsh word he threw my way.

"I—" My mind drew a blank.

"Mama, I gotta pee." The one thing that could pull me out of my trance broke through my mental haze.

Aiden tugged on my hand, and I was brought back to reality. He moved from behind me, and I watched as Ace looked from me to my son at my side. His eyes widened, allowing me to see the totality of his grey irises.

The ferocity of his stare was something that I never forgot. But to see it up close after all this time was still breathtaking.

Then he narrowed them again as he returned his gaze to mine. The accusation was written all over his expression.

"Mama," Aiden whined again as he began squirming.

I peered down to see him doing the dance he does when he has to go.

I glanced over at the bar and spotted a bartender.

"Where's your restroom?"

"Down that way. To the left," the bartender pointed.

"Thanks." Without looking, I clutched Aiden's hand closer to me and side-stepped the man in front of me to scurry down through the central area of the bar, around the corner, to the bathroom.

Pleased when I realized it was a one-stall bathroom, I pulled Aiden inside and slammed the door behind us, locking it. Aiden went to the toilet to take care of his business, and I lowered my face to my palm.

Of course. Not even thirty minutes back in Harlington and I run into Ace.

"Done," Aiden announced once he finished.

"Wash your hands." I pointed at the sink while still gathering my thoughts. "And don't forget to sing your ABCs," I told him.

"Twice. I know. I know," he said with a roll of his eyes.

I couldn't go back out there, and I couldn't stand there and wait for the ground to swallow me up.

While Aiden sang the ABCs as he washed his hands, I noticed an outlet underneath the sink. I pulled out my phone and cord and prayed my plug would fit into the outlet.

Thankfully, it did.

"All done." Aiden held out his dripping wet hands. "See?"

I nodded in the direction of the paper towel holder. He sauntered over and grabbed way more paper towels than he needed, but I didn't bother saying anything about it. I eyed my phone as it charged.

Luckily, I had reception, and I pulled out my AAA card to dial the number for assistance. I gave the operator the name of the bar, which I spotted when we first entered.

"The Rustic," I told her.

I let out a relieved breath when she relayed that the driver of the truck that was on the way knew exactly where it was.

"He should be there in about twenty minutes."

Things could be worse, I reminded myself as I hung up the phone.

"Why are we still in the bathroom?" Aiden asked.

I held up my phone. "Charging. Does your tablet have any battery left?"

He nodded.

"You can play your game for a bit while we wait for my phone to finish, and then we'll wait out in the car, okay?"

All Aiden heard was me allowing him to play on his tablet long past usual hours, and he lost interest in anything I said after that. He hopped up on the counter next to the sink and started playing.

As for me, I paced back and forth with my phone in my hand, trying to hold it together. I couldn't release the look on Ace's face from my mind.

For the past decade and a half, I often wondered what our son would've looked like if he had lived. I got my answer standing in the middle of The Rustic while waiting for a tow truck to come and change my flat tire.

AJ, or Ace Junior, as I had named him, would have features just like his father. With brown, silky hair, an angular jaw and pink lips, and matching grey eyes.

I bet he would've been the mirror image of Ace.

"Mama, your phone's ringing."

I blinked and peered down at my phone to see it was indeed ringing. "Hello?"

"Ma'am, this is Chuck from Triple AAA," the man said. "I'm in the parking lot of The Rustic, but I don't see anyone out here waiting."

"We're inside," I told him. "Coming right out."

I hung up and gathered my things, and grabbed Aiden to exit. I braced myself before pulling the door open and quickly leaving. This time Aiden dragged behind me, not because he was half asleep, but because of the speed at which I walked. I didn't look around the bar or try to make eye contact with anyone.

I held my breath until I made it to the door. Only once we exited did I exhale. I saw the tow truck right away and rushed over to greet Chuck.

Nerves washed through me as he fixed the tire, and I continued to peer over my shoulder every other minute. I presume it didn't take long, but it felt like an eternity. I didn't sense that Ace was still around, but I refused to stop and check.

Chuck changed the tire, and I practically threw a tip at him before jumping in the car. When Aiden was all buckled in, I peeled out of the parking lot. No need to stick around The Rustic any longer.

I had only one goal in mind for my time in Harlington: to meet with my grandmother's estate attorney, retrieve the inheritance she supposedly left me, and get the hell out of town and back to my regular life back East.

CHAPTER 2

avannah

    After a sleepless night, I found myself wide awake, staring at the blank television screen in our hotel room. Aiden would often awaken in the middle of the night with a nightmare, but not last night, keeping me up.

I'd dreamt of grey, piercing eyes, sunflowers, and the sound of doctors' voices telling me there was nothing more they could do. Obviously, seeing Ace again had done a number on my senses.

With a sigh, I pushed up from the bed, to sit up. I had another thirty minutes before I needed to awaken Aiden so that we could get ready to go to the lawyer's office.

In an attempt to shake free of the memories from my dreams, I cupped my face and shook my head. That only served to bring as a reminder of the first time I met my husband.

THEN

"Who is that knocking on my door?" my grandmother asked, her feet brushing against the uneven wooden boards of our trailer as she came up the hallway.

"I don't know." I shrugged and brushed aside one of the yellowing curtains to peer out the tiny window.

"It's some girl." I didn't know the girl who stood on the other side of our door, but she appeared to be my age. My grandmother had told me there were a few teens who lived in the trailer park.

"Go ahead and answer. She's probably one of the neighbors." My grandmother turned and headed back down the hall.

"Hey," the girl with long brown hair and a broad smile said as I opened the door.

"Hey," I replied with a wrinkled brow.

"I'm Kate." She pressed a palm to her chest. "You're new here, right?"

I nodded.

"Thought so. I saw you a couple times this week but never before."

"I just moved in to live with my grandmother."

"Oh." Kate nodded. "That makes sense. How old are you? I'm sixteen, and I'll be a junior in the fall."

"Me too."

"Cool." She lifted on her tiptoes as if excited to meet someone else her age. "What's your name?"

"Savannah."

"Savannah, do you want to come and hang out with a few of us down at Gaines River?"

I glanced down at my jean shorts and T-shirt. "I don't have a swimsuit."

Kate waved a hand. "No problem. It's hot as Hades outside. If you get wet, you'll dry off fast. Come on," she urged. "We're meeting at this cool spot right underneath Tucker Bridge."

I hesitated and glanced over my shoulder. My grandmother had told me to stay away from Tucker Bridge. Well, not so much the bridge, but from the people who lived on the other side of it.

I worked for them people all my life, she'd told me. They hated when that bridge was built. Didn't want their kids going to school with our kind.

Our kind, meaning those whose parents couldn't afford homes with actual foundations built into the ground.

But I was sixteen, and sitting inside all summer watching reruns of courtroom dramas wasn't how I wanted to spend my time, either.

It didn't matter that I didn't know Kate; I wanted to go out. Even braving it out in the Texas sun beat staring at the TV or worse, the framed picture of my mother that sat on the wall directly over the TV.

I missed her so much.

"Hold on," I told Kate while holding up a finger.

I left the door open before going down to my grandmother's bedroom. "Grandma, I'm going out with Kate for a little while."

She pressed the mute button on her remote, silencing her tiny black-and-white television. I didn't even know they still made those things. "Where are y'all going?"

"To grab a slice of pizza," I lied.

My grandmother looked me up and down. "Hm, hm. Just don't go over by that bridge. I have to work tonight, so I probably won't be around when you get back. Take your key."

"Yes, ma'am."

I felt a small pulse of guilt for lying to my grandmother, but I was just going to hang out for a little while. Hopefully, Kate and I had something in common besides our age, and at the very least, I'd make a new friend.

It's the least I could ask for, given the past few months.

Kate led the way to a dirt trail behind our trailer park. It led to an opening that followed along the Gaines River. Kate talked non-stop on the fifteen-minute trek. Thankfully, the shade of the trees protected us from the sun.

She talked about everything from fashion to what electives she was looking forward to taking as a junior and what teachers to be on the lookout for.

Her non-stop chatter suited me just fine since it took me more than a few sentences to open up to others.

"There they are." She pointed a ways down the trail once we'd walked about a mile or so. There was a clearing. A perfect grassy knoll by the river right beneath a giant oak tree.

I peered down to see about four other teens hanging out at the side of the river. There were three girls and one boy who had his shirt off as if he'd just come out of the water. They were spread out a blanket under the tree.

One of the girls leaned out, stretching her legs in front of her and shaking her long blond locks. She looked over at us as we approached.

"That's Carol Anne," Kate whispered as we got closer. "She's a total bitch. She thinks she's better than everyone. Her dad's like, some famous heart doctor or something. Heather's next to her. That's her best friend, but Heather's not too bad when Kate isn't around."

One by one, Kate pointed out all of the other kids, naming them along with some interesting piece of information about each one.

"That's Stephen and Clarke." She pointed at the two boys swimming on the other side of the river.

We were at a spot where the river narrowed, so they were only about twenty-five feet away.

I watched the two boys splash and yelp while they play-fought in the water.

"Hey, Carol Anne, why don't you get in?" one of them taunted.

"No way," she answered, shaking her head for emphasis.

I looked past her, over to the river again and beyond the two boys. On the far side of the river, I spotted a rope swing hanging from the branch of a tree. A beat later, a large figure stepped from behind the tree and grabbed the rope swing.

I couldn't take my eyes off of him. Whoever he was stood there in a pair of red swimming trunks and nothing else. His stomach muscles clenched as he reached up to take hold of the rope.

"Who's that?" The question came out of my lips without my brain fully registering.

Kate glanced over.

"Oh," she giggled. "That's Ace."

"Ace," I repeated in a whisper.

"He's hot, right?"

Hot didn't describe Ace at all. He had to be at least six-foot, with bronzed skin and well-formed muscles, though he wasn't bulky.

"Ace Townsend. Every girl in our junior class wants him. Hell, every girl *in our high school wants him. Those grey eyes are dreamy." Kate swooned beside me.*

I felt her get closer, but I kept my eyes pinned on the boy stepping back from the river with the swing in his hands.

"He's the reason Carol Anne shows up here every day. Even though she hates swimming."

"Cannonball!" Ace yelled as he swung high in the air and released the rope before tucking himself in a ball and crashing into the water below.

The splash his body made was loud and stole my breath. I gasped, surprised at first and then searching the water with my eyes, waiting for him to emerge.

"Is it safe to do that?" I asked Kate, eyes still glued to the river. Ace hadn't come up yet.

She laughed, but that didn't ease my fright.

"He's always doing that. His nickname is Cannonball. Don't worry, that part of the river goes really deep."

I barely heard Kate's words. Relief didn't come until about ten seconds later when Ace finally broke through the water. His deep laughter filled the air, over and above the whooping and clapping of his two friends and the cheers from the other girls.

"Come on. Let me introduce you to everyone."

I allowed Kate to lead me toward the group of teens seated at the river-bank. We made the introductions, and I could feel Carol Anne eye me up and down. Though she smiled at me, her eyes were dismissive as they trailed over my shoulder.

"Who's this?"

Those two words sent a shiver down my spine.

I turned and came face to face with Ace Townsend. He was even more magnificent up close. The sun stood high in the sky behind me and reflected off his grey irises. An intriguing smile tugged at his pink lips.

Droplets of water fell from his brown hair and onto his chest, cascading their way down his abdomen. My mouth became as dry as Texas grass in August.

"This is Savannah," Kate introduced me.

Ace's gaze flickered over to Kate and then back to me.

"Savannah," he said.

Another shiver coursed through my body.

"Ace, that was some cannonball. You should do it again," a voice said from behind me. I recognized it as coming from Carol Anne.

But he continued to peer down at me. "Are you new here?" he asked.

I nodded.

"She lives down on Woodmill Road. Right next to Kate," Carol Anne said.

If I'd been paying closer attention to her, I would've taken offense to the sneer in her tone as she said my street name. Like the people who lived on Woodmill Road were the annoying gum that gets stuck to the bottom of your shoe.

But the only thing capturing my attention was Ace.

"You're new to Harlington?" he asked.

I nodded.

His smile widened, and he folded his arms over his chest. "So, what do you think of Harlington so far?" He asked as if my opinion mattered.

I glanced out toward the river, breaking eye contact because it was too hard to think with him looking at me like that. The image of him swinging high in the air and jumping in the water to not come up for such a long time replayed in my mind.

He'd done it on purpose. To scare everyone, as a joke.

Then I said the only thing that came to mind.

"I think it was pretty stupid to submerge yourself underwater just to play a prank on everyone."

I sucked in a breath when I heard someone gasping behind me. At times, I tended to get snarky when I felt out of place.

"Who does she think she is?" Carol Anne demanded behind me.

"You don't like tricks?" Ace asked with a lifted eyebrow.

"I don't like playing about death." The muscles in my stomach tightened. "Life is already scary and dangerous enough."

I hadn't meant to say that last part out loud. My mother's recent death had left such a hole in my heart that I found myself blurting out things that I often wanted to keep quiet.

Ace cocked his head to the side. There was a gleam in his eyes. "Life's not safe... It's wondrous but not for the timid."

That comment made me roll my eyes and huff. "Q said that after killing eighteen members of the fleet."

"But he prepared them for the Borg. Without his actions, they wouldn't have known what was coming, and many more could've died."

"I—" I paused and widened my eyes.

Ace's smirk grew into a smile. As if we both realized what was happening.

"You're a Trekkie?" we asked at the same time.

"I used to watch with my mom," I said before clamping my lips shut. I didn't want to talk about her.

Ace's eyes narrowed before he said, "No one else gets it when I say that line."

I shrugged. "I don't like Q, but he had his place, I guess."

It was hard finding fans of my favorite sci-fi show, Star Trek, that were my age. What were the chances that this beautiful boy standing before me was a fellow Trekkie?

"Live long and prosper," we said at the same time while holding up our hands and making the famous Vulcan salute.

"No way, man," one of the boys from the group came over. He wrapped his arm around Ace's neck. "You found a chick into the same sci-fi crap as you," he said.

Ace's face changed from grinning to anger in a flash as he pushed the boy away from him.

"Her name's Savannah." He turned back to me. "Right?"

I nodded. "Uh-huh, like the city in Georgia."

He gave the guy another dismissive look before turning back to me. "Is that where you're from?" he asked, moving in closer.

"I was born there, but mostly lived in Atlanta."

"What brought you to Texas?" he asked as if interested. Not only that, but it was like I held his full attention.

I bit my bottom lip, not wanting to talk about why. Instead, I shrugged. "Life, I guess."

His gaze softened, as if he could read between the lines. He stepped closer and looked down at me as if we were the only two people out there by the river.

"Which is your favorite Star Trek film?"

"I haven't seen them," I replied.

"Oh man, you've got to watch them in order," Ace said.

"No way," I said, a few minutes later, with a shake f my head. "Everyone knows Picard is the best Captain the Starfleet has ever seen."

Ace huffed. "Everyone says that, but it's bullshit. Kirk is where it's at," he insisted. He looked at me with a light in his eyes. "When I'm a pilot, I'm going to be as kickass as Kirk."

"A pilot?"

He nodded, self-assured. "In the Air Force." He stopped talking and tilted his head as if an idea had formed. "Do you have time? I want to show you something."

"Yeah, sure." I had no idea where this was going, but I wanted to follow wherever he led.

Ace took my hand in his and helped me to stand. My insides flooded with a rush of hormone-induced warmth. I'd had crushes on boys before, but nothing like this.

"We're leaving," Ace said to the group with a wave of his free hand. He continued to hold onto my hand with his other one.

He only released my hand to put on his shirt and shoes that sat next to the blanket.

"Where are we going?" I asked, following closely behind him, up a trail leading away from the river. The pathway was surrounded by the tallest, most beautiful sunflowers I'd ever seen.

"I want to show you something cool."

"It better be cool," I griped as he trudged up the rocky trail.

"We're almost there," Ace said, taking hold of my waist to steady me.

We walked up and down a sort of winding trail for probably another fifteen minutes. The other kids were long gone, and I couldn't even hear their laughter or voices anymore.

"We're here," he said when we came to a clearing.

I glanced around and saw that it was an overlook. We could see down into the town of Harlington. While the spot was nice, it was deserted and not unique in any way that I could see, save for the view.

I turned to Ace. "What's this?"

"Hang on." He held up a hand.

It grew quiet between us. I heard the noise of car engines and horns some-where in the distance, but that was it. We weren't far from a road. Then, after about a minute of waiting, a rumbling started. The sound grew louder and louder. The earth beneath our feet rattled.

I glanced upward and shielded my eyes from the sun. Through squinted eyes, I could make out a black figure in the sky.

Ace's laughter beside me caught my attention. "There it is." I watched him as he watched the fighter pilot fly over our heads. He spun around and followed the plane with his gaze until it was out of our sight.

"That's going to be me," he turned and said, squeezing my hand.

I dropped my gaze and looked at our clasped hands. "You'll make an amazing pilot." There wasn't a doubt in my mind.

His smile widened. Ace ran his thumb against the knuckles of my hand. I shuddered.

"What do you want to be?" he asked.

"A doctor," I replied without hesitating.

"You can be my doctor."

I laughed at that until he told me he was dead serious.

"Well," I said, off-handedly, "it'll be the least I can do since you're sacri-ficing yourself for our country and all."

We stayed up on that overlook, laughing, debating which episode of Star Trek *was the best, and watching fighter pilots fly overhead until it got dark.*

Ace walked me home, and when he wrapped his fingers around my chin and pressed a kiss to my lips before I went inside, I knew I'd fallen for the beautiful boy that lived across the bridge.

A WEEK after that first kiss, Ace told me he had changed his mind about letting me be his doctor.

"I don't think doctors are allowed to treat their spouses. Or some-thing like that." He'd shrugged.

I'd given him a curious look. "What's that mean?"

He took my hand while we walked down the street toward a local pizza spot. "It means you're going to be my wife, Savannah. I can't be your patient because I'll be your husband."

He'd said the words so casually, but there wasn't a hint of laughter or joking in his voice. He'd meant it one hundred percent.

And less than two years later, Ace made good on his word.

I roused myself from my reverie. What Ace and I had was years ago. We were two kids who thought we could make something last that wasn't supposed to.

Wasn't it? I jerked at the question my subconscious quickly shot back at me. But I shook it off as wishful thinking. I'd made my decision when I walked away. If nothing else, the look I saw the night before in Ace's eyes spoke of the betrayal and hurt I'd left in my wake.

"C'mon, Aiden. Time to get up."

I shook him a little in the bed beside me.

"Morning, Mama," he croaked out while rubbing his eyes.

"Morning. We have to get showered and changed so we can have breakfast before meeting with the lawyer."

Aiden yawned but didn't protest. I watched him pull himself from the bed and drearily pad his way to the bathroom. His curly, silky, almost-black hair was mussed and growing back from his latest haircut.

When we got back to Philadelphia, I would have to make an appointment with his barber. The thought of returning to the city where we lived caused my stomach to fill with dread.

I'd lived there for over a decade, but with the recent loss of my job and with Aiden's birth father resurfacing, I couldn't say I was looking forward to getting back to the city.

That feeling of needing to rebuild my life started to overcome me. Even as I showered and changed, ate breakfast with Aiden, and drove over to the lawyer's office in the heart of Harlington, the feeling remained with me.

By early morning, Aiden and I entered the office of Jason Wolcott, my grandmother's estate attorney. I checked in with his receptionist and took a seat in the lobby. We were the only two people waiting since it was first thing in the morning. I hoped we could wrap all of this up quickly so I could book our return flight for the next day.

"Mama, why are we here?" Aiden asked.

"Remember I told you that my grandmother passed away last year?"

He nodded with his copper eyes wide.

I tried not to keep secrets from Aiden. Unfortunately, he understood death better than most children his age.

"Well, she left what's called an inheritance, and we're here to talk to the lawyer about it."

Though, I wasn't sure how this would help. I didn't even know my grandmother had enough money to be put into a trust. Hopefully, it was enough to buy me some time to find a job and come up with a plan.

I left the part out that I hoped whatever my grandmother left, I could use it to pay off the man who threatened to tell Aiden's birth father about him. That was one secret I had to keep from my son.

"Ms. Greyson?"

I stood after a male voice called my name.

"Mr. Wolcott," I greeted, sticking out my hand.

"Pleasure to meet you. Of course, I wish it were under better circumstances," the older man said.

"I'm Aiden." He waved at the attorney.

"Nice to meet you, too." He stepped to the side. "Please, let's go to my office."

A minute later, we entered Jason Wolcott's office.

"Aiden, you can sit here and play with your tablet." I pointed to the leather couch on the far end of the office while I took a seat in the chair directly across from Mr. Wolcott's desk.

"Ms. Greyson, I'm glad you were finally able to make it down to Texas to meet in person."

My smile dipped, but I tried to hold onto it. I didn't bother telling this lawyer that, at this point, I had no other option but to meet with him. Any inheritance I might receive from my grandmother was my last-ditch effort to pay off the man blackmailing me in exchange for keeping Aiden's birth father away from him.

"Yes, well, you know. The life of a single mother is always busy," I told him. "I haven't had the opportunity to take any time off until recently."

He nodded. "I'm sure." He opened a folder. "Let's see here." He glanced over whatever the form in his hand was.

"Your grandmother set up a trust for you. All of her assets, which include the money from the sale of her trailer and money from her investment accounts, are to go to you."

It was on the tip of my tongue to ask how much it was worth, but I withheld, not wanting to sound too eager. My grandmother and I were never close.

Not even after I went to live with her after my mother died. I knew she blamed me for my mother's death.

Once Ace and I started dating, she often told me how he was just using me.

I never believed that because I had nothing he could use me for. Sex? Ace could have had any girl in our high school. Aside from that, the first nine months we dated, I didn't sleep with him.

I'd wanted to, but I also wanted to wait. And Ace was incredibly patient with me, even as a sixteen-year-old boy. I knew he wanted to have sex, but he would always tell me it would happen whenever I was ready.

We have the rest of our lives for sex, baby.

"Ms. Greyson?"

I blinked and zeroed in on the lawyer in front of me. It was only then that I realized I'd gotten lost in thoughts of my past.

"I'm sorry. We had a long travel day yesterday," I explained. "What did you say?"

"That's not a problem," Mr. Wolcott said. "I said the total value of your grandmother's assets amounts to approximately $250,000."

My eyes ballooned. "A quarter of a million dollars?"

He nodded. "Yes, your grandmother was very conservative with her money after she sold her trailer."

I knew my grandmother had sold the home on Woodmill Road about a decade earlier and moved into a retirement complex.

"I don't... how does she have that much money?"

Wolcott smiled. "Your grandmother got lucky. A land developer purchased the trailer park where your grandmother lived and paid her a nice amount to vacate her lease early and for the trailer."

I nodded, knowing that my grandmother had sold her trailer. "She used that money to move into the retirement complex, didn't she?"

Wolcott nodded. "Yes, but she didn't live extravagantly, and she also invested for years into a retirement account."

"I didn't know that," I whispered. My grandmother and I never talked about money.

I kept in touch with her and visited from time to time to make sure she was all right. The retirement community allowed her to live her final days surrounded by people her age with whom she got along while also having her medical needs met.

A feeling of relief started to overcome me for the first time in weeks. Not only could I use the money to pay off my blackmailer, but I could live off the leftover funds until I got a new job.

It wouldn't take me too long to find a new job. Most doctor's offices, hospital floors, and urgent care clinics needed physician assistants. I had options, which was a great thing. And the pay was excellent.

It was just that I needed this money fast.

Maybe instead of immediately looking for a job, I would take Aiden on a trip to Disneyworld like he wanted.

"There is one stipulation, however."

That statement caught my attention, halting my daydreams. "What's that?"

"To receive the money, your grandmother had one requirement," Jason Wolcott said.

A pit in my belly formed. "What's that?"

"You have to divorce your husband."

CHAPTER 3

*A**ce*   I stood from the desk in our debrief room and stretched, working the kinks out of my neck. My squadron had an overnight training flight, followed by hours of debriefing.

We spent tons of time analyzing the five percent of our training that didn't go well. It was tedious, but it served a double purpose that morning. Not only did it improve my flight skills, but it also kept me from thinking about Savannah.

A week later and I still hadn't moved past the fact that she'd casually walked into The Rustic that night.

I ran my hand through my hair, ready to take my ass home, eat, and get into bed for the next eight hours. Hopefully, I was tired enough not to think about her while dozing off.

"Hell of a sortie, Cannon," my wingman, Maple, said, slapping me on the shoulder from behind.

I nodded in his direction. "Did you expect anything less?"

He chuckled. "And they say fighter pilots have egos."

"We're humble as shit," I lied.

He laughed louder.

We made our way to the room where we kept our personal

belongings and retrieved our packs before heading to the front of the office building to sign out.

"You've been quiet for the past few days," Maple said, eyeing me as we walked down the hall.

I frowned at him. "What? You want to talk about your feelings or something?"

He held up his hand. "I got a wife for that, but you don't."

I tightened my hold around my pack but didn't say anything.

He shrugged. "Just thought something might be up."

"Nothing's up," I told him. Maple and I had flown together for three years. He was a hell of a wingman. He, like every other guy in my squadron, didn't know everything about my past. I planned to keep it that way, too.

"Hi, Ace," Tricia, one of the administrative support specialists and a past fling of mine, purred as we approached her desk.

I had to keep myself from rolling my eyes.

"How was your flight last night?" she asked, leaning over just enough to expose an untasteful amount of cleavage.

"Hello too, Tricia," Maple interrupted.

I chuckled.

Tricia gave Maple a quick wave but then turned back to me as I signed out.

"Ace, I wanted to know if I could speak with you for a minute?"

I shook my head before she even finished. "Can't. Maybe next time."

I moved around her desk and quickly exited the building, leaving Maple to follow closely behind. His laughter echoed through the doorway.

"Why'd you leave that girl hanging like that?" He elbowed me.

"Like what?" I asked as I slid my aviators over my eyes to block out the bright sun.

It was a perfect day. Not a cloud in sight. Beautiful day for flying. A piece of me wished I had an afternoon flight instead of another night flight. It would serve to keep the thoughts of Savannah at bay.

"You know she still likes you," Maple continued, talking about Tricia. "Maybe you should give her another chance?"

"The hell are you?" I asked as we approached Maple's SUV and my motorcycle parked next to it. "A dating coach?"

"I should be," he replied. "You need one. When's the last time you were on an actual date? Hell, when's the last time you were in a real relationship?"

"Why?" I lowered my glasses, peering over the rim at Maple. "Is that an invitation?"

He shot me a middle finger. "Remember, I'm the one who's married. You could take a lesson or two from me."

I snorted and placed my helmet over my head. "You have no idea what you're talking about."

"Been married for ten years. I might know a little something." He winked like the goofball he was. "Also, you want that instructor position down by San Antonio, don't you?"

I stopped and cocked my head sideways.

"Come on, Cannon. You know as much as I do, the brass likes to promote settled guys, with families and shit."

I shook my head. "I'm transferring overseas in six months." I knew what Maple said was true. It was an unspoken and unofficial rule that Airmen who were married and had families tended to fare better when it came to career options.

But I'd done just fine in the Air Force.

I liked the constant moving every three to four years. It worked for me. Even though I'd started to have doubts about relocating to Germany.

With my family still in Harlington, this was the one place I wasn't so gung-ho about leaving again.

I chose not to reveal any of that to Maple. And I definitely wouldn't tell Maple that my own marriage preceded his by six years. I'd been married for sixteen years, though only on paper.

"Maybe you should give Tricia a chance again. She's cute."

"Yeah, but she's a pain in the ass." Tricia and I had gone out for a few months, and she was fun for a little while. Not bad in bed, but she wasn't a keeper. Which was what she wanted to be.

I didn't do long-term. A fact that I made clear from the beginning.

"Fine, give someone else a shot."

"Here's an idea: Take all that advice you're trying to give me, wrap it up in a bow and shove it up your ass. I'm going home. You should do the same since you have a wife and all."

The last thing I heard was Maple's chuckle as I revved up my bike and peeled out of the base's parking lot.

I did my best to let the wind whipping against my face, and thoughts about my earlier training flight, push out ideas about dating and women. One woman in particular.

She has a kid.

That one thought pushed through all of the rest. Savannah had come back to Harlington, but she wasn't alone. A little boy was with her. A boy who distinctly called her *Mama.*

He appeared to be around eight or nine.

She'd gone and had a kid with someone else. I tightened my hold on the handles of my bike and forced myself to calm down. But the anger continued to boil inside of me.

I made it home in record time, noting that I'd done well over the speed limit the entire way. I entered the house through my garage and slammed my door shut if for no other reason than I needed to work out my aggression.

I stripped out of my flight suit and changed into a pair of gym shorts and nothing else. I headed down to my basement gym, gloved up, and started wailing on my punching bag.

Physically, I was exhausted from work, but the emotions coursing through me were too raw to let me sleep.

Thirty minutes in my home gym should work well enough.

I trudged back upstairs after my gym session and toweled off while entering the kitchen to grab a bottle of water. As I took my first sip, the doorbell rang.

I grabbed my phone from the counter and opened the app

connected to my video security system. I almost dropped the damn thing when I saw who was standing at my door.

What the fuck is she doing here? I wondered.

For days since that night at The Rustic, I debated whether or not to go look her up. To find out where she was and why she was back in town. But I decided against it. She was the one who had walked away, and the way she barely acknowledged me, hid in the restroom, and then high-tailed her ass out of the bar that night, I figured she wasn't back in town to see me.

Now she stood on my doorstep.

There was only one way to find out what she wanted.

I yanked my front door open. "What the hell are you doing at my house?" I demanded through clenched teeth.

Savannah startled and stumbled backward a couple of steps. She tripped off the stair but righted herself before she fell.

I firmed my hold on my doorknob as I glared down at her. I didn't want to, but my eyes traveled over her face, taking her in. She had the same soft-looking dark brown skin as the first day we met, a perfect oval face, button nose, and lips that were so full I couldn't take my eyes off them.

At five-foot-six, she stood about average height.

Her weight was something she'd been conscious of while we were in high school. But I appreciated every inch of her back then and made it a point to tell her so. She'd gained some weight over the years but, I hated to admit it, she looked good.

Too fucking good, standing there dressed in a cream sleeveless top and blue jeans.

She cleared her throat, pushed back her shoulders, and stood taller. "I'm sorry for disturbing you, Ace."

I narrowed my gaze as I stepped forward. I wanted more than an *I'm sorry for disturbing you.* But I wouldn't beg her for a damned thing.

"What do you want?" I folded my arms across my still bare chest.

She briefly closed her eyes then opened them. "I-I don't have a lot of time, but there is something that I need to ask you."

"Spit it out."

She cleared her throat again then looked over her shoulder.

I glanced up to see a car parked in front of my house. From my vantage point, I could see her little boy sitting in the backseat. My stomach hurt at the sight of him.

"I wouldn't be here if this wasn't important."

I grunted. "What the fuck do you want, Savannah?"

She pushed out a breath. "A divorce. I need you to sign these divorce papers." She held out papers in my direction, but I didn't bother looking at them.

All I saw was red.

I moved closer, causing her to take a step backward. "You show up at my doorstep after sixteen years without even a fucking hello and demand I sign divorce papers?" The growl in my voice was something even I hadn't heard before.

Savannah bit her bottom lip but didn't look away. "I told you. If this weren't important, I wouldn't be here."

"Of course, you wouldn't be here. Because you fucking ran away."

A current of satisfaction ran through me when she flinched at my statement.

"You ran away, and like a coward, you left your key on the bed for me to find."

I watched as she visibly swallowed. She turned her head away, not looking at me. She blinked a few times, and if I were dumb enough to have fallen for the act, I would've believed she was trying to push away tears.

But I wasn't a fool for her. Not anymore.

"We can talk about what happened back then if you want."

"I don't want shit from you."

She turned and looked at me, her eyes narrowing and lips pinching. A flash of anger. I could see it, feel it, but she bit her tongue.

"Look, I recognize this—me coming here like this—isn't an ideal situation for either of us. But I need you to sign these papers."

A mix between a snort and a laugh escaped out of my mouth. "You show up here after sixteen years. No word or any sort of communication and demand that I sign those bullshit papers."

"I'm not demanding. I'm asking you. Please?"

I would've sworn there was a desperation in her plea, but I pushed that thought right out of my mind. Savannah was nothing if not manipulative. How else could I have believed her lies of forever?

Never again.

"*Please*," I mimicked. "Why? So you can go off and marry whatever sucker you had a kid with?"

Savannah gasped, her lips falling ajar.

"What? Are you trying to lie your way into another ring when having his kid didn't work?"

"Mama didn't have me."

The kid's voice jolted through me, surprising me. Next to Savannah stood the same little boy from the night at The Rustic. He had big copper eyes, shiny jet-black curls, and a very fair, golden complexion.

I searched his face to see any hint of his mother in it.

"Mama's not my birth mom. My real mommy died when I was four. She was friends with Miss Savannah. But after she died, Miss Savannah adopted me, and she's my Mama now," he explained.

"Aiden," Savannah scolded in a whisper. "I told you to wait in the car."

"I was, but it got hot, and my battery died." He held up the tablet as proof of why he hadn't followed her directions.

"Go back in the car. Turn the air conditioner on and use my phone to watch videos while I talk to Mr. Ace."

Something heavy sat on my chest during this exchange between the two of them. It made sense why I couldn't find a hint of Savannah in the little boy's features.

"Is that true?" I asked as the boy got back in the car. "Did you adopt him?"

"Yes, but he's every bit my son as..." She trailed off.

I didn't want to hear the last part of that comment.

My gaze bounced between Savannah and the car where the boy sat. I stared down at her as she shifted from one foot to the other.

"You want a divorce?"

She paused but then nodded.

I ignored the piercing feeling that went through my chest. I had every mind to slam the door in her face, but suddenly a second idea formed. Maple's reminder from earlier about how having a family looked good to the upper levels of our branch.

Maybe I could get something out of this.

I stepped closer to Savannah. "I'll sign divorce papers under one condition."

Her forehead wrinkled as I stepped forward. "Everyone has conditions," she mumbled and sighed. "What are yours?"

"You will give me the next six months of your life."

A confused expression passed over her face. "Say that again?"

"Has your hearing faltered in the last sixteen years?"

Her lips pinched, but she swallowed down her retort. "Please repeat yourself."

I leaned in, getting in her face. "You will give me the next six months of your life in exchange for my signature on those papers. Otherwise, I will make your life a living hell."

This time around, the ball was in my court, and I planned to play the game to its fullest.

I would use this time to my own career advantage.

"The decision is yours, but I suggest you make the right one," I taunted, folding my arms over my chest.

CHAPTER 4

*S*avannah

Not for the first time, life had decided to toss me around like a ragdoll. A week after Ace issued his ultimatum, I found myself lugging suitcases out of the backseat of my Mazda.

Obviously, I conceded and decided to give in, in exchange for his signature on those divorce papers.

Aside from the fact that we had to pack up our entire lives, I resented that I'd dragged Aiden into this chaos. I'd lied to him and said that we were moving to Texas because I found a job down here, and Mr. Ace was kind enough to let us stay with him.

"Yeah, right," I muttered as I rolled my suitcase toward the front door.

I paused and peered up at the two-story house. It sat at a spacious thirty-five hundred square feet with stone siding and a sizeable front yard. I could only assume that the backyard was significant as well.

In the early days of our marriage, Ace and I often daydreamed about buying our first house together. Tears filled my eyes upon recognizing that was yet another dream he'd fulfilled without me.

"Dammit." I cursed myself for getting emotional.

"That's my last suitcase, Mama," Aiden said, plopping his Superman suitcase on the floor just inside the door.

"Where am I going to put my stuff?" Aiden asked as I glanced around the house, still trying to get ahold of my new reality.

"Your bedroom's on the second floor, down the hall, to the left," Ace's deep baritone said, emerging from the living room.

"Thanks, Mr. Ace," Aiden said as he went to run off, but I grabbed his arm, stopping him.

"You know better than to run in the house," I scolded, trying to assert some sort of control over the situation.

"Sorry, Mama. Sorry, Mr. Ace," Aiden said, shifting his body to look behind me to where Ace stood. I could feel his presence back there, but I refused to turn to look at him.

"No problem, kid," Ace replied.

"It is a problem," I shot back. "He knows better than to run wild in someone's home."

Ace moved around me, coming to stand in front. He cocked his head to the side and lifted an eyebrow. He didn't say anything but the look was challenging enough.

"This is his home for now."

My belly quivered at hearing Ace calling his home Aiden's. But then I remembered what was truly happening. Ace was holding me hostage in exchange for his signature on the dotted line of the divorce papers.

A signature I desperately needed if I was to gain the inheritance from my grandmother and pay off Vincent Reyes, the man black-mailing me.

"Hey, kid. Why don't you head upstairs to check out your room?" Ace suggested.

Aiden looked to me, silently asking for permission. Slowly, I released his arm and nodded.

He took off, but before I could remind him of the no-running-in-the-house rule, Ace stepped closer. He got in my space, but I didn't back down.

I squared my shoulders and looked him in the eyes. No matter how difficult it was to look into those windows to his soul and see the venom that stared back at me.

"I won't let you undermine me when it comes to him," I said, unable to think of anything else. "He's a child that needs to keep in mind the importance of respecting other people's property."

Ace snorted. "Whatever." He waved a dismissive hand.

"Whatever," I mocked, feeling just as childish as he was right then. "Listen, since I agreed to this bullshit arrangement of yours, I felt it would suit us both to agree on some terms."

I pulled a folded piece of paper out of my shoulder bag and handed it to Ace.

"You and your fucking terms." He snorted and shook his head at the same time he snatched the paper from my hand.

I watched as he unfolded it and read its contents.

He eyed me over the paper. "You expect me to sign this?"

"It's a perfectly reasonable request," I said, nodding. "It's an agreement that once these six months are up, you will sign the divorce papers and not give me problems about doing so."

"I'm pretty good with reading comprehension." His tone dripped with sarcasm and disdain.

"Then you should recognize that by signing this agreement, you aren't giving anything up. We both get what we want."

"We do?" Both of his eyebrows lifted.

I nodded slowly.

He moved, and that time, I did take a step back. He held up the form I'd given him and tore it in half before tossing it on the floor.

"Unlike you, I keep my word. If I say I'm going to do something, I do it."

I clenched my fists at my side. "You're being impossible."

He shrugged.

"Asshole," I mumbled.

That made him smile. A genuine smile.

"And what is it that you want, Savannah?" he asked, harkening back to my earlier comment.

"You already know what I want." My voice came out much lower than I anticipated.

Ace shook his head. "You want a divorce, but that doesn't tell me shit about why. Why the hell after sixteen years are you coming to me with this?"

My mind grasped for bits and pieces of lies that I could tell him. He didn't want to know the truth of why I came back after all these years. He hated me and wanted to use anything I said to continue to stoke the flames of his anger.

"I think it's time that we finally get the divorce out of the way," I finally said.

Ace lowered his face only inches from mine. "Your nose still flares when you lie." His voice was menacing. "Lie to me again, and I'll add another month."

I bulged my eyes.

"You've got ten seconds to give me a straight answer." He paused and stepped back. He pivoted on his heels. "Ten..." he counted over his should as he headed toward the kitchen.

"Nine..."

I couldn't give him seven months. Hell, six months was pushing it.

"Because it's a stipulation of my grandmother's trust that I divorce you before I can receive what she left for me," I blurted out behind him.

He spun on his heels, giving me an incredulous look. It was so full of surprise, malice, and disgust that I would've preferred he slapped me across the face than look at me that way.

"Money?" His tone was stern. "That is why you're here?"

I looked away, unable to take the expression on his face and the harshness of his voice at the same time.

Not for the first time in the past sixteen years did I yearn for the boy I fell in love with and married. The one who was my protector.

But in his stead before me stood the man who'd come to hate me.

"Yes," I whispered, giving him the answer he wanted.

"Of course," he sneered.

"What about you?" The question came out of my anger. Why I was pissed, I didn't know, but it propelled me to ask questions of my own. "What are you getting out of this?"

Ace stepped forward. When I thought he would stop, he continued to advance on me, forcing me back against the kitchen wall. His hand shot up, cupping the lower part of my face.

His movements were so swift, I didn't have time to react before his mouth covered mine. His kiss was bruising, even more punishing than the words he'd thrown at me seconds earlier. But a small spark went off deep in my belly.

Somehow, I ended up kissing him back. And as soon as I did, Ace pulled away from me.

With his hand still around my face, he looked me right in the eye and said, "In six months, I'll get what I want from this marriage." He paused. "And then I get to forget all about you. I won't ever think about you again. You will be dead to me."

I didn't think there could have been more words in any other language as cold and painful as the ones he just spat in my face.

I tried to search those grey irises for a glimpse of the old Ace. The one who would've never said anything remotely close to this to me.

"I get to forget you ever existed." He pushed the dagger through my heart one more inch.

I sank into the wall behind me. Over the past sixteen years, I believed I'd cried every tear I had to give over the end of our relationship. But that old feeling of wanting to bury my head in my pillow and let the tears flow came over me again.

"Answer your phone."

I blinked. "What?"

He dipped his head toward my shoulder bag, which was now on the floor. "Your phone is ringing," he said before exiting the kitchen.

I steadied my breathing before digging through my bag.

"H-hello?" I answered my phone right before it went to voicemail.

"I was hoping you weren't planning on ignoring me."

My shoulders deflated at the sound of Vincent Reyes' voice on the other end of the line. Hadn't my heart just been shredded enough for one day?

Now, here was the guy blackmailing me in order to keep my son safe, calling.

"Hold on. I have to step outside."

* * *

I SHUT the door behind me as I exited the house. Slowly, I brought the phone back to my ear while rubbing my temple with my free hand. No matter how hard I tried, I couldn't seem to catch a break.

"Hello?"

"You do know who this is, don't you?" the male voice asked with a sneer in his tone.

"Vincent," I said, hating even the sound of his name.

"Did you believe you could hide from me by moving to Texas?"

"I moved to Texas for personal reasons," I said.

He let out a chuckle, but there was no humor in it. "Ms. Greyson, do you think I'm an idiot? I gave you one month from when I showed up at your apartment door to get my money. Time's up."

I turned to stare at Ace's house and decided I was still too close to have this conversation. I moved away from the front door toward the edge of the front yard.

"I'm working on getting the money, but I told you I would need more time."

A lot more time, as it turned out.

"A hundred and fifty thousand dollars is a lot of money," I added.

He made a sound on the other end. "It shouldn't be for someone in your profession. Don't you have any money saved?"

I sighed. "I told you when you first brought this up that I spent a significant amount of my income paying off all of my student debt for the past few years. And raising my son."

He snorted. "Not quite your son."

"You son of a bitch," I hissed. "He's my child, and I won't let you or anyone else hurt him."

"We'll have to see what his biological father has to say about that," Reyes threw back at me. "Maybe I should give him a call and ask him."

I pinched the bridge of my nose and slowly exhaled.

Yvette, what did you get me into?

Yvette Burgos was Aiden's birth mother and had turned from a former patient to somewhat of a little sister to me. I met her when I started working as a CNA at the same hospital where I eventually became a PA. She came into the hospital's clinic for prenatal care.

She was young and had very little money or means to care for herself. I related to her so much that I made it a point to check in on her when I could. That grew into a friendship and me becoming Aiden's godmother, though she never told me who his biological father was.

I accepted we all had secrets. I never shared with her that I was married. A few months after Aiden's fourth birthday, Yvette passed out in the middle of a grocery store. Weeks later, after many tests, she was diagnosed with an aggressive brain tumor.

We cried our eyes out together, and Yvette begged me to take care of Aiden once she was gone.

But the asshole on the other end of the phone didn't care about any of that. He wanted money, plain and simple.

"I don't fucking like excuses, and neither does my client," Reyes continued.

I sniffed. "Your client. How do I even know you're telling the truth?" I whispered harshly into the phone.

This guy, Vincent, was waiting inside my apartment one morning after I'd dropped Aiden off at school. He said he worked for Marco Flores. As in, Senator Marco Flores from the state of Florida. Vincent was there on behalf of Senator Flores to clean up a little problem he had.

That was how he referred to Aiden. As the Senator's *little problem*.

"You don't believe my client is that little shit's father?"

"Watch how you refer to my son," I seethed.

"It appears Ms. Greyson does have a backbone. Good to know. But do not be mistaken, backbone or not, my client intends to get his answers regarding this child. I'm willing to hold him off for a while, but that is contingent upon you giving me my money."

I silently fumed. This bastard was playing both sides. Flores hired Vincent Reyes to clean up any dirty laundry of the Senator's. Flores was popular in his home state of Florida and ran on a campaign of family values. He was eyeing a potential run for President within the next election cycle. It wouldn't look good for an illegitimate child to become known to the public, in that case.

Not to mention, by my calculations, Yvette had only been seventeen years old when Aiden was conceived.

But Vincent was a double timer. He'd offered to lie to the senator and tell him that Aiden had either died or that he couldn't locate him —if I were willing to pay.

"I-I could go public about this," I blurted out.

There was silence on the other end.

"Yeah," I continued. "I could go to the press and tell all about how the Senator had an affair with a teenage girl, got her pregnant and is now threatening his own child's very safety."

I stood up straight, feeling a balance of power shift as the thought formulated in my mind. "How do you think the Senator's constituents would feel about that?"

Another beat of silence. And then a deep, throaty laugh pushed through Reyes' throat.

"Do you think it would be that simple?"

My shoulders sagged at the mockery I heard in his voice. Just like that, my confidence deflated like a seven day old balloon.

"You can't actually believe the Senator would cave to your demands, do you?" He made a disbelieving sound. "That's not how this works. The Senator and his people ae deeply connected to a whole world you know nothing about, Ms. Greyson. Press or no press, your son wouldn't be safe. In fact, by going public, you would be placing him in even greater danger. Trust me on that."

A cold chill raced down my spine. I didn't know anything about Vincent Reyes beyond the fact that he was the man sent to do harm to my son. Yet, when he made that declaration, I believed every word.

Not even the public knowing could keep us safe.

I swallowed the lump in my throat. "I-I'll have your money, but I need more time," I whispered.

"How much more time?"

"Six months."

"Did you now just hear what I said?" He demanded, sounding wildly frustrated. "Are you playing with me?"

I shook my head. "Look, I know it's a lot of time. More than we discussed but I don't have the money right now, and I won't be able to get it for another six months."

There was silence on the other end.

"Hello?"

"Okay, here's the deal. You want me to wait an additional six months, then the price is going up by a hundred grand."

"You can't be serious."

"I'm deathly serious," he said darkly. "You will now pay me two-hundred and fifty grand to keep your son alive."

My heart squeezed in my chest.

"Don't try to disappear. There is nowhere that you can go that I won't find you. You sleep tight tonight."

The phone went silent. I pressed my hand to my chest, willing my heartbeat to slow down. The next six months had to go smoothly, or I wouldn't get the money, and Aiden's life was in danger.

I still didn't know how all of this had happened. Yvette rarely shared anything about her life before we met. All she would say about Aiden's father was that he was an evil man and had no interest in being in her son's life.

When Vincent Reyes first showed up at my door, I all but called him a liar when he said that Marco Flores was Aiden's father. That was when he pulled out pictures of Yvette and the Senator together.

There were photos of my friend, so young looking, sitting on the senator's lap.

Then there was the uncanny resemblance Aiden had to Flores. Vincent went so far as to show me an image of Flores' youngest son, Oscar, and place it next to a picture of Aiden. It was almost like looking at twins. There was no way the two boys weren't related.

No matter how fucked up this situation was, I couldn't let the Senator or Vincent Reyes get anywhere near Aiden. I'd lost one son. I'd be damned if I was going to lose another.

"Hey, Mama, come look. You have to see this."

I peered up to see Aiden standing at the front door, waving me inside. My heart squeezed in my chest.

"Coming." I moved to the door, staring at the excitement in Aiden 's eyes. "What's up?" I asked.

"Look." He grabbed my hand and pulled me to follow him down the hall and up the stairs to his bedroom.

He pushed the door open, granting me a first-time view of his new room.

"Mr. Ace decorated the room for me."

I took in the vast mural of the world map, painted on the far wall of the bedroom, the hanging wooden chair a few feet from the bed, which sat across from a window nook that was perfect for reading or playing on his tablet. A desk sat along the opposite wall, and on it were various model airplanes.

Displayed on walls devoid of the mural were planes of different shapes and sizes.

"Isn't this so cool?" Aiden said, his voice sounding in awe. "Look. This is the type of plane Mr. Ace flies, right?" he asked.

I spun around to see Ace leaning against the doorframe. His stern glare remained on me, but when he lowered his gaze to peer down at Aiden, his eyes softened.

"That's a model of the F-35. I used to fly those," Ace told Aiden in a voice much softer than the one he used with me.

"Which one do you fly now?"

Ace pushed away from the door and strolled over to the desk. "The F-16," he said, handing the model of the F-16 to Aiden.

"Woah, so cool," Aiden whispered. "Could you take me to fly with you sometime?"

Ace let out a laugh, and it sounded sincere. He shook his head. "Sorry, kid. Even the flight crew doesn't get to ride in the F-16."

Aiden pouted. "How come?"

Ace tapped the front window of the model plane that Aiden still held. "The F-16 is a single-seater. There's only room for the pilot."

"Aw, man." Aiden's entire face dropped as if he genuinely believed that he would've gotten the chance to ride in an actual fighter jet.

"Maybe you'll just have to grow up and learn to fly one for yourself," Ace said.

Aiden perked up. "You think I can?"

Ace shrugged. "I don't see why not." He stopped and looked over at me, finally. "I did."

Just like I knew you would. It was on the tip of my tongue to say, but I held back.

"Mama, can I fly fighter planes when I grow up?"

A smile touched my lips for the first time all day. "Not if you don't learn to brush your teeth before bed and eat all the vegetables I feed you at dinner."

Aiden's wide-eyed expression dropped. "Aw, man. I hate broccoli."

I stifled the laugh I wanted to let out. "Aiden, tell Mr. Ace thank you for your cool new room, and then go downstairs to bring up your bags."

"Thanks, Mr. Ace," Aiden said before racing out of the room.

I went to tell him to stop running, but it was no use. He was halfway down the hallway. I looked around the bedroom. It would be any little boy's dream. And it was twice the size of the bedroom Aiden had back at our apartment in Philadelphia.

The air around me shifted, and I lifted my gaze, realizing that Ace continued to stand there, watching me. My mind went back to that kiss in the kitchen. Could it even be called a kiss?

It was more like a mauling. Or a warning of things to come. It was nothing like the kisses we shared all those years ago.

"Thank you," I said.

Ace didn't respond. His grey-eyed gaze slowly passed down the length of my body, pausing at the slight amount of cleavage left exposed by the V-neck T-shirt I wore. They roamed lower, again stopping at my hips and the apex of my thighs.

Then he peered back up at my face.

"I didn't do it for you." His tone was as hard as concrete.

Another verbal slap in the face.

But I didn't flinch that time. "Thank you anyway."

A muscle in his jaw ticked. He took a step back. "You'll move your bags into my bedroom. It's at the other end of the hallway." He exited the bedroom without a second look.

Did he order me to take my stuff to his bedroom?

We hadn't discussed where I would be sleeping during these six months. Why I'd thought it would be in some sort of guestroom was beyond reason, apparently.

In six months, I'll get what I want from this marriage...And then I get to forget all about you. I recalled what he said downstairs in the kitchen.

So was sleeping with me part of his plan to forget me? My breathing began to grow shallow at the thought of Ace forgetting me. His words shouldn't have affected me as much as they did.

"Should I put my clothes away?"

I came back to the present moment, realizing that Aiden stood before me with his Superman suitcase by his side.

"Yes." I nodded toward the white wooden dresser that stood against the wall. "Put your clothes away and I'll get dinner started."

I headed down to the kitchen, Ace's words replaying in my mind. Luckily, he wasn't around. I had no idea where he went but I wouldn't try looking for him. I needed my head to stop spinning.

What the hell had my life become?

CHAPTER 5

Ace

My life no longer felt like my own. In the two weeks since Savannah and Aiden had moved in, I felt like a stranger in my own house. That wasn't the reason I made her move in with me at all.

I needed to reestablish my equilibrium and get back to working her out of my system.

I would get on that as soon as I woke up. I was dead tired from another training flight and debrief. The hours we spent going over seemingly miniscule details were sometimes as grueling as the flights themselves.

If only I could apply that same damn tenacity to working Savannah out of my system, I thought as I entered through my front door.

I dropped my bag by the front door and pushed it to the side with my foot before heel-toeing my boots off. It was quiet, since it was after midnight. Savannah and Aiden were probably asleep.

I suppressed the urge to go up to my bedroom and stare at her from the doorway. I found myself doing that more times than I cared to admit over the past two weeks and I cursed myself every time I did it.

Instead of going up to the bedroom, I went to the kitchen. It was late but I still needed to eat and hydrate. We had another training flight later on in the week, which meant I needed to be vigilant about keeping a regular schedule as far as eating and drinking water were concerned.

The button on the oven caught my eye and I saw that the oven was set to *warm*. Against my better judgment I pulled the oven door open to find a plate of food covered in foil.

My stomach roiled both in hunger and in anger. I stuffed my hand in an oven mitt and removed the plate of food, uncovering it. Meatloaf, homemade cheesy mashed potatoes, and broccoli sat on the plate, staring at me.

I wanted to ignore the zing of pleasure that raced up my spine, knowing that Savannah had left this plate of food to keep warm just for me. It was something she'd come to do since she moved in. Every night when I came in from a late training or work, there was a version of whatever dinner she'd prepared for her and Aiden waiting for me.

As much as I wanted to forget the gesture, I'd taken to skipping my usual pickup from whatever local restaurant was still open, to have dinner at home. Prepared by my wife.

I shook my head. Not my fucking wife. Only on paper was she my spouse.

I made myself remember that this wasn't a real marriage and Savannah wasn't my wife in any real sense of the word. That, within a few short months' time, she wouldn't even be my wife on paper.

And it was all so she could get money that her grandmother left to her.

"Pssh," I grunted as I took a bite of the last piece of meatloaf on my plate. The reminder of why Savannah had come back into my life after all of these years was all I needed to let go of any softening I felt toward her.

So what if she left me dinner in the oven, and if, on really late nights, my mind whispered to me that she looked right lying in my bed? Or that, since she started sleeping in it, my bed had taken on a lavender scent that I'd spent years trying to forget?

Fuck all of that bullshit.

Savannah was back for the money. And she needed me to sign divorce papers in order to get it. Therefore, the power was in my hands. When I finally got everything I wanted from her and was able to extinguish her from my memory, I would grant her that fucking signature and say good riddance.

The rest of the house was semi-dark as I passed from the kitchen into the living room. The television had been left on and I would've bet that Aiden had forgotten to turn it off. I felt something like a smile break out on my face.

The kid wasn't too bad. He had a lot of energy, which I remembered having at nine years old, as well. Savannah was constantly reminding him not to run in the house.

I shut the television off and started to head upstairs toward my bedroom, but my foot caught on something and I bumped my leg into the coffee table.

"Shit," I grunted as I bent to rub my shin. I kicked whatever I'd tripped over and realized it was another cardboard box.

It was Savannah's, of course. She'd moved a bunch of her belongings into storage but a few boxes lingered around the living room. If I remembered correctly, this particular box had the words *Personal. Not For Storage* written on it in black marker.

Since it was dark in the living room with the TV off, I couldn't see clearly.

"Dammit." Some of the contents from the box had spilled out when I knocked it over.

I pulled out my cell phone and turned on the flashlight app to see what the hell I was doing. I grabbed an old sweater and stuffed it back in the box, followed by a framed picture. My heart damn near stopped when I shined my light on the picture.

The image was of a young couple smiling at one another as they stood, face to face, underneath a huge oak tree. It was us, Savannah and me, on the day we got married.

She wore a long white dress with a crown of sunflowers around her head, while I was dressed in a black tux that Micah loaned me. The backdrop of Tucker Bridge peeked out overhead.

It was the spot where we first met. Down by Gaines River. That was where we got married, in a gazebo constructed not too far from the area.

My mother was the one who took the picture.

I could barely bring myself to look at the beaming smiles on our faces. We appeared as if we had the whole world laid at our feet.

Instead of continuing to look, I threw the picture into the box and went to pick up the next item, a small, silver chain. Attached to it was a heart-shaped, sterling silver locket. The first gift I'd ever given Savannah.

I opened the locket, and an unfamiliar sound came out of my mouth. On one side was a picture of a woman in her mid-twenties. She was young but I knew her face.

It was Savannah's mother. The picture of her that she always kept with her. But it was the image on the right side of the locket that caused a fury to well up in me. A small infant cradled in a light blue blanket.

He appeared to be asleep, but I knew he wasn't.

"AJ."

This was a picture of our son. The hospital staff took this photo of him nestled in a blanket after he was born. It was for us to have something to remember him by, but how the hell could I forget my own son? I adamantly refused the picture. I knew he wasn't asleep in it.

He was dead. Never to open his eyes.

Savannah had kept it.

Anger propelled me to my feet and I stormed up the stairs with the locket in my hand.

I pushed through the bedroom door, closing it behind me and cut on the light.

"Why the hell would you leave this laying around for me to find?" I barked.

Savannah sat up in the bed with wide eyes, looking around. "What-what's happening? Aiden?" she called, sounding distressed.

I didn't let her fear or whatever innocent image she was attempting to portray persuade me.

"Aiden's fine. Why did you leave this laying out?" I demanded, holding the locket up.

She blinked, reorienting herself, then stared at the locket.

"Are you going through my belongings?" she shot back, ignoring my question.

"Don't play games with me, Savannah," I growled.

And playing games was what she was doing. She had to be, because why, of all things, would she leave a box of belongings with a picture of our wedding day and the locket I gave her with an image of our son inside, for me to find?

She was fucking with me.

"Ace, I have no idea what you're talking about."

"You know what this is." I jutted the locket into her face. I'd made it across the room in three steps, glaring down at her.

"It's my necklace."

"Not just any necklace," I reminded her.

She shook her head. "It was in my box of belongings."

"A box you conveniently left in the living room for me to trip over and find."

She tilted her head to the side as she came to stand to her full height. "You cannot be serious." She snorted and shook her head. "You believe that I purposely left my stuff for you to find—to what? Get upset over?"

"Why don't you tell me what your intentions were?"

"I would," she replied, "except I didn't have any intentions. I left the box downstairs because I forgot to bring it upstairs after I took the rest of my boxes over to storage."

I frowned down at her, a piece of me urging me to believe her, but I wouldn't let it drop so easily. Why did she still have these items after all of these years? And why did she keep them in a box marked as *Personal, not for storage*?

She was the one who'd left me. It didn't make sense for her to hold on to keepsakes from a relationship she walked away from.

"Give me my necklace." She reached for the locket, but I snatched it away right before she could grab it.

"No."

"It's mine," she said, her voice sounding slightly higher-pitched than normal.

I shook my head and held it just out of range as she went for it again.

"Ace, you're being ridiculous."

"Fuck yeah, I am." I knew it too but she drove me crazy and seeing her struggle to get the locket gave me more than a little bit of delight in an otherwise undelightful situation.

"It's mine and I want it back," she argued.

"Come and take it," I demanded, moving again.

She leapt at me, trying to get to the chain, but instead of landing cleanly, she landed on my foot and stumbled.

I caught her body and brought her flush against mine. I pressed her back against a wall and leaned into her. We both breathed harshly as if we'd just got done racing up the stairs.

My gaze dropped to the tops of her breasts, which were on display from the silk nightgown she wore that reached down to the tops of her thighs. I pressed my knee in between her legs, forcing my way closer into her center.

"I don't know what the hell happened to you, but you're a son of a bitch now," she said through gritted teeth.

"You fucking happened to me."

I crushed my lips against hers. Something inside of my chest eased open at the contact. I ignored it and instead sought to dominate Savannah with my kiss. I felt her hand press against my chest but I didn't move.

She gasped and her lips parted. I found my entry and breached her open mouth, deepening the kiss. A yearning for more started in the pit of my stomach. It was made even worse when the hint of a moan escaped Savannah's mouth.

Her hand went from pushing against my chest to wrapping around my neck. I adjusted and lowered my hand to lift one of her thighs around my hip. I pressed my hips against hers and this time the sound of her moan was unmistakable.

Even though I still wore my flight suit which restricted my erection, the bulge was enough to press against her. She wasn't bare down there. The panties she wore were another barrier between our bodies, but our clothes didn't stand a chance.

I pushed away from Savannah, breaking the kiss. My free hand lowered to wrap around her neck. I peered into her eyes, searching for something. She did the same to mine.

"Is this what pretending to be married looks like?" she asked, breathless.

"Yes." I kissed her again, this time bringing both of her thighs to wrap around my waist as I carried her to the bed.

Savannah's hands weren't idle as she searched for the zipper on my flight suit. I helped her along, lowering the zipper and allowing the top half of the jumper to slide down my arms.

Her hands moved down my arms, completely freeing them of the sleeves. I lowered both of our bodies to the bed, continuing to join our lips. The nightgown of hers was easy to dispose of, leaving her in nothing but a pair of cotton panties.

I pressed away to take a full glimpse of her body. A body that I had known so well. Her full breasts tempted me with each rise and fall of her breathing. I cupped them, enjoying the way they fit perfectly into my larger than average-sized hands.

"Oh," she sighed when I squeezed them, pinching her dark brown nipples. A noticeable shiver ran through her body.

"You're still sensitive here," I said aloud, although I'd meant to keep that observation to myself.

She nodded, her eyelids half closed. She didn't say anything, which was a good thing. There were too many unnamed and uncontrollable emotions that flowed through me. Hearing her voice would've only set something off that I wasn't ready to explore.

"Turn over," I ordered.

She frowned. "What?"

"This is too close," I said. "Turn over." I didn't give her time. Instead, I adjusted my body and moved her around onto all fours. Her ample ass was perched high in the air.

I stared at it as I stripped the rest of the way out of my flight suit and reached into my night stand for a condom.

Within seconds, I was sliding inside of her. Savannah's back arched, allowing me to penetrate deeper.

She cursed and beat her fist against the bed. I tightened the hold I had on her hips, stilling myself. My vision became blurry and I needed a moment to get my shit together.

"Ace," she panted.

I shook my head. "Don't say my name. Not while I'm fucking you."

This wasn't about reconnecting or any second chance bullshit.

"This is about forgetting you," I said through gritted teeth as I rammed into her again. Her ass jiggled and bounced each time I pounded into her.

I reached around and felt in between her thighs, searching for her button. I knew the moment I found it because Savannah's entire body convulsed.

I leaned over her and grabbed a handful of her hair. I pulled her head back, causing her back to arch even more. I plowed into her body repeatedly.

Savannah bit her bottom lip, moaning but cutting herself off. I recognized her trying to keep silent as to not awaken her sleeping son. I would've cursed myself for having forgotten all about the boy if I weren't so far gone.

"Come now," I said low in her ear. This wasn't about connection but I still needed to see her come on my cock.

"Now, Savannah," I ordered as I massaged my thumb against her clit while stroking her walls with my dick.

A second later a tremble moved through her body and she pressed against me. Every muscle in her back tightened and I felt her pussy clamp down around me. Heat spread throughout my body as she came, sparking my orgasm.

I bit down on my tongue almost harsh enough to draw blood as I pounded her out while coming. The orgasm was quick and ferocious, passing through me like a lightning bolt.

When it was over, I pulled out of Savannah.

She flipped over, turning to look up at me. The both of us stared at one another, panting. Her eyes were saucers, searching mine for answers to questions I didn't want any part of.

"Mama," a tiny cry broke through the awkwardness of the moment.

Savannah gasped. "Oh my God. We woke him up."

She hurried off of the bed and ran over to the dresser, pulling out a pair of joggers and a T-shirt. She redressed and ran out of the room just as Aiden yelled for her again, louder this time around.

I took a step in her direction but stopped myself. There was no need for me to follow. She wasn't really my wife, and the boy down the hall wasn't my son. I headed for the private bathroom instead, shutting the door behind me and stripped myself of the used condom.

I needed a shower and to take my ass to sleep. Those were the only two tasks I would allow myself to focus on.

By the time I got out of the shower, Savannah hadn't returned. The smell of sex still lingered in the air. I stared down at the crumpled sheets and comforter and at Savannah's nightgown that rested on the floor by the bed. The locket and broken chain were left next to her sleepwear.

I picked it up and tucked it into my palm. Sleeping in that bed didn't feel right.

On a sigh, I exited my bedroom and carried my ass downstairs to the guest room.

The last thought I had for the night was that I'd just fucked my wife for the first time in sixteen years. And for the life of me, I wanted to do it again.

CHAPTER 6

Savannah

"The Air Force family picnic is this Saturday."

I spun around from the counter, butter knife still in my hand, to look at Ace. Those were the first words he'd spoken to me in the past week. Since the night he accused me of running some type of game on him because he went snooping through my belongings, and we'd had sex in his bed.

"What did you say?" I asked, knowing what he said but wanting him to repeat himself, if only to piss him off a little.

"You heard me." He barely looked at me as he adjusted the collar of his uniform.

While I didn't want to admit it, he looked damn good dressed in his ABUs with his pants tucked into his combat boots. They were second best to seeing him dressed in his flight suit. But he also looked great in a regular pair of blue jeans and a white T-shirt. Then there was...

I shook my head.

"And you expect what?" I asked, shaking myself free of thoughts of how good he looked.

"I expect you to attend." He stepped closer, his boots making a soft thud against the hardwood floors as he did. "Just like a proper military wife."

"What am I supposed to do with Aiden?" The school year was just about over when we moved here, but I'd signed Aiden up for a day camp hosted by the school he would be attending in the fall. The camp was five days a week, with weekends off.

Ace frowned as he crossed his arms over his chest. "It's a family picnic. Other children will be there," he said as if I were two cards short of a full deck.

I narrowed my eyes. Not only had he forced me to move in with him to play this charade of marriage, but now he expected me to drag my son out in public to be a part of this game.

"And what are you going to tell everyone? How are you going to explain suddenly popping up with a wife and son?" I knew he hadn't told members of his squadron that he was married, and they knew he wasn't a father. Ace had all but told me as much.

"I'm not explaining shit to anyone," he replied as if that settled the matter. He stepped back and slapped his hat on his head, completing his uniform. "The picnic starts at eleven. We'll leave here around ten thirty. Be ready," he ordered as if I were one of his subordinates.

I was about to tell him what he could do with his orders, but Aiden interrupted.

"Morning, Mr. Ace," Aiden said as he raced into the kitchen. "Morning, Mama." Aiden leaped up as I bent low for him to plant his usual good morning kiss on my cheek.

"Morning, sweetie."

"Morning, kid. Enjoy your breakfast," Ace told him right before exiting the kitchen and heading out for the day. He didn't give me so much as a backward glance.

"Asshole," I grumbled.

"What?"

I stood straight and turned to look at Aiden. "Nothing. Go take a seat at the table." I went back to the counter to finish buttering Aiden's toast and plated his scrambled eggs.

"Thank you," he said as I sat his plate down in front of him.

I ran my fingers through his hair. "You didn't have any more bad dreams last night, did you?"

He shook his head. "No."

"Good."

A week earlier, the night I thought he'd heard Ace and me, it turned out Aiden had another one of his nightmares. He said that he couldn't remember what the dream was about but that it was scary.

He'd begged me not to leave him, which was how I ended up sleeping in his bed for the rest of the night.

Not that I minded. The last place I wanted to go back to was Ace's bedroom after what we did. I was just relieved that we hadn't awakened Aiden. I already felt guilty enough for dragging him into this.

For his part, though, Aiden adjusted well to his new environment. He was intrigued that Ace was a fighter pilot. Early on, he'd had a million and one questions for me about the types of planes Ace flew and how big they were, and how long he'd been flying.

Ace was better suited to answer those questions, but I didn't approach him about it. The more I managed to keep my distance from him over the next six months, the better.

"We've got about fifteen minutes before we need to leave for camp," I told Aiden. "Go up and brush your teeth and then come down and put your shoes on."

While Aiden headed upstairs, I finished my breakfast of scrambled egg whites with spinach and mushroom and toast with extra butter.

I'd made a massive cup of coffee and hoped it was enough to carry me through the rest of the morning.

After I dropped Aiden off at camp, I had plans to look for a job. There were a couple of urgent care facilities in the city of Harlington where I wanted to apply.

I figured it was best to get a job as soon as possible for Aiden and me to live off of when this was all over.

"Ready," Aiden declared as soon as I dropped my plate into the sink.

"Me too. Let's go."

We made it out the door in good time, and the drive from Ace's home to Aiden's summer camp was only about ten minutes. I dropped him off with a wave and a kiss and headed to the first urgent care office I had on my list.

I knew in this day and age, most people sent résumés via online applications, but I speculated that applying in person would help me stand out amongst the other applicants.

The third office I drove into had a filled parking lot. I doubted I would be able to speak with any of the hiring managers or staff, by the looks of the outer office. Patients lined every single one of the ten chairs, and a few were left standing.

I scanned the patients, observing a woman who had a pretty nasty cough. A toddler played on the floor beside her. My childhood memory of waiting with my mother in a similar office while she coughed and coughed floated to mind.

I was much older than this little girl, though. But I was still useless to help my mother. Only a week later, she died of undiagnosed pneumonia.

With a shake of my head, I released that thought from my mind and pressed ahead to the front counter.

"Good morning," I said cheerily to the receptionist behind the desk.

She glanced up and gave me a half-smile. She was cute, looked to be about in her late twenties or early thirties, and wore dark brown and blond box braids.

"Hi," she greeted. "Please fill out one of these forms and then take a seat in the lobby."

"Oh no." I shook my head. "I recognize you're busy, but I wanted to drop off my résumé. I saw online your facility is hiring for a physician assistant."

Her forehead wrinkled. "Um, I think so."

Before she could continue, another woman, this one tall and dressed in a white lab coat, entered the receptionist's office from the back, where I assumed her office and examination rooms were.

"Reese, can you make a note for Gwen to order more supplies later today?"

"Sure thing, Dr. Pierce," the receptionist said.

On a whim, I decided to go for it. "Hi," I called through the receptionist's window. When the doctor turned around, I glanced down at her lab coat. "Dr. Pierce, I'm Savannah Greyson. I saw online that your clinic is looking to hire a physician assistant." I stuck out the folder in my hand.

"I know this is a bit unorthodox—"

"We like unorthodox here," she said, cutting me off.

I smiled. "Well, I'm certainly that. Anyway, I'm a licensed PA with just under five years' experience in the emergency room."

"That would make a shift to urgent care easy," Dr. Pierce noted as she scanned my résumé.

"Yes, it would," I rushed on. "I live only about ten minutes from here, and I can be flexible." I stopped short. "I mean, I do have a nine-year-old son, but your online job description said you were looking for someone for day hours."

"We are," she said.

I pushed out a sigh of relief. "Great. As you can see, my references are excellent."

"What would you do in the case of a patient presenting with shortness of breath or unexplained wheezing?" she quizzed.

I inhaled and ran through the numerous medical scenarios that could cause a patient to present with those symptoms.

"It depends on the patient, of course. I would do my best to get a medical history to rule out asthma or any other possible chronic condition. But you said unexplained wheezing, so in all likelihood, the patient hasn't experienced it before. In which case, I could be led to believe possible cardiac arrest. But the necessary testing should be run to be sure."

"Which we don't have here," Dr. Pierce noted.

I paused and glanced around. "I would follow the proper protocols to get the patient transported to the nearest emergency department, which is Carson Medical Center, so they can be tested and get the treatment they need."

Dr. Pierce nodded. "All viable solutions. What are you doing tomorrow morning at nine?"

"Nothing." Hope welled up in my chest.

"Can you be down here for a formal interview? My wife and co-owner of Brightside will be available then."

"Absolutely. I will see both of you then." I stuck out my hand for her to shake. "Thank you so much, Dr. Peirce. Thank you," I said to Reese, the receptionist.

She gave me a giant smile and thumbs up.

"If this works out, we'll have you to thank," Dr. Pierce said. "We've been short-staffed for a while now."

"I look forward to the opportunity."

A few minutes later, I exited Brightside Clinic feeling a little taller than when I walked in. Brightside was the urgent care facility that was number one on my list. Though the salary was on the lower end of the spectrum of what I could make, it was still enough for Aiden and me to live comfortably, once we moved out of Ace's house.

I'd already started to think about rebuilding my life down there in Harlington. I didn't want to pull Aiden out of school in the middle of the year, and if I could find a job doing what I loved and serving the people I most wanted to, it would be a win-win.

Brightside Clinic served those who were uninsured or underinsured. Due to that, the staff salary wasn't the same as one would make at a higher-end facility or even working in a hospital, which was likely why they had trouble with staffing.

But this was the population I'd always wanted to work with. It was why I'd had my heart set on going into medicine since I was a teenager.

While the rest of my life might have been a complete mess, things were looking up in my career. All I needed to do was bide my time with Ace, get him to sign the divorce papers so that I could inherit my grandmother's trust, pay off Vincent Reyes, and hope that was enough to keep Aiden out of his biological father's crosshairs.

CHAPTER 7

Savannah

The sun nearly blinded me as we pulled into the parking lot for the Air Force summer picnic. It was a beautiful day with not a cloud in sight, despite the predicted late afternoon thunderstorms.

It was still early in the summer, but the temperatures reached the high eighties. I would bet the temps would rise at least another ten degrees before the day was over if the rain didn't come.

"Look, they have kites," Aiden said excitedly as he jumped out of the backseat of Ace's truck.

"Can I fly one?"

I turned to answer him but realized Aiden was looking up at Ace.

Ace briefly turned his head in my direction. His expression was unreadable, with his eyes hidden behind his aviators. I swore he'd worn them on purpose so that he could conceal his expression from me.

"You have to ask your mother."

"Mama, can I?"

"We'll see," I told Aiden, taking him by the hand.

The state park was about an hour outside of Harlington. A shallow river ran throughout, and the area had an open field for children to run around and play in.

From the looks of it, several different games had been set up already.

It was a little after eleven, and others were still arriving.

"Hey Cannon, can't believe you showed up to one of these," a guy called.

I turned around to see a tall, bald Black man with a massive grin on his face. He wore the same aviators that Ace wore covering his eyes. I knew right off the bat that this guy was another fighter pilot.

Obviously, a member of Ace's squadron. They all had a specific look about them. A confidence that wasn't easy to emulate or fake.

It was probably the assurance of knowing you were highly trained in flying some of the most advanced air technology in the world. But, in all honesty, Ace had always had that confidence. It'd only grown with age.

"Maple," Ace said. "'Sup." They slapped hands.

The guy Ace called Maple looked toward me. I saw his eyebrows lift above the rim of his sunglasses. "Hello."

"Hi."

"This is my wife."

Maple had to work on his poker face because the way his jaw fell open, it was apparent that he wasn't expecting that sentence to come out of Ace's mouth.

"Your wife," Maple said as he peered his down the brim of his nose.

"Dennis, don't be rude," a petite woman with caramel skin and a beautiful high-puff said as she moved next to Maple.

"My bad. I, uh, didn't know Cannon was married." He cocked his head to the side, to stare at Ace.

I cleared my throat, bringing their attention back to me. "Savannah," I said, sticking out my hand.

"Sabrina," the other woman said. "And this is my husband, Dennis."

Ace didn't say a word during the awkward introductions. I guess he meant it when he said that he didn't plan on explaining anything to his teammates or anyone else. I certainly wasn't about to give these strangers the rundown on our relationship.

Which wasn't actually a relationship.

"Mama, I wanna fly kites," Aiden whined, reminding me that he was still standing there.

Out of the corner of my eye, I watched Maple's face drop again. His head snapped over in Ace's direction.

"Okay, sweetie," I said, taking Aiden by the hand. If Ace didn't feel the need to explain any of this, I sure as hell wasn't going to.

"He can play with James and Angel," Sabrina said as she called her children over.

I nodded and followed her over to where some of the other participants set up the kites. I glanced back over my shoulder to see Ace staring in my direction. Maple was saying something to him, but he stared straight at me.

A few other men walked over, and Maple told them something. The next thing I knew, all eyes were on me. Ace continued to stand there like a statue. I turned, shaking my head.

"James, be careful," Sabrina yelled at her son. "If yours is anything like mine, you have to remind him not to play so rough."

I laughed. "Only fifty times a day. How old is yours?"

"Eight. And Aiden?"

"Nine."

"Hey Sabrina," another woman greeted with a wave. She was cute with short brown hair and a baby on her hip.

"Rach, hey. This is Savannah. Cannon's wife."

Naturally, Rachel gave Sabrina the same shocked expression Maple gave me earlier.

"Wife?" she asked as if someone knocked the wind out of her.

"Savannah," I introduced with my hand outstretched.

She eyed me before shaking my hand. Little by little, more women trickled over to our group, and with every new person, it was the same thing. They all stared from time to time as if expecting me to share my life story with them.

It was strange enough being the newcomer in a group of women who knew each other well, but being introduced as the wife of someone they'd known for years?

It was like being the odd man out in high school all over again. Only, back in high school, I had Ace at my side to help keep the awkwardness at bay. He had a way of always making me feel safe.

That was no longer the case. I stood amongst the women, making conversation here and there. But when their questions bordered on too personal, I not-so-discreetly redirected the conversation.

"Tricia, I wondered if you planned on coming," Rachel said about forty minutes later when another woman joined us. "Trish, this is Ace's wife, Savannah," Rachel introduced as she held her hand in my direction.

There was something in her tone that I didn't like.

This new woman openly gawked at me.

"Wife?" she said while her hazel eyes looked me up and down. Her top lip curled on a sneer.

It didn't take the knowledge necessary to fly F-16s to recognize that Tricia took an instant disliking to me. Again, memories from high school rushed back. This woman, with her slim hips, hazel upturned eyes, and thick, long hair, was beautiful.

She was the type of woman few men would pass up, given the opportunity.

"How are you his wife?" she asked, not even bothering to say hello or introduce herself formally.

"It's simple, really," I retorted just as tersely. "We stood in front of a pastor, said our vows, exchanged rings, and signed the license."

Albeit, sixteen years ago, with very few years of even seeing one another in between, but what were details when I was in the mood to be just as catty?

"I think I'm going to get a hot dog," I said, excusing myself from the group.

As an introvert, the group interaction was already beginning to wear on me, but coupled with that woman's response to finding out who I was and the whispers I could overhear as I walked away, I needed my distance.

I watched as Aiden climbed to the top of one of the jungle gyms, preparing to slide down. He looked like he was having fun. In the distance, I spotted Ace in the light pink Polo he had on with a pair of light blue jeans. He was in a group of men and a few women. All of whom had that look.

"Birds of a feather."

I turned away from the grill to see Sabrina smiling at me. She nudged her head in the direction of the men. "They tend to group like that. The pilots and the flight crew."

I nodded. "I figured. They all have that look about them."

Sabrina laughed. "They do, don't they?" She turned and glanced over her shoulder. "The wives or hopeful wives on the other side."

I followed her gaze with my own before turning back to the grill.

"Don't worry about Rachel and the others," Sabrina said, surprising me. "In this life, the wives tend to be, um, how should I say it?"

"Cliquey as all hell?" I asked with a lifted brow.

She let out a laugh. "That's one way to put it."

"Not my problem."

It wasn't like I was going to be around for much longer anyway. I didn't see the need to try and get the other women to like me. But I did like Sabrina. She seemed nice and was a lot warmer than the other women who wanted to know the story behind Ace and me.

"Plus, Rachel and Tricia are cousins, so…" She paused when I gave her a funny look. "Anyway, I think they're about to start the tug-of-war. You should come play."

I waved my hand in the air. "I don't think so." I pointed to the floral print, sleeveless summer dress I opted to wear for the day. "Grass stains don't go with the look."

She shrugged. "Suit yourself."

I watched as she headed off in the direction where a couple of the Airmen laid out a long rope. Sabrina waved her son, James, over, and I looked over to the last place that I'd seen Aiden.

He was no longer over by the slide.

I scoured the crowd, noting the various groups of women and men mingling about. Children ran in different directions. Some still had kites while others played with balls in their hands, while a few of the younger kids had balloons. Thank goodness for the trees and the pavilion, blocking out some of the sun's rays.

Aiden was amongst a crowd of three other boys. From my vantage point, it looked like he was having a good time, so I opted to let him be. Hopefully, when this was all over with Ace and me, and we were settled in our permanent home, somewhere, he'd have time to make real friends at his school.

I ignored the ache in my chest at the reminder that that would mean Ace and I were legally divorced. Officially not a couple any longer, although we hadn't been a real couple in years.

I swung my attention in the opposite direction to Ace with the same group, talking and laughing. There was an ease about him as he stood with one hand in his jeans' pocket, the other cupping a red Solo cup. His smile was genuine, but it wasn't unguarded like the smiles he used to give me back when we were the real thing.

God, I miss his smiles.

They always had a way of putting me at ease. And I could've used the comfort at the moment.

"You two seem distant," a female voice came up behind me, breaking into my thoughts.

The roll of my eyes was automatic as I instantly recognized Tricia's voice.

"Excuse me?" I asked.

Her expression was none too friendly. "You and your...*husband*," she sneered. "You two have barely spoken since I got here." She eyed me over the rim of her plastic cup as she took a sip of whatever she was drinking.

"Do you make it a point to track the conversations of every couple you come across, or just me and my husband?"

Tricia's face scowled at the last two words of my question. "Since when is Ace your husband? He wasn't married last week."

I let out a humorless laugh. "Are you sure about that?"

Her face reddened, and I was sure it wasn't from the summer heat. "He wasn't married when we slept together."

I almost dropped the plate in my hand. Unwittingly, I took a step back as if she'd pushed me. The ache in my belly worsened when a triumphant smile broke through her lips.

But I wouldn't let her get the best of my emotions.

I hadn't seen Ace in sixteen years. He was an attractive and successful man. Of course he hadn't remained single all this time.

Nor had I. The difference was, none of the men I dated were rubbing our relationship in his face at the moment.

I placed the plate on the table next to the unmanned grill and got in Tricia's face.

"A separation isn't the same as a divorce. Whatever you two had was nothing special, since you're in my face right now, trying to size me up instead of over there talking to him. I bet he won't even give you the time of day anymore."

I wanted to say more but feared that if I did, the conversation would take a complete left and would get real ugly quickly.

But Tricia wasn't done. She snorted.

"Hm. The only reason he's bringing you around now is because he's looking to get out of that transfer to Germany at the end of the year. He's angling for the instructor pilot position, and a ready-made family looks good to the higher ranks."

I sucked in a breath, trying to piece together everything she just spat at me. Ace hadn't mentioned a transfer out of the country at the end of the year. Nor did he tell me anything about wanting a new job.

Not like I expected him to, though.

It stung that this woman knew more about my husband than I did. I didn't have a right or any actual claim over him. But could it be true? Was he using our marriage as a tool to get a promotion?

He mentioned something about getting what he wanted out of the next six months.

With a considerable amount of restraint, I stepped back and moved around Tricia to find my son. I wasn't about to let this woman see my anger.

It was a fight to suppress the heat running through my veins. When I spotted Aiden, I waved him over at the same time I picked up my steps to get to him.

"Come on, sweetie. We're leaving." I grabbed him by the arm and began pulling him in the direction of the parking lot.

"Why're we leaving so soon?" he asked, but I didn't bother to stop to answer his question.

"Shit," I cursed under my breath when I remembered that Ace was the one who had driven us to the park. I stopped short next to his truck.

"What are you doing?"

I spun around to face Ace. His expression was placid as usual whenever he looked at me.

"We're leaving," I said firmly. "Give me your keys. You can find a ride back with one of your teammates or something."

He folded his arms across the chest. "You're not leaving." His tone brokered no argument. "Aiden, why don't you go play with the other kids while I talk to your Mama."

Aiden recognized the directive in Ace's comment because he took off running in the direction of another group of kids.

"What is this all about?" Ace leveled me with a look.

"This is about your little whore girlfriend getting in my face." My tone was just as sharp as his. How dare he bring me to an event where he knew she would more than likely be there?

"You've met Tricia." His tone was deadpan, almost bored.

"At least you didn't deny it."

"What do I have to lie about?" he retorted. "We dated, and now we don't."

"Whatever, Ace." I rolled my eyes. "And now you're forcing me into this pretend marriage so that you can look good to your squadron for a new job."

I almost demanded to know why he hadn't told me he was supposed to transfer out of the country in a few months.

But that wasn't my business. If all went according to plan, in a few short months, I'd have the divorce papers signed, and we would no longer be one another's problem, anyway.

A muscle in his jaw ticked. "It's just about the same as asking for a divorce after sixteen years so you can inherit money."

I grilled him with a glare. "You have no idea what you're talking about."

He shrugged. "Neither do you, sweetie. We're staying until the end of the picnic. Get used to it."

He turned and started for the crowd. I was left standing there fuming all by myself. I wanted to yell at the sky in frustration.

After a few deep breaths, I slowly started in the direction of the field again. I spotted Aiden standing alone with his head bowed.

Confused, I started for my son, knowing something was the matter. Ace and I reached him at the same time.

I stooped low. "Aiden, why aren't you playing with the other kids?"

He looked at me with sad eyes. "William said I couldn't play touch football because I don't have a daddy."

"What?" I blurted out with ballooning eyes. "Since when do you need a dad to play touch football?"

"They're playing in teams of dads and sons." Aiden shrugged. "Since I don't have one..." he trailed off.

My heart lurched against my ribcage. Ordinarily, I would've busted all up in that game and either demanded they let my son play or let me substitute as the parent, but my sundress wasn't suitable for a game of football.

As I tried to figure out how to make this situation right for him, I felt Ace lower next to me.

"William talks too much," he said. "Just like his daddy."

Aiden perked up a little from Ace's comment.

"I've wanted to play a game of touch football all day. Would it be okay if I played with you?"

I gawked at Ace. His tone was so tender. Sweet almost.

"You want to be my pretend daddy?" Aiden questioned with his eyes wide.

Ace hesitated and then looked over at me. He shrugged. "Just for the afternoon. I don't see the harm in that, right?" he asked Aiden.

"We can, right, Mama?"

A piece of me wanted to say hell no. Ace wasn't his pretend daddy, not even for the afternoon. He only wanted us here to paint an image so he could get a promotion. But the excitement in Aiden's voice stopped me. I couldn't let him down.

I nodded. "Just be careful, all right?" I looked at Ace as I said that.

He gave me a slight nod before standing and taking Aiden by the hand. I looked on as they headed in the direction of where the other men gathered.

This is only pretend, Savannah.

I reminded myself. I couldn't let Aiden or me get caught up in the fantasy that we were somehow a real family. It would be too devastating to both of us when that bubble burst.

CHAPTER 8

ce I pushed through the door to exit the building where a few of my squadron mates and I finished flight simulation training. I heard footsteps behind me.

"Hey, man. Good shit today," Maple said, patting me on the back.

I nodded and pounded Maple's fist with my own. "Always."

"It was good seeing you this Saturday too. Even if you did have a surprise none of us were expecting."

I paused and gave him a look.

"Still not talking, huh?" He laughed. "Whatever, man. Your business. But look, you know Tricia's pissed."

"Am I supposed to give a shit about her being upset about my personal life?"

"No." He shook his head. "But she seems like the vengeful type. You know, a woman scorned and all of that."

I gave him a dismissive look. I wasn't worried about what Tricia could do, but I did need to correct her about something. I hadn't seen her since the picnic that weekend.

"Anyway, Sabrina said she liked Savannah."

I snorted.

I could picture Sabrina and Savannah getting along. Maple's wife was kind and down-to-Earth.

"She did say she wasn't too talkative, though. Like she felt out of place."

"Yeah, we'll work on that. Listen, we need to go over those notes from the debrief," I said, redirecting his attention to work instead of personal matters.

The truth was, I was too fucked up in the head about Savannah to even reveal to myself what was going on between us. I hadn't slept in my damn bed since that night we were together. I knew if I did, the chances of me keeping my hands to myself was like asking a fox to guard the henhouse.

I'd told Savannah sex with her was part of my process to forget her, and I still meant it. I just needed to get my head on straight before I touched her again.

Maple and I talked for another minute as we walked to our vehicles. Right when I started to hop on my bike, Tricia came up to me out of nowhere.

"I need to speak with you," she said, sounding breathless as if she'd run to catch up with me.

I gave Maple a nod. "See you tomorrow."

He raised an eyebrow but got in his car, saying nothing.

"That makes two of us," I said, turning to Tricia as I slid my eyeglasses off of my face. I wanted her to see the look in my eyes as I said what I needed to.

She must've taken the move as a good sign because she smiled. "Good. I mean—"

"I'll go first," I said, interrupting. "I don't know what the fuck you thought you were doing on Saturday, but you have one more time to say another word to my wife, and I promise you, you're going to regret it."

Tricia's facial expression dropped immediately. "What the hell, Ace? Your wife? Do you even hear what you're saying?"

"Did you hear me stutter?"

"What are you even talking about? How long have you been married? When did you run off and get married?"

"I never ran off anywhere. She's been my wife for years."

Tricia gasped. "How?" Her tone rose to almost shrill.

I pinched the bridge of my nose, reining in my anger. I supposed Tricia did deserve some sort of explanation.

"Savannah and I are…complicated."

"Complicated? That's the best excuse you can give me after breaking my heart?" There were tears in her eyes. They had little impact on me.

"We dated for a few months. I never made any promises to you, and I've been clear for the past few weeks that you and I are through." I gritted my teeth as I said the following phrase. "I'm sorry if you felt led on, but it's time to let it go."

"Let it go?" She insisted, pulling me by the arm when I went to get on my bike. She let out a shrill laugh. "Ace, we both know the only reason you're parading her around right now is so you will look good for that instructor position down in San Antonio."

"You really should stop while you're behind."

I snatched my arm away from her.

Tricia's eyes widened and she took a step back. After watching me for a beat, a superior look crossed her face.

"I bet it wouldn't look good for Mr. Family Man, all of a sudden, to have news get out that he was whoring around on his wife and stepson or whatever that fucking kid is to you."

She gasped when I got directly in her face.

"I told you to stop talking while you were behind. You don't fucking listen. Let me remind you one final time: keep my wife and Aiden's name out of your mouth. Don't talk about them. If you see either of them, cross the street. Don't even dream about them because if you do, you'll wake up to one very pissed Townsend."

My top lip trembled with anger.

"Trust me when I say the last thing you want is to see me when I'm irate." I took a step back and grabbed my motorcycle helmet. "Enjoy the rest of your day."

I slammed my helmet over my head and got on my bike, revving it up. I peeled out of my parking spot, still fuming.

Tricia was the last person to whom I felt the need to defend my marriage. She knew our relationship wasn't going anywhere. Hell, no woman I dated over the past sixteen years was ever destined to be anything more than temporary.

Savannah had burnt that bridge for any other woman. And now she was back, seeking a divorce so she could get money from her grandmother's estate. I huffed and flicked my wrist to rev my bike up to go faster.

The thought of Savannah and divorce brought on memories of the very day we said our I do's.

* * *

THEN

Ace

I looked out onto the sparkling water of the Gaines River, thinking back to the first time Savannah and I met. The sky above was a brilliant blue with not a cloud on the horizon. One of those perfect spring days that only Texas could deliver.

May ninth. Our wedding day.

I peered down the road, shifting my weight from one foot to the other. Nerves like I'd never experienced before crashed through my entire body. My stomach felt like I'd just gotten off a roller coaster.

"Maybe you shouldn't have had that BBQ for lunch," Micah said as he stood beside me in the parking lot.

I elbowed him. "Shut the fuck up," I growled, feeling every bit of my anxiety.

"You need to be nicer. I am your witness for this. If I'm not here, there's no proof you went through with it."

We stood in the parking lot of a park that led down to an opening by Gaines River. In the center of the park was a white gazebo. This spot wasn't too far from where Savannah and I first met, and it was the location of where we were to get married.

"She'll be here." Micah placed a comforting hand on my shoulder.

No less than thirty seconds later did a Taxi pull up. I exhaled as Savannah got out of the car. All of the tension in my body fell away, but then my heartbeat kicked up for a different reason.

Savannah stood there next to the taxi, smiling at me. She looked like an angel dressed in a white dress that stopped a few inches above her ankles. It was a simple dress, but she'd paired it with a crown made of her favorite flower. Sunflowers.

She'd straightened her hair and wore it long.

"After the rain comes the sunshine. Sunflowers remind me of the sunshine," she'd told me once when explaining why they were her favorite flower.

"Damn, my wife is beautiful."

"She's not your wife yet," Micah reminded me.

"She will be," I said with all the confidence in the world. As I took a step closer to the taxi, I noticed the passenger side door open. "Mom?" I couldn't believe she was there.

"You didn't think I'd miss your big day, did you?" my mother asked, looking at me with soft eyes.

I moved closer, taking her by the elbow to hold her steady. She was so weak from the cancer that riddled her body. I wondered how she was even able to get out of bed some days.

"How did you...?" I trailed off.

My mother turned to look over at Savannah. "Your fiancée invited me."

"I'm sorry. I didn't think you would come," I told her, honestly.

My mother cupped my cheek. I lowered so she could press a kiss to it. "I wouldn't have missed this for the world." She pulled back. "Savannah needs to speak with you first," she whispered.

Out of the corner of my eyes, I saw Micah move to our mother's side and help her walk toward the direction of the pavilion.

I turned back to Savannah.

"I called her earlier today and told her we were doing this," she confessed. "I wanted her blessing, and I knew she would've wanted to be here." Her voice was almost apologetic.

I cupped her face and brought our lips to touch. "Thank you."

Those were the only two words I could manage. Between Savannah's beauty in the white dress and my mother's presence, I was overwhelmed.

We were young, eighteen years old, and had a few months before we would even graduate high school. My parents, mostly Joel and Savannah's grandmother, had repeatedly told us that we were too young to have the feelings we had, but I knew better.

"Come on," I said, taking Savannah by the hand to get this started.

At six in the evening, the sun was still high in the air with Tucker Bridge in the distance behind us. It was the perfect backdrop to say our vows.

"Wait." Savannah tugged on my hand, not moving.

"What is it?"

Her eyes dropped to the ground, and she glanced around, looking at everything but me.

"Babe." I lifted her chin for her to look me in the eye. "What's wrong?"

She bit her bottom lip before asking, "Are you sure we should do this?"

"You don't want to marry me?" It hurt even to ask.

"I do," she quickly said. "It's just that..." She sighed. "There are so many people who disagree, who would freak out if they knew what're about to do."

"They can jump off of Tucker Bridge for all I care."

She tugged at my hand, which was still tightly wound around hers. "Ace, don't say that. One of those people is your dad. He's going to flip when he finds out we got married."

"I'll handle my father. He won't say shit to you."

She shook her head. "I'm not afraid of him. I just..." She stopped. "Are we making the right decision?" She looked at me as if she were looking through to my soul, seeking out my most profound truth.

"Baby, nothing has ever felt more right in my life," I assured. "Not even when I got my acceptance letter to the Academy." And I'd wanted to be an Air Force pilot since I was six years old. Even that dream took a backseat to making Savannah my wife.

"That's just it," she protested. "How is this going to work? You off at the Academy and me at school back East? And then there's medical school if I make it in."

"You'll get in. And we will figure it all out together. As long as it's you and me." I squeezed her hand. "Forever."

"Forever," she whispered. A small smile touched her lips, and I let out a sigh. "Okay."

"Jesus, baby. You're going to give me grey hairs. Scaring me like that."

She laughed, and I held firmly to her hand as I walked her to the gazebo where my mother, Micah, and the pastor of my mother's church stood.

"I think we're ready," my mother said, looking from Savannah and me to the pastor.

Micah stood behind me while our mother remained seated. Pastor Jacobs stood at the center of the pavilion with the Gaines River behind him. Savannah and I stood before him.

"We are gathered here today," started Pastor Jacobs.

I couldn't take my eyes off of Savannah. She had the widest smile on her face as Pastor Jacobs spoke. I glanced down to see the silver locket that hung around Savannah's neck. The one I'd given her a year before. She never took it off once I placed it around her neck. She'd added a picture of her mother to one side.

It was her way of having her mother with us on our wedding day.

"We are blessed to be here on this beautiful day, surrounded by God's glory. In the distance stands Tucker Bridge. A bridge meant to bring both sides of Harlington together. A passageway for the city to become one."

Pastor Jacobs looked between Savannah and me.

"Today, you two become one. Let love be your bridge. Always remember that love is patient. Love is kind. And yet, it is unyielding. When you find it difficult to come back to one another, remember the love that you share today, at this moment. And you will find your way back home. Back to this union."

Tears ran down Savannah's cheeks. I wiped them away, one by one. Then it was she who wiped my tears away after she recited her vows and placed the ring on my finger.

"Ace, you may now kiss your bride," Pastor Jacobs declared.

The first kiss we shared as a married couple was nothing short of magical. Savannah's eyes sparkled with joy as I pulled away from the kiss.

"Thank you," I whispered to her.

"You're welcome," she mouthed and laughed.

"I now present to you Mr. and Mrs. Ace Naiche Townsend," Pastor Jacobs said, *using my full name.*

We held our clasped hands up high while Mama and Micah applauded. Our audience was small, but none of that mattered. I knew we'd have problems to face as a young married couple, but the world could bring them on. Our love was ready for anything.

Or so I thought.

CHAPTER 9

avannah

I smiled at the woman sitting before me in one of the examination rooms of Brightside Urgent Care.

"It looks like you have a bit of a respiratory infection. I'm going to give you a prescription that should help with that."

"How much will it cost?" Mrs. Baker asked while she toiled with a handkerchief in her hands.

My heart squeezed. I knew that look too well. Not only had I seen it on the faces of numerous patients, but I'd seen the same worry in my mother's eyes when we went to the clinic shortly before her death.

I patted her hands with mine.

"This one is the generic brand of the medication, and your insurance should cover it."

She still didn't look too relieved.

"If it doesn't or if there's an issue, give us a call, and we'll see what we can do about it. Okay?"

She nodded.

"I'm serious. Please don't forego getting this filled. I know you can't take off work to rest as you should, but the prescription will help you recover. Brightside has a lot of options for our patients. Don't hesitate to call us."

"All right." She hoisted herself from the exam table with a heavy sigh.

Once she left, I took the time to fill out the chart and make a note to give her a call in a few days to follow up. After two weeks at Brightside, I was still working on figuring out the lay of the land.

The good news was that while the clinic was always busy, most of the cases I tended to were minor compared to what I saw when working in the ER.

"I need to see my wife," I heard his voice boom through the open exam room door.

"Ace?" I said to myself since no one else was in the room. I was sure that was his voice as I got up from my stool and headed in the direction of the lobby.

Sure enough, as I rounded the corner, I saw Ace standing at the front counter with a scowl on his face.

I pushed through the door that separated the lobby from the exam rooms. "What are you doing here?"

Ace stormed over to me and grabbed me by the arm. It wasn't too tight or painful, but his grip was firm.

"What are you doing?" I whispered as not to alarm the patients who waited.

"Savannah, are you okay?" Reese asked. The wrinkle in her brow read concerned. "I can call the police."

Ace glared at her over his shoulder before turning back to me. His face looked as if he dared me to tell her yes, call the police.

"It's okay, Reese." I held my free hand up. "He's my husband."

I turned and pulled open the door that led to the exam rooms. Ace kept ahold of my arm, trailing me as we entered the room.

He shut the door behind us.

"Why did you do it?" he demanded before I could ask him what this was all about.

"Do what?"

"Marry me. Why the hell did you bother marrying me when you didn't want to?"

I took a step back, needing to put space between our bodies. "How could you ever think that?" I shook my head in disbelief.

"You all but said it right before we made our vows."

I thought back to that day, showing up in the cab with his mother.

"You gave me every excuse not to get married. You were hesitant, but you still went through with it. Why? Why the fuck would you do that if you were just going to walk away?"

The question came out strained. A strain that spoke of the underlying feeling of betrayal. It was that tone that cut me more profoundly than his vitriol.

"I never would've said those vows if I didn't mean every single word."

My voice trembled with emotion. I could still picture us in that gazebo, young but so in love. I'd choked up while reciting my vows because my body had felt like it overflowed with the love I felt for him.

"You used every excuse you could think of to get out of marrying me."

"Ace, that's not even remotely true."

"Then what the hell was that conversation about before our vows?"

"I was scared," I yelled, forgetting I was at work. "I went to my grandmother the day before our wedding and told her we were getting married. Do you know what she did?" I paused.

Ace just looked at me.

"She slapped the hell out of me. Told me I was making the biggest mistake of my life. Just like my mother did when she had me."

I didn't bother telling him the rest of what my grandmother said. That she'd told me Ace was just using me for a good time and that he'd soon tire of me and leave me deserted. Probably with a baby, like my father did to my mother.

"I called your mother and told her we were getting married because I wanted the blessing from at least one of our parents." I swiped angrily at the stupid tear that fell from my eye. "I wanted her to be there, and I knew you needed her to be there. Whether you knew it or not."

My chest heaved, and I had to turn away from Ace. Reliving the past was painful enough when I did it in my head, but staring him in the face as I did was almost unbearable.

"I went to your grandmother," he said, "after you left me."

I turned to face him again as my mouth fell open.

His demeanor was an almost one-hundred-eighty-degree difference from when he first entered the clinic. His voice was lower, less angry but still riddled with pain.

"She told me that it was probably for the best." He speared me with his gaze. "That our son…" He stopped.

I covered my mouth with my hand and gasped.

I could imagine my grandmother saying something like that to me. But hearing that she told it to Ace felt like someone yanking my heart out of my chest. I hadn't even told her I was pregnant until well into my second trimester. That was only a couple of weeks before AJ died.

"I went to her to look for you."

"I NEVER WENT BACK TO HER," I whispered. My grandmother's home was the last place I wanted to go after deciding to leave Ace.

"Where did you go?" he asked, his voice sincere yet resigned.

I shrugged. "I went back to Georgia for a little while. I stayed in a homeless shelter for almost a year." But the memories of living in Georgia with my mom became too much for me.

"Then I took a bus up to Philadelphia to stay with a cousin for a little while."

"Homeless shelters? You chose to stay in a shelter rather than live with me?" The hurt was back in his voice.

I shook my head. And my eyes watered even more. I couldn't wipe all the tears away as they streamed down my cheeks. How could I explain that I'd felt like being homeless was what I deserved? That I'd been the catalyst of his pain, just like I'd been the impetus of my mother's pain and, eventually, her death?

"You deserved better," I whispered, unable to look at him. "I'm just sorry my leaving the way I did made you hate me so much."

"I don't hate you, Savannah," he said, his voice thick with emotion. "I never hated you. Even when I tried to hate you, I couldn't."

He moved closer. "Everything would be so much easier if I could just fucking hate you."

I closed my eyes against his words. He was right. A piece of me wished he hated me, too.

When I opened my eyes, Ace stood before me, much closer. He raised his hand to cup my face and leaned in. The kiss was slow at first, tender as if he was feeling out new territory.

I melted into the soft brush of his lips against mine. He followed that by a lick of his tongue against my bottom lip.

I released a sigh, and he brought our bodies even closer. His arm slipped around my waist, pulling me into him. This wasn't like our previous kisses. Those were filled with anger and resentment.

This kiss was more like the way we used to kiss. Where Ace led and I followed, savoring every second of our skin brushing against each other's. This felt like a kiss from the old Ace.

My Ace. My husband.

"Savannah," Reese called through the door.

I startled and pulled back from Ace. "Shit."

I had completely forgotten where I was and that I should've been seeing patients.

Ace took a step back as if he needed to reorient himself as well. He didn't say anything as he moved to open the door.

There stood a wide-eyed Reese, glancing between the two of us.

"I'll see you at home," he said, his voice gruff.

"Home," I repeated in a low tone, needing to make sure I heard him correctly. Not once in the past six weeks had he referred to his house as my home.

I nodded.

"Sorry for the interruption," he told Reese before exiting.

I watched him walk away and fought my legs to remain where they were. I wanted to follow him but I couldn't.

"Gwen asked for you," Reese said.

I pushed out a breath with my hand pressed to my chest. Gwen was a nurse practitioner at the clinic, and she was married to Dr. Pierce. They co-owned the urgent care facility and were partial owners in the medical office connected to the urgent care clinic.

"I'll be right there."

Reese eyed me but remained silent. She simply nodded and went back up the hallway. I watched her as she limped away. Though curious, I never asked her what caused her disability.

I shook off the wayward emotions still streaming through my body and pushed them down. I would have to work them out at a later time. Even as I went back to work, it was like I could still feel Ace's lips on mine. That kiss had been even more intimate than that night we had sex in his bed.

That tryst that came on the heel of an argument was cold and distant, even if pleasurable. What happened in the examination room was different.

More intimate. My heart, body, and soul started to crave more.

CHAPTER 10

Ace

About a week after my impromptu visit to Savannah's workplace, I entered my home to the sound of laughter. A child's laughter followed by the throaty amusement of Savannah's.

My chest expanded, my body suddenly shaking off the tiredness I felt after a long-ass work shift. I hadn't flown that day, but we'd undergone more rigorous training and reviewed our previous training flights. I was happy to have the evening off for the first time in a few weeks.

That was, until I walked right into the middle of Savannah and Aiden, cooking in the kitchen. After dropping off my bag and heel-toeing my shoes off by the door, I instinctively followed the peels of giggles and music in the direction of the kitchen.

Neither one of them saw me at first. Without thinking, I leaned against the wall and silently watched as Savannah shook her hips in time with the music. She danced while bending over to open the oven. A blast of heat filled the air, accompanied by the smell of garlic, onion, and rosemary.

"Is it done?" Aiden asked, coming to stand next to her in front of the oven.

"Not quite. A few more minutes." Her voice was so delicate and sweet when she spoke to him, even when reprimanding him for running in the house.

I swallowed the lump in my throat. My mind flashed with a memory of Savannah speaking to our son like that while pregnant.

"Let's dance," she suddenly said. She took Aiden by the arms and swayed from side to side, tossing his arms high in the air.

He broke out in laughter.

With a shake of my head, I stood away from the wall to leave.

"Mr. Ace, you're home," Aiden said, stopping me in my tracks.

"Oh," Savannah commented, turning to me. Her eyes widened briefly. "No night flight tonight?"

I cleared my throat and shook my head. For the past seven days, I'd done my absolute best to avoid Savannah. My head had been even more fucked up since I kissed her in that damn examination room.

I'd barged into her job to get answers. To demand to know why she walked out on me. I hoped that whatever answer she gave would resolve something inside of me. I thought it would finally allow me to hate her the way I wished I could.

Instead, I found myself wanting her even more.

When she'd whispered with tears in her eyes that I deserved better, I could feel the rust shake lose off of the protective instinct I always had for her. Rather than pushing her away, it made me want to reel her in and keep her close.

If we hadn't been in her place of work, I know for a fact, I would've taken her right where she stood.

"Are you joining us for dinner?" Aiden asked, breaking my thoughts.

I stood a little taller and peered down at the boy. There was a look of hope in his eyes. Again, my chest tingled with something foreign.

In lieu of an immediate answer, I floated my gaze over to Savannah. She stared back at me.

"I've made plenty of food."

I knew she would've. While I had avoided eating dinner with them most nights, she still left a plate of food for me in the oven to keep it warm.

Just like old times.

I pushed that thought down and took a step back. "Probably not a good idea," I commented.

"Mama made baked chicken with rosemary," Aiden said, his eyes glittering with excitement. "It's delicious." He sounded as if he was trying to persuade me.

Savannah didn't say anything.

My stomach took that opportunity to growl. Loudly.

I hadn't eaten lunch that day, and my hunger suddenly became apparent to all of us.

"I helped with the mashed potatoes," Aiden continued. "And we've been dancing." His smile grew. "Mama says you can't trust the food of anyone who..."

"...doesn't dance while they cook," I finished at the same time Aiden did.

His eyes widened. "How did you know?"

Unconsciously, I looked over at Savannah. "She used to say the same thing to me."

I lost count of the number of times I came home to my wife dancing in the kitchen. Her motto was that anyone who didn't dance while they cooked didn't deserve to have their food eaten.

"Dancing makes the meal taste better," I mumbled.

A smile touched Savannah's lips. It was small, and just that quickly, I wanted to see her smile wider.

"I'll join you," I heard myself say.

"Yay," Aiden cheered.

"You can help set the table?" Savannah asked.

"I'm still pretty good at that." Our eyes connected again. That was always my job when we lived together. Savannah did the cooking because she loved it, and I set the table and cleaned up after the meal.

Aiden chattered about school and his new teachers as I put the utensils and plates out and Savannah finished cooking. A warm feeling invaded my body as I listened to him talk about his favorite class, which was math.

"I need to be good at math if I'm going to be a pilot, right, Mr. Ace?"

Savannah and I both stopped to look at Aiden.

I nodded and swallowed. "All subjects are important."

"It's such a cool job, and I'll get to fly planes and protect our country, right, Mr. Ace?"

I gave him a half smile. He reminded me a little of myself when I was a kid and first learned what a fighter pilot was.

"Something like that."

Aiden nodded as if it were a done deal.

Savannah turned off the music that'd been playing.

We sat down a few minutes later, plates full and appearing delicious. My stomach growled as if telling me that I'd better not pull out of eating this meal. I had already started thinking of ways to excuse myself from dinner, but my hunger and that feeling in my chest wouldn't allow me.

"Mama said there was a movie that you watched that made you want to become a pilot."

I shot Savannah a look.

Her lips twitched.

I narrowed my eyes at her across the table. "That was supposed to be a secret."

She finally did laugh. "It slipped out."

I rolled my eyes and looked over at Aiden. "Yeah, there was, but don't tell anyone. That's just between the two," I paused and glanced across the table, "three of us," I corrected.

Aiden nodded. "What was it?"

"*Top Gun* with Tom Cruise."

For years when I was younger, my family teased me that a movie was what had spurred my dream of being a pilot. To counter their teasing, I lied and said I barely even remembered the movie.

I told them that meeting a pilot at an air show at age ten that encouraged my dream of being a pilot.

Savannah was the only person to whom I'd told the truth. That movie imprinted on me at six years old, and ever since there was nothing else I wanted to be.

"Can we watch it?" Aiden asked.

"He can get you to watch a movie you never heard of, but I've begged you to watch *Star Trek* and you consistently turn me down," Savannah chimed in.

Aiden held up his hands. "*Star Trek* is boring," he griped.

"Take that back," Savannah said, laughing.

"Whoa, kid," I added. "*Star Trek* is quality TV. Captain Kirk is top tier."

Savannah snorted. "He means Captain Picard is the best captain Star Fleet has ever or will ever see."

"Oh, man." I shook my head. "We're still on this nonsense."

Aiden's head ping-ponged between Savannah and me as we debated the merits of which captain was best.

"Wait, so can we watch *Top Gun*?" he asked again.

"Whenever you're ready, kid." I pointed my fork at him. "But you have to give *Star Trek* at least one try."

He frowned but waved his hand. "Fine. Can we watch the movie tonight?"

I lifted an eyebrow in Savannah's direction.

"I'm sure Mr. Ace is tired after a long day. Maybe another night."

"I'm good," I said, interrupting her. "And I'm always game to watch *Top Gun*."

"Yes," Aiden cheered.

"Finish your dinner first. You don't eat while watching TV."

The pace at which Aiden ate increased noticeably. Savannah and I both laughed as we watched him shovel a spoonful of sweet potatoes into his mouth.

After Savannah warned Aiden multiple times against the danger of choking, we finished dinner and were in the living room within minutes.

Aiden sat between the two of us on the couch. Again, that warmth shrouded my chest and the air, and I couldn't shake the feeling that something bigger than me was happening without my permission.

Aiden was a champion and was able to stay awake for the entire movie. He cheered at the end when Tom Cruise, a.k.a. Maverick, reengaged in the fight to help his fellow pilot. That part always got to me, too.

By the time the credits rolled, I peered down into my lap to see Aiden's head in it. His eyes were closed, his breathing even. Just that quickly, he'd conked out.

"He falls asleep in the blink of an eye," Savannah commented as she stood. "I'll take him." She reached for him, but my hand covered hers.

I barely managed to ignore the tingle that shot through me at the skin-to-skin contact. I noticed Savannah's breath hitch. That caused my heartbeat to quicken.

"I'll take him to his room." My voice came out low and deep.

She nodded and stepped back.

Slowly, I released her wrist and maneuvered to stand in the way that allowed me to carry Aiden without awakening him. Savannah's footsteps were soft behind me as she trailed me up the stairs to his bedroom.

Somehow, I had managed to change him into his PJs without disturbing him too much, but as I tried to leave, he caught me by the hand.

"Can you read to me?" Aiden mumbled.

I grabbed the top book on the stand next to his bed. It was a story-book about a boy who had a father who was a pilot in the Air Force.

I stopped and stared at the book. I hated the way my eyes watered. Looking up, I caught Savannah standing at the door. She shifted her weight from one foot to the other.

"He picked that one out when we went to the library last week." There was a slight shake in her voice as if she were nervous. "I can read to him if you're too tired."

I waved her off and opened the book. "No problem, kid." I read page after page of the story. Every page or so, Aiden would mumble about how cool something was.

When I was satisfied that he had finally fallen asleep, I put the book back where it was and tiptoed out of the room.

Savannah stood in the hallway as I shut the door behind me. I'd thought she'd gone downstairs to finish cleaning up the kitchen.

"Thank you for doing that."

I shook my head. "No thanks needed." I peered back at the door. "He's a good kid."

She gave me a tight smile.

We stood there silently for an awkwardly long time, but I couldn't stop looking at her. For years, in my most private thoughts, I'd wished she was standing there, right in front of me. Now that she was, I couldn't tear my eyes away from her.

"I couldn't have deserved better," I said out of nowhere.

She frowned, her forehead wrinkling up the way it always did when she had a question.

"Last week," I explained, "you said I deserved better. That's a lie."

She visibly swallowed. "Ace..."

"It never mattered to me," I continued. "Where you came from. Where I came from. Opposite sides of the bridge, too young, different races, whatever all the bullshit everyone else said why we shouldn't be. You were it for me."

I had no idea why I was admitting everything, but it felt like it needed to be said.

Savannah's eyes watered, and I grinned. With a step forward, I used my thumb to wipe a tear that fell. A small chuckle fell from my lips.

"You're still a crybaby."

She laughed and pushed at my shoulder. "Shut up. It's still your fault I am." She wiped her tears and cleared her throat.

We fell into silence again. But it was easier this time, less awkward.

"I'm proud of you," she almost whispered.

"Say that again. Louder this time," I commanded, needing to hear the words again.

She looked me directly in the eyes. "You've accomplished everything you wanted to do." She gave me a shaky smile. "I never doubted you would, but I wanted to tell you that I'm proud of you."

I stepped so close that it forced her to back into the wall behind her. When I cupped the side of her face and brought our lips together, it wasn't out of anger or even a need to protect her. It was the burn in my chest that drove me.

I bit Savannah's bottom lip. It was a light bite, but she let out a soft moan that shot to my cock. The thoughts and ideas I had about creating more space between us vanished.

The last thing I wanted with Savannah, right then, was distance. I wanted her writhing beneath me, preferably in a bed but up against a wall, in a chair, on the couch, anywhere would've been fine with me.

"Mama."

I heard the tiny voice somewhere in the back of my mind, but I was too far gone to make out what it was.

"Mama."

Savannah pulled back, panting with wide eyes. "Aiden," she said as if, she too, realized what that noise was. She broke out of my hold and moved around me toward Aiden's bedroom door.

I inhaled deeply in an attempt to get my shit together.

"He must've had another nightmare," Savannah mumbled.

Before she entered the room, I caught her by the hand. "Next week is the Air Force Ball."

She squinted. "You want me to go with you."

"Of course. You're my wife."

"O-okay," she muttered before turning away from me to tend to Aiden, who called for her again.

I ran my hand through my hair, stopping myself from going into that room with her. They had each other. They didn't need my help.

I was supposed to be working toward forgetting Savannah. Not getting caught up with her and her son. That's all this was.

Me exorcising her from my system.

I had four and a half more months to let her go. That was it. I reminded myself of that repeatedly as I changed and headed down to my basement for a late workout.

CHAPTER 11

*S*avannah

I stared at myself in the floor-length mirror, turning from side to side to observe all angles of my body. The silver one-shoulder, A-line dress I wore went past my ankles. Every move of my leg left the dress flowing a little and exposed a portion of my thigh as the dress contained a high split.

That evening was the ball, and I was Ace's date for the night.

I smiled at my reflection, enjoying how the silver dress glinted against my coffee complexion.

"You look pretty," Aiden said from the doorway of Ace's bedroom.

"Thanks, baby."

He rolled his eyes. "I'm not a baby anymore." He pouted as he entered the room with his shoulders slumped.

I refrained from telling him how much like a baby he looked when he poked his bottom lip out like that.

"I'm sorry. I forgot."

"Get used to it, kid," Ace said as he stepped into the doorway. "Mothers will always let you know you're still their baby." His grey eyes shifted over to me, and he gave me a genuine smile.

I'd been on the receiving end of more of those since that encounter in my office two weeks earlier.

"But I'm nine years old," Aiden whined.

"You'll still be my baby when you're fifty," I told him.

He gave me the most dramatic sigh, making both Ace and me laugh. Our eyes connected for a moment, but we shared something in that brief exchange.

Not for the first time that night, I let my eyes travel down the length of Ace's body. He looked damn good in his dress blues. The uniform fit him perfectly, and each ribbon, or signifier of his accomplishments within the Air Force, left me a little in awe.

A pang of sadness filled my belly also.

Seeing him in the uniform reminded me of all of the years that I'd missed with him. We were high schoolers when he dreamed about being a pilot. I'd envisioned being there as he went through his training and early days in the military.

Yet, I wasn't present for any of it.

"Does that button mean you were in a war?" Aiden asked, pulling me out of my thoughts. He pointed at one of the badges on the left side of Ace's chest.

Ace looked down at Aiden and tapped the silver wings. "These symbolize my position as an Air Force pilot." He moved closer, stooping low to give Aiden a better view.

"Can I touch them?" My son asked.

"Aiden," I called.

But Ace looked up at me. "It's okay. Sure you can."

Aiden ran his finger against the emblem that Ace worked so hard to achieve.

"So cool," Aiden whispered.

Ace told him a little more about what the different ribbon stripes and metal emblems on his suit meant. Aiden's attention was glued to him the entire time. My throat tightened up with emotion from watching the interactions between them.

Ace was so good with him. He patiently answered every question Aiden had.

I cleared my throat. "Melissa will be here soon. We should probably head downstairs."

Ace nodded at the same time the doorbell rang.

"There she is," I said.

Melissa was a babysitter that Ace's squadron member, Maple, and his wife Sabrina, often used. She would pick up Aiden and take him over to Maple and Sabrina's home, a few blocks away, to watch all of the kids together.

"Do you have to stay out all night, Mama?" Aiden asked as we walked down the hall.

I heard the worry in his voice. Pausing, I turned to get closer to him. "What's wrong, sweetie? You don't want me to go out?"

The ball was being hosted at a resort hotel down in San Antonio, about a thirty-minute drive away. Ace had chosen to rent a room for the night. A thought that both excited me and made me nervous.

He nodded vigorously. "I do. Mr. Ace needs you to be his date, but it's just that..." He peered down the hall as if making sure Ace wasn't around. "What if I fall asleep and have another nightmare?" he whispered.

I heard Ace open the door to let Melissa in.

"Sweetie, have you been having more nightmares?" Aiden hadn't woken up in a few days from another bad as far as I knew.

"No, but what if I do over there? Everyone will think I'm a baby."

I shook my head. "No one will think that," I assured. "Listen, if you get scared, you know you can always call me. No matter what time it is. If you need me to come and pick you up, I will be there, no questions asked." I cupped his chin. "Okay?"

He glanced over his shoulder downstairs before nodding.

I stood and watched as my son turned and headed down to meet the babysitter. I wondered about his nightmares. He always said he couldn't remember any of them, but a part of me questioned whether he was honest about that.

"Ready?" Ace asked, once Melissa and Aiden headed out. He held out his arm for me to take.

I wrapped the black shawl I wore around my shoulders and took his arm. We fell in step with one another as we walked to the car.

"Aiden's right, by the way," Ace said as he held the car door open for me. "You look beautiful." A genuine compliment. I could tell from the sparkle in his eyes.

"Thank you." My voice sounded breathy. We'd shared multiple kisses since that day at the clinic. The slow, lingering kind that always left me wanting more. Something had shifted in our relationship. We'd gone from resentment-filled ships passing in the night, at times bumping into one another, to a more relaxed state.

We talked casually as we drove to the hotel. Ace told me about his different squadron members and the women and men that made up his flight crew.

"There are three female pilots in your squadron?"

He nodded. "Snake, Piper and Lockjaw."

"Not their real names," I said.

He chuckled and shook his head. "I sometimes forget we have real names."

"I bet."

"Now that you've performed as Flight Lead for your unit and been doing what you love for a while, are you as big a fan of Captain Kirk's style of leadership?"

"One hundred percent."

I rolled my eyes. "Of course you are."

Ace had a lot in common with the famed *Star Trek* captain. He was charismatic when he wanted to be, good-looking as hell, loyal. But he could break rank and buck against tradition when he felt it was right.

He'd done precisely that by asking me to marry him when we were only eighteen.

The conversation was easy between us.

When we arrived at the hotel, there was a stream of guests entering the main entrance, obviously heading toward the ball. It was hard to miss all of the navy-blue uniforms.

"Thank you for agreeing to come with me tonight," Ace said as he helped me out of the truck.

"I wouldn't miss an opportunity to see this up close," I joked. I swallowed down my unease when my mind reminded me that part of the reason Ace invited me was to be able to show those in the upper ranks that he was a "family man."

He hadn't answered me that day in the park when I accused him of using our marriage to gain an advantage in his quest for the instructor position. But deep down, I knew it was true. That, and he wanted to forget me. The only reason he was holding out to sign those divorce papers.

I glanced around the room, taken aback by how beautiful it was. The theme was apparently *A Midsummer Night's Dream*, since we were entering the final weeks of the summer. Along the walls of the room were imitation tree limbs outfitted with hanging candles. The candles, instead of the ceiling's overhead fixture, provided light throughout the ballroom. White tea candles lit each table, accompanied by vases filled with flowers that were unique to Texas.

"Looking good, Cannon," another airman commented behind us.

"I always look good," Ace said to his friend.

Ace briefly introduced me to Ted, who was a member of his squadron's flight crew.

"Been a part of the flight crew for years," Ted said to me. "Tried to get this guy to take me up for a flight, but he no longer flies the F-35s. Chump."

Ace snorted and laughed.

"It sucks not being able to take one of the crew up in a flight," he told me once Ted and his date moved on.

"Because the F-16 is only a single-seater, right?" I asked to make sure I had it right.

He smirked. "Right. I used to do it once or twice a year in the F-35. It helps lift their spirits."

"How so?" I asked, interested.

"Without them, we can't do our job. Some crew teams spend years working to make sure we're as safe as possible. It's nice to get to show them what they spend hours working on from the air." He got a gleam in his eye. "Nothing looks the same once you've experienced it from fifty-thousand feet."

"Is it everything you thought it would be?" I thought about the times he'd taken me to that overlook to watch planes fly in and out of the base.

"Almost everything." His gaze dropped to meet mine.

A crackle in the air vibrated around us.

I was the first to break eye contact. "It's lovely in here. Whoever decorated did a great job with the theme."

"Why, thank you," a female voice commented.

I turned, and my smile dropped before I could help myself. "Rachel," I commented. Of course, she was the one in charge of setting up the decor.

Ace and Rachel's husband, Mike, greeted one another.

"It's stunning in here. You should be proud," I told Rachel.

It was Ace's and his fellow Airmen and women's night. There was no need for me to be catty.

"Well." She waved her hand like she was a contestant on Miss America. "I can't take all of the credit. Most of the other wives helped out also." She looked me up and down as if to ask where I had been when they needed help.

A few more Airmen approached our group with their dates for the evening. Eventually, Ace, Mike, and the rest excused themselves to talk amongst the rest of their squadron, leaving Rachel and me and a few other women.

More of Rachel's friends trickled in. They talked about how difficult it had been to find particular decor to match one another and all types of stuff I didn't care too much about.

"Look at Sheila," Rachel said to a blond-haired woman standing beside her. "She's draped all over Conner like he still wants her. Everybody knows he's got one foot out of the door."

"So pathetic," the other woman said.

Two of the other women nodded.

"And what is it that you do, Savannah?" Rachel asked, staring in my direction.

All of a sudden, I became the focal point of the group.

"I mean, we tried to get Cannon to give us your number so that we could invite you on as part of the decorating committee." She flipped her hair over her shoulder. "But Mike told me you work during the day."

"That's right." I took a sip from the champagne flute in my hand that Ace grabbed for me from a passing waiter before he left. "I'm a PA."

"A personal assistant?" one of the women asked.

"Well, you got the assistant part right," another voice answered for me.

I gritted my teeth when Tricia appeared next to her cousin. She gave me a smug smile. "The P stands for physician. Savannah is a physician assistant, isn't that right?" she asked like she already knew the answer.

"Yes, it is." I took another sip of champagne and glanced around the room.

"So, you're not actually a doctor?" Rachel asked.

The urge to smack her and her cousin overcame me. I had a lot of regrets in life. It took a while to get over the fact that I never went to medical school as planned. But being a physician assistant was the right job for me. I knew it.

Yet the snobbish way Rachel hurled her question in my direction with Tricia watching with a glint in her hazel eyes pissed me off. Old feelings of not being good enough resurfaced.

"I bet you two were the mean girls in your high school, huh?" I blurted out. "The ones who got whatever or whoever they wanted?" I paused and looked at Tricia up and down with the same disgust she threw at me. "Too bad neither one of you ever grew up."

I rolled my eyes and held up my empty glass. "I need a refill. Excuse me."

"Simple bitches," I grumbled underneath my breath as I walked away.

By the time I made it halfway across the room, Ace had approached me with a wrinkle in his forehead.

"Hey." He glanced over my shoulder, his eyes narrowing. "Did she say something to you?"

"Nothing of importance." I shook my head. It was apparent what game Tricia was playing.

"Are you sure? I'd handle her if she disrespected you."

My stomach muscles tensed at hearing the protectiveness in his voice.

"We won't allow her to ruin our night." Up until that point, I hadn't thought of it as *our* night. Ace had needed a date for the ball, and though he'd been much nicer about it than with the picnic earlier in the summer, he still assumed that I'd attend with him. To keep up the charade.

"Let's dance," I suggested.

He slowly brought his gaze from over my shoulder down to meet mine, and nodded.

He took me into his arms like he'd done so many times in the past. We naturally fit together, as if I were made to fit perfectly against him.

When he lowered his arm to my waist and brought us closer together, I inhaled the woodsy scent of his cologne. He hadn't worn cologne much when we were younger, but this scent suited him. It reminded me of the grown man he'd become, older, more mature, and accomplished.

I lifted my arms to his shoulders and glanced up to find him staring down at me. Our eyes locked. As cliché as it sounds, everyone else in the room fell away. It was only Ace and me, standing there, holding one another, dancing to the instrumental music in the background.

"What's that smile about?" I asked.

"This isn't the typical pop music you listen to."

I let out a laugh and shrugged. "It's not my party. I didn't have a say in the music. But it'll do, I guess."

"As long as you don't ask me to sing for you," he said, smirking.

"Would you if I asked?" I lifted my eyebrows, hopeful.

"Hell no."

We both laughed at that.

A doozy of a memory came back to mind as I laid my head against his chest.

* * *

THEN

I belted out the lyrics of Mariah Carey's "We Belong Together" as I browned the ground beef in the frying pan. I shook and swayed in time with the music, turning it up to drown out the sound of my voice.

I wasn't a singer by any means, but I loved dancing and singing while cooking. My mother always said the food tasted better when prepared by someone who made it with joy.

To me, that meant dancing and singing.

Suddenly, I heard a deep chuckle behind me. I spun on my heels and quickly lost my balance, forgetting that, due to my new body, my equilibrium was still off.

"Oh, shit," I screeched as I reached for the counter to my left to steady myself.

Ace made it to me before I could get ahold of it. His strong arms came around my waist, preventing my fall.

"Phew." I blew out a breath and held my belly with one hand while I rested the other on Ace's shoulder.

"Careful, baby. Are you all right?" he asked, concern marking the creases in his eyebrows.

I nodded and smiled. "I'm fine." I tapped my belly. "This little guy just throws off my balance sometimes."

Ace placed a loving hand against my five months' pregnant belly. "As long as my two favorite people are okay."

"You scared me." I slapped his shoulder. "I told you about secretly watching me while I'm dancing."

That grin that always made my lower belly flutter appeared on his face. Not for the first time, I stared into his grey eyes and wondered how in the hell I'd lucked up enough to have been fortunate to marry this man.

His eyes glittered in mischief. "I'm going to be watching you dance in the kitchen when we're eighty years old."

Those butterflies in my stomach turned to full on quaking, and it wasn't from our son kicking me. Ace planted a kiss on my lips.

"How was work?"

He frowned and shrugged. "Boring as usual." His eyes roved over my shoulder. "What's for dinner?"

"Spaghetti."

His shoulders dropped. "Again?"

"Don't say it like that," I chirped. I moved to the stove and removed the lid from the frying pan. "Tonight, we have ground beef. I splurged a little at the grocery store today."

Ace loved beef. He could eat steak every day, but with our tight budget, we couldn't afford that. We'd had spaghetti at least three times within the last two weeks. I always gave the leftovers to him the next day for lunch at work. It was a cheap and easy meal to make.

"Thanks, babe," he said, his hand moving to grasp my ass and squeeze it.

"Taste the sauce and let me know if it needs anything," I said as I moved to turn the volume down on the radio I'd placed on the windowsill.

Ace used the wooden spoon and tasted the sauce that was bubbling in the saucepan. "Little more oregano."

I topped the sauce off with some more oregano and turned it low before putting the pasta water on to boil.

"I love this song." It was The Pussycat Dolls' "Don't Cha."

I shimmied and shook around Ace, making him laugh out loud. I loved the sound of his laughter more than anything.

"Dance with me," I encouraged when he just stood there. Not waiting for him, I took his hand into mine and twirled around, rubbing my backside against his front, dipping it low.

"If you go too low, you won't be able to get back up," he joked at the same time his hand came around to tap my belly.

I tossed my head back against his chest, laughing. "You're probably right."

I flicked my left hand in the air, and out of the corner of my eye, I saw something go flying. I heard it as it cracked against the ground.

I glanced down at my hand, and my mouth dropped open when I saw the cubic zirconia from my engagement ring had fallen out.

"The hell?" Ace groaned as he took my hand in his, peering down at the

ring. He searched the beat-up tiles of our kitchen floor and found the stone lying right next to the garbage can in the corner. "Son of a bitch," he said as he picked it up.

"It's okay." I went to reach for the stone.

"It's not," he retorted. The pinch in his forehead between his eyebrows signaled his anger. "This damn stone shouldn't have come out like that. Fuck. I'm sorry, Savannah."

"Hey." I cupped his face in between my hands. "I said it's fine." I shook his face a little. "Really. It's just a ring."

"I'm going to get it fixed first thing in the morning."

"No." I shook my head. "We need to save that money. Between classes for next semester and rent and our hope of buying a new car once AJ is born, the last thing we need to spend money on is this ring."

Ace pushed out a hefty breath, his shoulders slumping. He stared down at me.

I hated the look on his face. Ace was always protective over me. I could see that he felt like he wasn't doing his job as my husband.

"When I'm done with school, and I finally get my wings, I'm gonna buy you the biggest diamond I can find," he promised, not for the first time.

I placed his free hand against my belly while I placed my other hand on his chest.

"As long as my two favorite people are okay, I'm okay," I said.

He smiled. It was a slight grin, but it was there.

"Finish dancing with me." I held out my arms.

He stuffed the stone in the pocket of his jeans and took the lead, per usual, sweeping me into his arms.

"You know what would make me feel better?" I said after a while.

"What?"

My smile widened. "Sing for me."

He groaned and tilted his head skyward.

"You want me to feel better, right?" I asked with a mock pout.

"What happened to 'as long as my favorite two people are okay, I'm okay'?"

I laughed. "What happened to 'I'll do anything for you'?" I retorted, reminding him of the many times he'd said that.

111

He squinted. "I don't remember that being a part of the vows."

"They were. Right after you called me your forever," I lied and giggled.

He groaned again.

"Come on. The baby likes it when you sing." I poked him with my belly for good measure.

Ace had a beautiful singing voice, even if he hated admitting it. His mother had taken him to lessons when he was a little boy after she discovered he could sing. By the time he turned twelve, she had allowed him to quit, but he sang for me once on our six-month anniversary date.

Ever since then, I was a sucker for his voice.

"I doubt he can even hear me in there."

I shrugged. "Well, I like it when you sing, and what I like, the baby likes."

He frowned. "You liked that spicy chili dog you had last week, but from what I recall, AJ didn't respond too well to it."

It was my turn to groan. "Don't remind me." I was up half of the night after eating that damn chili dog with gas and heartburn.

"Sing. Please," I pleaded.

"What song?"

"*NSYNC, 'God Must've Spent a Little More Time.'"

He sang it for me once before, and I cried like a baby.

He inhaled deeply and started on a hum before singing the first lyrics. My entire body lit up as he sang. To me, he sounded even better than Justin Timberlake or JC Chasez.

If he hadn't had his heart set on becoming a fighter pilot in the Air Force, I would've encouraged him to go into music.

Ace looked me directly in the eyes when he sang that God must've spent a little more time on you. My vision blurred from the tears. They streamed down my face as he continued singing.

I laid my head again his chest and knew I was soaking his shirt from my tears. This always happened when he sang. I closed my eyes and felt the vibrations in his chest as he sang.

I knew that we'd be singing and dancing just like this when we were eighty years old.

When the song was over, I lifted my head.

Ace swiped a few tears with his thumb.

"You're such a crybaby." He chuckled.

"It's your fault." I sniffled and wiped the tears away.

"You are the love of my life," he said. It was the same comment he'd made every day in the seven months that we'd been married.

He leaned down and kissed me with all the passion he had in his body. A blanket of heated desire started at the top of my head and raced down the length of my body. My knees would've buckled if he hadn't held me up.

His hands slid down to my hips, pulling me into his hardness.

"Wait." I pulled back.

He grunted, obviously not liking that.

"I have to turn the food off."

I knew where this was going, and the last thing we could afford was to burn up our dinner because we'd gotten too carried away having sex.

I turned off the two burners that were still going.

"Where were we?" I turned back to Ace, lifting my arms to his shoulders again.

"Right here," he said as he lifted my legs to wrap around his waist.

He was so strong that he picked me up like I weighed nothing. Even with the extra weight of my pregnancy, he didn't flinch as he carried me down to our bedroom. Ace worked out six days a week as part of his regimen to get and stay in shape for his future career in the military.

We spent half of that night in bed. If I hadn't already been five months pregnant, that night would've done it.

Or any night since we'd married, honestly.

The pregnancy had been an accident. I was on birth control but forgot to take the pills for a couple of days. And Ace and I were like two jackrabbits. I supposed it was inevitable, and after the initial shock and fear calmed down, I didn't have any regrets.

I knew we'd be happy together forever.

CHAPTER 12

*S*avannah
"What are you thinking about?" His deep voice pulled me out of the memory.

A pang in my chest started, realizing that we weren't that young, innocent, and hopeful couple we used to be. For years, I managed to suppress my desire to go back to those days. We were young and struggling to keep our heads above water financially, but every time I looked into my husband's eyes, the fears fell away.

I didn't know how it all would work out, but I didn't doubt that Ace would do everything in his power to fix whatever the problem was.

That was, until I realized his biggest problem was me.

I pasted on a phony smile. "Just enjoying how beautiful this decor is," I said, glancing around the ballroom, mainly to avoid looking him in the eye.

He stopped moving.

"Your nostrils are flaring."

That stupid tell of mine. I thought I'd broken out of that habit. But then again, nobody in my life had ever watched me as closely as Ace.

No one had ever brought up to me that my nostrils flared when I lied. Not until him.

"I—"

"Jane. Jane, what's the matter?" A man's shrill, scared voice blasted me out of whatever story I was about to make up.

I glanced around and found a couple standing not too far from us. The Airmen wore the same uniform as Ace, while the woman with him wore a black ball gown.

He called her name again, his voice cracking that time.

I looked over at Ace. "Call 9-11." I gave him the order before heading over to the couple.

"Jane, talk to me," the older Airman called again as I reached them.

"Sir, what's wrong?" I asked.

He looked at me with worried eyes. "My wife. She's babbling, and I can't understand what she's saying."

I looked toward the woman who appeared to be in her early to mid-fifties. "Ma'am, my name is Savannah. I'm a physician assistant. Can you do me a favor and recite the ABCs?"

She opened her mouth and a slur of incoherent babblings poured out. Before I could ask her my next question, she stumbled. Her husband and I both took either side of her and guided her over to an empty chair.

Once she sat, I kneeled in front of her.

"Jane, can you smile for me?" I asked.

She attempted a smile, and my stomach dropped when I saw only half of her mouth move upward. I looked up to my right and saw Ace on the phone standing over me.

"Is that 9-11?"

He nodded.

"Sir," I turned to the woman's husband. "How old is your wife?"

"She just celebrated her fifty-third birthday last week."

I nodded. "Can you tell me how Jane was feeling today? How was she when you arrived?" I asked him, looking between the couple.

"She said she was feeling a little lightheaded when we arrived. I

115

thought that was because she forgot to eat." He paced a little. "You're always forgetting to eat, honey."

"And how long ago was that?" I asked, bringing his attention back to me.

"How long ago was what?"

"When you arrived, how long ago?"

"Uh, around eight, I think."

I looked at the time on my watch. "Okay, that was thirty minutes ago." I patted Jane's hand, getting her to look at me. "You're going to be all right, okay?" I encouraged. "Help is on the way."

I stood and took the phone from Ace. "Hello?"

"Ma'am," the operator said.

"Yes, we have an emergency. Jane…" I glanced over at the lapel on the man's breast pocket. "Caldwell." I assumed her last name was the same as his. "Jane Caldwell, age fifty-three. She's unable to recite her ABCs. Only half of her face is mobile. Husband says she began experiencing symptoms about thirty minutes ago."

I relayed all the information to the operator, knowing she would feed whatever I gave her to the paramedics that were on the way.

"Is she breathing?"

"Yes, but it's shallow. How far out are the 'medics?"

"Three minutes," the operator responded.

"They'll need to take her to Sam Welles Memorial. It's the closest hospital," I instructed, as if I had any say over the matter. I already knew Welles had the best facilities to handle what I highly suspected to be a stroke.

"It's going to be okay, Mrs. Caldwell," I told her again. Her eyelids started to droop. "Here." I gave the phone back to Ace and helped Mrs. Caldwell's husband lower her to the ground when she began slumping even more, unable to support her body weight in the seated position.

I checked for a pulse and was relieved when I found it. Again, I took the phone from Ace and told the operator Mrs. Caldwell's beats per minute.

It probably felt longer than it was before the paramedics arrived. There was an outbreak of movement around me once they did. All of the guests paused to watch as the paramedics loaded her onto the stretcher.

Her husband fell in line at her side, and I rushed behind the stretcher, telling them all of the details I could think of to give them the best information I could.

I stood outside of the ambulance as they loaded her and her husband inside and pulled off. I said a silent prayer that they got her to the hospital fast enough to get the necessary tests.

"Is she going to be okay?"

I turned and saw Ace standing beside me. A few people had piled outside of the door, watching the ambulance disappear into the distance.

"Hope so." I sighed. "It's been less than an hour since her symptoms started, and the hospital is nearby."

He lifted an eyebrow.

I shrugged. "There's no way to be certain without a CT, but I think she's having a stroke. Her husband said she wasn't on any medications. If the hospital responds as quickly as I think they will, they'll be able to diagnose and treat her within the window. She should have a good chance of making it through this."

I stared in the direction the ambulance took. It had disappeared, and I could no longer hear the sirens.

Ace reached out and pulled me to his side. I glanced up at him.

"Ready to go back inside?"

I nodded.

He held me close as we walked back inside the ballroom. A few of the other Airmen and their spouses patted me on the arm, either thanking me for my quick reaction or giving me a smile of appreciation.

It felt odd. I was simply doing what I'd been trained to do.

The rest of the evening went by in a sort of a blur. Half of my mind was still on Jane Caldwell and her prognosis. The other half of my brain felt as if it were malfunctioning from how closely Ace held me the rest of the night.

Even when we weren't dancing, he kept his arm around my waist or his hand on my arm, keeping me near. He never failed to introduce me as his wife to the rest of his squadron or his commanders.

Toward the end of the night, the higher-ranking officers gave out a series of awards to different Airmen. I clapped the loudest when Ace was acknowledged. He was recognized for his abilities as flight lead in his squadron and for being a team player, stepping up when necessary.

"Congratulations," I said as he returned to the table.

He gave me a brilliant smile that made the heat low in my belly burn hotter.

"Aiden's going to ask you a million questions about that now." I laughed and dipped my head toward the award in his hand.

"He can have it." He said it like the acknowledgment wasn't a big deal. It wasn't an official Air Force medal, but I knew it was special to have those around you acknowledge the work you put in.

"No," I said, placing my hand on his wrist. "It is a big deal. Really."

He peered down at me, and all of a sudden, the air around us crackled with electricity. That same feeling of being the only two people in the room came over me again. The sparkle in Ace's eyes told me that he felt it, too.

"It's time to go," he said in a low voice full of something that caused my nipples to harden.

I held my hand out for him to take. It was time to leave.

* * *

Ace

I wanted Savannah more than my next breath. Ever since I first saw her in that dress, I pictured her with it pooled around her ankles.

I secretly congratulated myself for making reservations at the hotel weeks in advance.

The hotel door slammed behind me and I whirled on Savannah. Her eyes were round and big, and she bit her bottom lip, a tentative expression as if she didn't know what to expect.

I took her into my arms, pulling her to me, and swayed our bodies, dancing. Though, there wasn't any music.

"What were you thinking about earlier?" I asked, placing my forehead against hers.

She tilted her head to the side.

"Right before Major Caldwell's wife got sick," I reminded her.

Her mind had taken her somewhere. I'd watched the far-off look invade her face, and I wanted to know what memory it was that made her face soften and let out the wisp of a smile I saw.

She rubbed her lips together as she looked over my shoulder. "That day in the kitchen when my engagement ring fell apart."

My insides tightened. That fucking ring.

"You were singing for me while we danced," she said before I could become too caught up in the thought about that ring.

I pressed a kiss to her forehead. I felt her shiver as she'd always done when I kissed her in that same spot.

"I'm proud of you, too," I told her.

She pulled back, blinking. "Why?"

I frowned. "What do you mean, why?" I asked. "The way you jumped into action to help Major Caldwell's wife."

She shrugged. "I was just doing my job."

"Exactly. Your job is saving lives and taking care of people."

I'd worked under the Major for some years but had never seen the look of fear in his eyes that I saw that night when he gawked at his ailing wife.

Savannah had helped ease his worries by taking over. Even with the other medical Air Force personnel in the room, she took control of the situation.

"If you get to tell me you're proud of me, then I get to return the favor," I said before leaning down to kiss her.

I brushed my tongue against her bottom lip, savoring the hint of wine she had with dinner. I lowered my hands and intertwined my fingers with hers before lifting her hands overhead.

I held out arms like that as I slowly walked our bodies back in the direction of the bedroom. With a kick of my leg, I pushed our way through the bedroom door and walked Savannah to the bed, her hands still suspended over her head.

"Don't move them," I instructed, looking her in the eyes.

Slowly, I spun her around so that her back was to me. I pulled the zipper of her dress down as if I were unwrapping a present on Christmas morning. The last time we had sex, it was heated and rushed, filled with anger.

This time, I wanted to savor it. Despite myself, a growing part of me wanted to remember these moments with Savannah.

"Lower your hands," I whispered in her ear from behind as I pushed the sides of her dress down her shoulders and arms.

I trailed my fingers down her back before I raised my hands again to undo the clasp of her strapless bra. It popped open as if revealing a gift to me. I greedily received it, wrapping my arms around her from behind and squeezing her ample breasts.

Savannah moaned and dropped the back of her head against my chest. Her boobs were always a sensitive spot for her.

I squeezed one nipple and then the other. Her moans grew louder. Leaning in, I dropped a kiss to her shoulder before moving lower. I licked my way up her back to her neck, then sucked the skin behind her ear between my lips.

Her moan turned into a groan, and she shivered. Before I could continue perusing her body with my mouth, Savannah spun around and started unbuttoning my uniform.

Her hands moved quickly, the look of hunger in her eyes likely mirroring my own. I let her strip me out of my jacket, shirt, and tie, leaving the top half of my body exposed. She ran her hands over my chest, fingering the strands of hair that resided there.

Meanwhile, I pushed her dress to the floor before moving to relieve her of her panties.

"I hope you weren't planning on getting to sleep anytime soon," I growled. "This won't be over quickly." I took both of her wrists in one hand, bringing her hands behind her back.

"It'd better not be over fast," she said breathlessly.

I leaned in and kissed her again before pushing her to the bed.

With my free hand, I reached between her legs, checking to see if she was ready. A sound between a growl and a moan came out of my mouth. The feel of the wetness between her thighs brought alive something animalistic inside of me.

"Ace..." she moaned with a lost, begging look in her eyes.

I had no choice but to answer that call. I peeled out of the rest of my clothing and pulled out my wallet, opening it with one hand.

The condom wrapper stood no chance against my rush to get inside of Savannah. Once sheathed, I brought her legs to wrap around my hips as I hovered above her. One final look was all the notice I gave before leaning in, licking her lips, and then thrusting inside of her, all in one move.

Savannah's back bowed almost entirely off the bed. I should've been more patient, given her more time to adjust to me, but my patience was hanging by a thin thread.

Still, I didn't move for long seconds, waiting to gauge Savannah's reaction to my invasion.

"Ace, it's okay. You can...you can," she said, out of breath.

That was all I needed to pull almost all of the way out before surging back in again. God, she felt so fucking good.

"Fuck." I didn't have the words to verbalize everything that ran through my body. Instead of talking, I lifted her legs from my waist to my shoulders. I hugged her thighs to my chest with both arms and pushed in even deeper, over and over.

Savannah dug her fingernails into my arms. I didn't feel any pain—only pure bliss from being inside her once again.

I released her thighs and positioned her legs back over my shoulders before leaning down. Savannah immediately sat up and wrapped her arms around my neck, pulling me into a kiss.

I allowed the feelings of joy that I'd done my best to suppress the last time I had her in this position to bubble to the surface. I stared down at Savannah, and only two words came to mind.

My wife.

Those two words shook me down to the depths of my soul, and I roared out my orgasm. Every inch of my body was overwhelmed with warmth. It almost entirely pushed out the coldness that'd settled around my heart for a decade and a half. Since the day she walked out on me.

This is only temporary.

My subconscious, evidently the more rational part of my brain, reminded me. Whatever this was between Savannah and me wouldn't last beyond the next few months. She'd come back to Harlington for one reason only: a divorce.

Even as her pussy muscles tightened around my cock, I fought to hold on to that knowledge. Savannah didn't want this marriage to go beyond the next few months.

Neither did I.

My one goal was to forget her.

"Ace," she crooned out my name while her body shivered from the aftershocks of her orgasm. The sound of her calling my name during sex was too familiar.

Too intimate. It had me slipping back into something that I promised I would never fall back into.

She gasped as I withdrew from her. Her eyes, half-closed, watched me as I pushed away from the bed in the direction of the bathroom.

I slammed the door shut and pressed a palm to the wall, forcing myself to gather my fraught emotions. I'd done a ton of shit since Savannah left me. I made it through college, Air Force ROTC, pilot training, and had seen combat.

But none of it stripped me bare the way being inside of her did.

"Pull your shit together, Cannon," I mumbled to myself.

With a deep inhale, I pulled myself up and grabbed a washcloth before heading back out to the bedroom. I didn't say anything as I cleaned both our bodies and climbed back into bed.

Savannah remained quiet as well, but I could feel her unease. She wanted to talk, but I wasn't ready for any of it.

"Sleep," I mumbled, wrapping my arm around her from behind. I made sure to keep our bodies separated while still holding onto her.

I fell into a restless sleep.

CHAPTER 13

Ace

I followed the smell of frying bacon down from the bedroom into the kitchen. It was a few days after the Air Force Ball and rarely had a night passed that I didn't find myself inside of Savannah. That is, the nights when I was home from work.

The more I touched, felt, and was inside of her, the more I wanted to be.

Which felt like the opposite of what should've been happening.

At least I had the entire day off. Savannah and Aiden would be at work and school, and I could do whatever I wanted.

I planned to head over to Joel's to spend the day riding my horse and helping out on the ranch.

"Morning," Savannah hummed as she turned from the stove.

I did my best to ignore the way my stomach filled with warmth from the sight of her smile.

"'Mornin'," I returned with a nod.

"I hope you're hungry. Chocolate chip pancakes, bacon, and eggs."

"Not spaghetti?" I teased, somehow falling into an easy banter, despite my desire to keep my emotional distance.

She turned and winked at me over her shoulder.

Dammit. There went those fucking butterflies again.

"I never forced you to eat spaghetti for breakfast."

"No. You just made me take leftovers every day," I replied.

She waved her hand, holding the spatula in the air. "You complain, but you secretly loved my spaghetti."

"I like spaghetti!" Aiden said as he ran into the kitchen.

"I know you do, buddy," Savannah said. "Come here. Smell check." She waved him over with her hand.

Aiden groaned. "Really? I'm not a little kid."

I watched with a grin as Savannah folded her arms and lifted her eyebrow, giving him a stern face. Aiden groaned again but marched over to Savannah. She bent low and sniffed behind his ears.

"Open," she ordered.

Aiden opened his mouth wide.

"Blow."

He blew out a breath.

"Mm. Minty fresh. You passed the sniff test. Good job. Go get your plate."

Aiden turned to me and rolled his eyes as if to say, *can you believe her?* A laugh spilled from my lips. I knew more than anyone how dirty little boys could be. I hated showering and washing up after coming inside or in the mornings. My mother always had to drag me into the shower or bathtub.

Joel would threaten me with whooping my ass with his belt to get me to listen. He never used it, though. His threats were incentive enough.

"Are you having breakfast with us, Mr. Ace?" Aiden asked.

"Yeah, guess so."

"Sweet," Aiden cheered.

"Aiden, don't pummel Ace with a million and one questions about being a pilot this morning," Savannah chided as she placed his plate in front of him.

His face dropped.

I chuckled. "It's not a problem, kid. Few things I like talking about more than being a pilot. Ask away."

"See, Mama." His face lit up as he peered at Savannah like he'd won a battle.

Savannah's phone rang before she could respond. I waved her away from the stove and took over fixing both of our plates.

She thanked me with a smile before answering.

I filled our plates with pancakes, bacon, and eggs before carrying them to the table.

"I would, but I don't have anyone to watch Aiden," Savannah said to whomever was on the other end of the line. "Are you sure?" Regret filled her voice. "Okay, bye."

I glanced over when she hung up. "What's up?"

"That was work." She twisted her lips in a disappointed frown. "Dr. Pierce had an emergency with another patient and won't be able to open the clinic this morning. That was Reese calling to see if I could come in an hour earlier than usual, but..." She trailed off and gestured toward Aiden.

I glanced down at Aiden as he cheerfully ate, staring at his tablet that sat on the table, playing some cartoon on the screen.

"What time does he have to be at school?" I asked.

Savannah's eyes went over to the clock on the wall. "Nine thirty. He has a delayed opening this morning."

It was a little before seven-thirty. Aiden's school was only a seven-minute drive from my house.

I shrugged. "I can take him."

Savannah perked up, but then shook her head. "I can't ask you to do that."

"You didn't ask." I reminded. "I'm volunteering."

"You don't have to go to the base today?"

With a shake of my head, I told her, "Took the day off since I have to head out for a two-week training next week. Didn't have much planned until later. I might head over to Joel's later."

Her eyebrows lifted. "Joel..." There was something strange in the way she said his name. She glanced between Aiden and me. "Are you sure it wouldn't be an inconvenience?"

The urge to take care of her needs filled my chest again. I pushed those feelings down and reminded myself this was no big deal. The boy's school was only a few minutes away, and I wasn't doing much of anything for the day.

"Okay." She let out a sigh. "Thank you so much." She went over to Aiden and rubbed the back of his head.

He looked up from his tablet.

"Sweetie, I have to go to work early." She glanced up at me. "Mr. Ace is going to take you to school this morning, all right?"

Aiden nodded. "Mm-hm."

"I'll be there to pick you up, as usual." She kissed his forehead. "Be good. I love you."

"Love you too, Mama."

I looked away, a burning pain pushing through my abdomen at watching the simple but delicate moment between a mother and son.

"Thank you," Savannah said, grasping my forearm before she headed out of the kitchen.

"Don't mention it," I said casually, but I had to push those three words out around the lump in my throat.

"It's just me and you, kid," I said, retaking my seat at the table to finish my breakfast.

Aiden smiled up at me, mouth full of pancakes.

"I think you're supposed to chew, then swallow," I teased as he went to stuff another forkful of pancakes into his mouth.

"They're so good," he commented. "Chocolate chip pancakes are my favorite. My second fave are pancakes with sprinkles. Have you ever had those?" he asked.

I paused, glancing upward as if trying to recall if I'd ever eaten the food he believed to be a delicacy. "No, I don't think I have."

"You should ask Mama to make them for you," Aiden recommended. "Hers are the best, I think. But she only makes them on my birthday."

"Is that right?" I asked.

He nodded. "Yup. I love pancakes."

I chuckled. "My kid brother is like you but with waffles. He only eats waffles for breakfast."

"Every day?" Aiden asked.

"Every. Day."

"Mama won't let me have the same thing every day. She says variety in food is important." He shrugged and wrinkled his forehead. "I don't know, for health or something."

I grinned and nudged with my head at the tablet. "What are you watching?"

"*The Loud House* on YouTube."

He went into great detail about the show featuring an eleven-year-old girl with ten siblings.

"I wish I had brothers and sisters," he said all of a sudden, his gaze lowering.

I cleared my throat. "I have two brothers, and the sh—it's not always all that great," I tried to reassure.

His frown deepened, and then he shrugged. "Still, I'd like a brother. I might even be okay with a sister."

I laughed.

"How come you don't have any kids?"

I almost choked on the last bite of my eggs that I'd just taken. I covered my mouth to cough up the eggs without spraying the table with them.

"Um, shit." I blinked, not remembering the time I felt this damn flustered. "Don't tell your mama I cursed."

He gave me a confused look.

"Anyway, how did you sleep?" A change in the subject was what was needed.

I thought it was a safe topic until he dropped his gaze, unable to look me in the eye any longer.

"What's up, kid?"

He hesitated before asking, "Are you ever afraid to fall asleep?"

I cocked my head to the side. "Scared? Like someone's going to get you in your sleep?"

A slight lift and lowering of his shoulders accompanied his response. "Maybe. But more like, I'm scared of my brain." He paused. "I have nightmares sometimes," he whispered.

I remembered a few times Savannah mentioned that Aiden had trouble sleeping and the few times he yelled for her late at night. Savannah said he always told her he couldn't remember the dreams when she asked him about them.

"Do you know what the nightmares are about?"

His eyes welled up with unshed tears. He nodded.

I leaned in, covering his hand with my much larger one, and squeezed. "Nightmares aren't anything to be ashamed of. I used to have killer dreams when I was a kid," I told him. "They frightened me so much that I would run down to my parents' room and sleep in bed with them."

"They never kicked you out?"

I let out a smile. "Joel tried once or twice, but my mother told him she'd kick him out of bed before she made me go back to my room."

"Who's Joel?"

"He's my father. We call him by his first name." I shook my head. "Don't ask."

"Mama always makes me feel better after a nightmare, too."

"But you've never told her what they're about."

"No." His lips pull downward. "I'm scared someone will take her away from me," he said in a voice so low, I almost had to ask him to repeat himself.

"Who would take her from you?" I finally asked.

"I don't know." He shrugged. "But my first mom died. What if the same thing happened to Mama Savannah? I would be all by myself, and I'm only a little kid." Tears filled his eyes.

Shit.

What the hell do you say to that? I knew more than most how painful it was to lose a parent before you were ready.

"I lost my mom, too," I admitted. "I was older than you are now, but still young."

The water in Aiden's eyes spilled over and he began crying. I found myself wrapping him up in my arms and pulling him onto my lap. I stroked his hair as he soaked the front of my T-shirt with his tears.

"I can't lose my mama," he croaked out. "She saved me."

"She saved me, too," I murmured.

I held onto Aiden until he stopped crying, then I wiped away the remaining tears. I checked the clock. We had plenty of time before he needed to be at school.

"Hey, how about you head upstairs and rewash your face while I put the dishes from breakfast away," I suggested. "Then there's something cool I want to show you."

He nodded and climbed down from my lap. I quickly cleaned up the kitchen and finished just as Aiden came running down the stairs.

"Where are we going?" he asked as he followed me out to the garage to my truck.

"It's a surprise. But it's someplace I used to go when I got scared or wanted to get away from my family," I told him. "Make sure to buckle your seatbelt."

We pulled out of the driveway. It took about twenty minutes to get to my planned destination. It was a spot outside of the base, but from the overlook, it was a perfect sight to see planes coming and going.

Overhead shone a brilliant blue sky with a few puffy clouds in the air. The temps were still in the high eighties. Down below, I could make out Gaines River and the sounds of traffic from the road we'd just veered off of. But we were the only ones up at the overlook.

While my squadron had the day off from flying, I knew a different unit planned a morning flight.

"We're here," I told Aiden when I pulled open the back door of my truck and took his hand. I held onto him as we rounded to the bed of the truck and lifted him inside.

"What's this?"

"This is the best view from outside of the cockpit," I replied. "It's also the spot I brought your mom to on the first day we met." I hadn't meant to let that piece of information slip out.

I pointed at the sky right as the thunderous roar of a fighter jet could be heard in the distance.

Aiden looked up, his mouth falling open as the incoming jet rushed over our heads.

"Never gets old," I mumbled.

"What type of plane is that?" Aiden asked a few minutes later when he spotted a much larger and slower plane.

"That's the tanker," I said. "We use those to refuel while in the air."

That answer prompted Aiden to ask many questions about how we could refuel our jets while still flying.

But as I told Savannah earlier, his questions didn't bother me. I think I had more fun than he did. I even managed to pull up a video on my phone of a jet refueling mid-air.

I'd seen this very sight hundreds, if not thousands, of times before. But seeing through Aiden's eyes was like experiencing it for the first time.

"Thanks for bringing me here, Mr. Ace." He hopped off the bed of my truck to the ground. "I wish we could go get ice cream."

I stuffed my phone back into my back pocket and lifted a brow, smirking. "Ice cream? It's like..." I paused to glance at my watch and bulged my eyes. "It's almost ten o'clock."

I was supposed to have Aiden at school thirty minutes ago. "I need to get you to school."

"Aw, man." He kicked a loose rock on the ground.

"I thought you liked school."

"I do." He continued to frown. "But hanging out with you is so much more fun."

"Are you trying to butter me up, kid?"

He giggled, and it brought me to laugh also. "I'll tell you what, how about we go and get that ice cream, and I'll have you at school by lunch?"

He nodded with wide eyes and a massive grin.

I knew Savannah probably wouldn't like my decision, but I couldn't deny that I'd grown a hell of a soft spot for this kid. I didn't want to send him off to school almost as much as he didn't want to go.

Fuck it. It was only one day of school. Not even a full day, at that.

Savannah would understand, I reasoned as I drove to the ice cream shop.

"Hey, Mr. Ace?" Aiden called as we pulled into the shop.

"Yeah?" I helped him down from the truck and held onto his hand as we entered the shop.

"What did you mean when you said my Mama saved you, too?"

I stopped short and peered down at him. He stared back at me with wide eyes, waiting for me to answer his inquiry. I hadn't even realized he'd heard me say that.

I thought back to the night Savannah saved me from myself.

* * *

THEN...

Savannah

My heartbeat quickened as we drove deeper into the woods, and I heard the revving of various engines. It was almost pitch-black outside, save for a few lights from houses scattered in the distance and headlights from cars.

"Aren't you going to get in trouble for being out this late?" Kate asked from behind the wheel of her old beat-up sedan.

"Yeah," I mumbled. My grandmother would certainly have my ass if she found out that I'd snuck out. But I didn't care right then. I knew Ace was out here somewhere.

He'd been avoiding me for a few days, which was highly unlike him. Ever since he got a call from Joel on his cell and he'd dropped me off early from our date at the movies, I hadn't heard from him.

I knew something was wrong. Ace never avoided me. And we hadn't gotten into a fight.

"Did you do the old clothes in the pillowcase under the sheets trick I taught you?" Kate asked, grinning.

She'd taught me the trick over a year ago when I complained about getting caught sneaking out to meet up with Ace the first time. She still worked late most nights and would sometimes stop by my room across from hers to check in on me.

But the clothes under the bedsheet had worked since that first time.

Either way, I didn't care. I needed to see my boyfriend. After almost a year of dating and talking every day, I knew this wasn't like him. He often said I was the first thought on his mind every morning and the last before bed.

I knew it was the truth because he called me every morning and every night before bed on the secret cell phone he'd bought for me nine months earlier.

I tightened my hold on the flip phone that he'd gifted me. The same one whose calls had remained unanswered when I called him for the past two days. He hadn't shown up at school, either.

I found out from some friends of his that he planned on being out in the woods that night, along with a few other kids who were known troublemakers.

"There they are," Kate said as we finally came to a clearing off the dirt road.

I squinted, almost blinded by the headlights of a few of the cars. I recognized Ace's bloodred Nissan Skyline. His car was used, but he'd spent hours with Joel maintaining it and upgrading it.

I'd know that car anywhere, given the many times I'd spent in its backseat.

I got out of Kate's car before she even put it in park. "Ace?" I yelled, running over to the driver's side.

He looked up from his seat behind the wheel, his eyes bulging when he saw me. His reaction was immediate as he turned the car off and jumped out. "What are you doing here?"

"What the hell are you doing here?" I threw back at him. "Why haven't you answered my calls?"

His lips turned downward. "I've been busy. You shouldn't be here, Savannah."

"We shouldn't be here." I emphasized the first word of that comment. "Since when are you too busy to answer my phone calls?" My voice shook with hurt. I hated that my eyes started to sting with tears. It always pissed me off that I cried so damn easily. But the idea of Ace brushing me off hurt more than anything.

Like always, he reached up and wiped my tear away.

"You ready, Townsend?" A guy I knew by the name of Kevin interrupted us.

My stomach plummeted. Kevin was bad news. He was supposed to grad-
uate two years earlier from our school but instead got kicked out when he got
caught selling drugs to other students.

"Yeah, give me a sec," Ace commented.

I grabbed Ace by the arm. "What are you doing with him?" I whispered.
"You know he's trouble. What's going on?" I demanded.

Ace stared at the ground.

"Look at me," I demanded.

He did. "You shouldn't be here. Go home, Savannah. I'll call you later."

He pulled away from me and walked back toward his car.

I watched as he slapped fives with Kevin. He gave me one last look before
he climbed back into his car.

"What's going on?" Kate came over to ask.

"I don't know." I shrugged.

"Sean said it's a race or something."

My heartbeat sped up as I watched Ace pull off. Behind him was the car
that Kevin drove. I didn't know what was happening, and I had the feeling
that I didn't want to watch it either, but I refused to leave.

"Stand back," another boy I didn't know well said, holding out his arms as
if he was a security guard ushering a crowd away from a celebrity or event.

The rest of the onlookers pushed back to either side of the road.

Ace drove far down to one end of the dirt road, while Kevin drove in the
opposite direction. When the two cars turned to face each other at the far
ends of the road, my knees almost buckled.

"They're playing Chicken," Kate said.

My stomach dropped to my feet. I knew what this game was. A boy a year
earlier had been killed in this stupid game of seeing who would give in first.

"On your mark," one of the guys yelled, standing halfway between Ace's
and Kevin's vehicles. "Get set." He paused for theatrics. "Go!"

Engines roared.

Dirt, rocks, and dust kicked up.

And tires peeled as the two cars raced in the direction of one another.

"Please stop," I quietly begged, not wanting to watch but unable to look
away. Every inch the cars grew closer to each other, my heart sank lower.
"Please," I begged as if Ace would magically hear me and slam on his brakes.

But it was too late.

He didn't hear me. He kept going.

If one or the other didn't swerve soon, they would smash in a head-on collision. At their speeds, death was almost guaranteed.

"Noo!" I yelled as tires screeched.

Kevin was the first to give in. But it was almost too late. By the time he swerved to avoid a direct hit, Ace's car was so close that Kevin clipped Ace's car with the back of his.

That time, my knees did give out. I collapsed to the ground, confident that Ace's car would flip over, killing him on impact.

My eyes squeezed shut against that reality. Instantly, images of walking into my apartment in Georgia and seeing my mom lying on the couch, cold and not breathing, pelted my mind.

"No, no, no," I repeatedly said, trying to escape those memories. I couldn't lose another person I loved.

"Savannah, get up." Kate pulled my arm, helping me to stand back up. "He's okay," she said.

Finally, I opened my eyes to see that Ace's car was right-side up. While there was a dent on the front end, he was okay as he stepped out of the car.

I took off running in his direction. My fear and anger urged me forward, and I pushed a few of the other onlookers out of my way to get to him.

"What the hell is wrong with you?!" I shouted as I shoved him so hard, he stumbled back against his car. I was well aware of the tears streaming down my cheeks, but I didn't care.

"Are you crazy?" I demanded. "You could've killed yourself."

"Jeez," Kevin said as he came up behind me. "Dramatic much? Fucking chicks. Oof!"

I gasped as Ace stepped forward, lightning fast, and socked the hell out of Kevin. He struck him so hard, the older boy fell to the ground.

"Talk to your fucking girlfriend like that. But don't ever do it to mine," Ace growled as he stood over Kevin with his fists clenched.

I stood there, confused, trying to figure out what was happening. He would knock out Kevin without a second thought for talking to me crazy, but he ignored my calls for days and had told me to leave.

"What is wrong with you?" I asked, grabbing his arm and turning him to face me.

He stood there, lips pinched, still as a statue.

"Fine," I said when he wouldn't talk.

I spun on my heels and started for Kate's car. "I don't need this shit," I said to myself angrily.

"Baby, wait." Ace came up behind me, stopping me.

"Don't touch me." I pulled out of his hold. "You could've fucking killed yourself," I screamed with all of the fear and emotion that welled up inside of me watching that damn race. "Why? Why would you do that to me?"

He knew more than anyone the pain losing my mother caused me. He was the one person who promised not to leave me. Now he was playing games with his life.

"I hate you." I pushed at his chest. He barely moved. "You're an asshole." I shoved him again. He stumbled back a few steps but didn't say anything. "You promised not to leave me." I pushed him again, but this time when I went to move away, he caught both of my wrists in his hands.

"I..." He blew out a breath. "I'm sorry."

"Save it. I don't want your apology. I don't want anything from you," I declared, trying to yank my hands free, but Ace held firm.

I didn't care that there were probably twenty to thirty other kids around, watching and whispering about us. All I knew was that the love of my life was out here taking risks with his own life. I couldn't wrap my head around it.

"My mom's dying," Ace said tightly. His voice was so low, I had to strain to make out his words over the sounds of other engines and people milling about.

"What?"

His hold on my wrists tightened. It wasn't painful, but it was more like he was holding on to garner strength.

"She's dying. That's what the call was about the other night," he confessed. I shook my head. "I-I thought the treatment was working."

Ace's mother had been diagnosed with breast cancer almost a year earlier. She'd endured rounds of chemo and radiation. At one point, it looked like her tumor was shrinking.

Ace shrugged. "Not anymore," he stammered. "They said she's only got a few months to live. She's dying, Savannah."

"Oh, Ace." I pulled free from his hold and threw my arms around his shoulders.

He hesitated but soon, his arms went around my waist, and he pulled me in tight. He buried his face into the crook of my neck. His shoulders began shaking as he cried.

Knowing he wouldn't want to be gawked at, I somehow guided us to the far side of the road, away from the crowd.

Ace continued to cry into my arms for I don't know how long. But I held him the entire time. When he finally pulled back, I cupped his face.

"You can't avoid this," I said.

He balled his face up in defiance.

I shook his head in my hands. "Listen to me. I would've given anything to have known that I was going to lose my mom before I did."

He knew the story of how my mom got the flu, and when it got worse, she went to a local health clinic. The doctor there dismissed her symptoms as I sat by and watched.

At sixteen, having grown up the daughter of a single parent who didn't make much money, I was used to doctors at the free clinic talking down to us in one way or another. The male physician had told my mother to drink fluids and stay in bed for the next day or two, and she'd be fine.

But my mother couldn't afford to stay home from work. And what the doctor failed to recognize was that my mother had a severe case of pneumonia from the flu she'd contracted. She died in our small, shitty apartment while I was at school.

"This shit ain't fair," Ace said.

"I know," I consoled. "I wish you didn't have to lose your mom, too."

Ace's mother was sweet. Ever since the first time I met her, she'd welcomed me into her home. She hadn't looked down on me because I was from the poorer side of town or because I was Black.

Ace's father was less welcoming.

His mother had been diagnosed with cancer not long before he and I met.

"But getting yourself killed isn't going to fix this," I said.

He wrapped his hands around my wrist and kissed the inside of my palm. "I'm sorry."

Two words that most people overused, but not Ace. If he apologized, I knew he meant it. At that moment, I realized he wasn't ignoring me because he was done with our relationship, but because he was scared.

"You're not alone in this." I remembered I'd never felt more forlorn in my life than when I came home and realized my mom had died.

Ace had his father and his brothers, but he also had me. He would never feel what I felt.

I wanted him to know that.

"Neither are you," he said, pulling me in for another hug. "I'm sorry I scared you," he said into the crook of my neck.

It didn't take much for me to forgive him. I'd been more scared than hurt.

"I love you," he mumbled.

"Love you, too. Even if you did scare the shit out of me." I wiped his tears away. "It's going to be all right," I promised, even though I knew there were more painful times ahead. I just didn't know how painful.

CHAPTER 14

S *avannah*

    I rolled away from the patient on the stool I sat on before standing up. "Now make sure to keep it covered for the next few days to avoid getting dirt or anything into the wound, okay?" I told the middle-aged man who'd come into the clinic.

I had one more hour before the end of my shift, and I'd go pick up Aiden from school. I thought about maybe taking him to get some ice cream and possibly inviting Ace to come with us. That is, if he was back from visiting with his father, like he planned to do earlier.

The thought of spending the late afternoon with those two brought a smile to my lips.

"Thanks, Dr. Greyson," my patient said as I held the door of the examination room open for him.

"Just Ms. Greyson is fine," I corrected, not wanting my patients to mistake me for the actual doctor.

I waved as he proceeded down the hallway.

"Savannah, how's it going?" Dr. Pierce asked, exiting her office.

"It's busy today."

She pushed out a breath. "I know. For some reason, Wednesdays seem to be our most hectic day," she commented. "Thanks again for coming in early. You were a lifesaver."

"How's your patient? The one that had the emergency."

"She's at the hospital with a burst appendix."

I hissed and made a pained expression. A burst appendix was painful as hell. I wouldn't wish it on anyone.

"Yeah, but she's being treated. Oh, that reminds me. Gwen and I were talking. We're thinking of expanding the clinic's services. To provide more care to patients who are on the bubble financially. It requires more money, naturally, and we're thinking of taking on a third investor. This person would become the third owner of Brightside.

She paused and looked at me.

I blinked and then pressed my hand to my chest. "You mean me?"

She nodded and shrugged. "Possibly. It's a lot to ask, I realize, but you've talked a lot about wanting to serve those who have trouble affording healthcare. This would be a way to do that in an even greater capacity."

"I don't know what to say. I would have to look into it more."

"Of course," Dr. Pierce said with a wave of her hand. "I wanted to put the bug in your ear. We'll circle back in a couple of months with some solid numbers and details."

"Okay, thanks."

"I'm off to the hospital to check on a few patients."

I nodded and watched Dr. Pierce stroll off, feeling honored she even thought to ask me about such a huge opportunity.

I headed up to the front of the office to ask Reese which patient was next. Hopefully, the lobby would be empty, and I could get to work on some charts I needed to complete before I left for the day.

"Hey Reese, how's it going?" I asked.

She smiled as she turned to face me from the chair she sat in at the front desk. "It's quieted down," she said.

I pushed out a breath. "Good."

"Yeah, I might make it out on time today," she commented.

I raised my eyebrows. "Got a hot date?" I inquired.

Reese dipped her head, the light brown, bob wig she wore, moved, covering her face, slight. Since I began working at Brightside, Reese changed her hairstyle at least six different times. I like the various looks on her.

She looked back up at me with an embarrassed half smile. "Yeah, right."

"Why is that such a silly question?" Reese was a pretty woman, in my opinion. She was a few inches shorter than my five-foot-six size and less ample in all the places I was, but she had a cute figure.

Her skin tone was a few shades darker than mine, but there was a glow about her skin that even the best Mac bronzers couldn't compete with.

She shrugged and peered down. "Men don't look at me. Not like that, anyway. I've made peace with it." She stood. "Anyway, I volunteer most evenings either for Meals on Wheels or at a nursing home not too far from here."

"That's kind of you," I told her while I plucked one of the patient files from the filing cabinet.

"Truthfully, I feel more comfortable around seniors than people my age. Anyway, tonight's a special occasion, and I'd like to get to the nursing home on time. To help set up."

I turned from the filing cabinet to ask her what the special occasion was, but my heart plummeted at the man who'd just walked into the clinic.

Vincent Reyes locked eyes with me as soon as he approached the front desk.

"Can I help you?" Reese asked.

His lips spread into an evil-looking grin. "I think Ms. Greyson knows why I'm here," he said, not breaking eye contact with me.

"Is he a patient of yours?" Reese asked.

I swallowed down the fear that rose in my throat.

"Are you here for a follow-up?" she continued before she reached for a stack of files.

"I'll take it from here, Reese." My voice shook a little, but I hoped she hadn't heard it. "R-right this way."

I stepped out of the front desk area and opened the door for Vincent to follow me down toward the examination room.

What the hell was he doing there? In the past few weeks, I almost started to believe he had been a figment of my imagination.

Reyes stepped inside behind me, and I closed the door but not all of the way.

"Long time no see," he said as he folded his arms in front of his body.

I kept my position right in front of the door. I couldn't see a gun, but that didn't mean he didn't have one.

"What are you doing here?"

That malicious smile grew, and my stomach curled in fear.

"Thought it was time to take a trip to Texas." He stepped forward. "It seems you think I'm playing about this money situation, Ms. Greyson."

"I told you I need time to get the money you're asking for."

"Time is a very scarce resource." His smile dropped, and the wrinkle in his forehead and frown on his lips conveyed his impatience. "Do you think I won't tell Senator Flores that I've located his son?" He stepped even closer. "Do you know what he wants me to do once I've found his illegitimate child?"

I shook my head, not because I didn't know, but I didn't want to think about the horrible task Vincent Reyes had been sent on by Marco Flores concerning Aiden.

"He wants me to kill him," Vincent said, obviously taking pleasure in my fear.

My heart just about stopped beating. I couldn't bear the thought of someone hurting my son.

"Many illegitimate children have taken down powerful politicians. My client does not want to be amongst those infamous groups."

"I won't let either of you harm my son," I growled, feeling rage at the mere thought of it.

He shrugged, an unbothered expression covering his face. "It is not my wish to harm your son. However, my silence requires payment."

"I told you, I will have your money in a few months."

He shook his head. "That's not good enough anymore. I need more of a guarantee. I need half of the money now."

I bulged my eyes. "That's over a hundred thousand dollars. I don't have that right now."

"Too bad." He started for the door. "Looks like I have a phone call to make."

"Wait," I insisted, standing tall in front of the door. "I have some money." I remembered some money I had saved in my old 401k. "It's only about fifty thousand dollars, but it's something."

He gave me a considering look.

It wasn't even half the amount he demanded, but it had to be enough. God, I wanted to reach for a syringe and plunge it into his carotid artery.

"I will need it by the end of the week," he finally said.

It was Wednesday. I had no idea how I was going to have that money within the next two days. But I pictured my son's face and knew I would have to figure it out. I couldn't let anything happen to him.

"I need more time than that," I said with my head raised. "It takes time to transfer money."

This time instead of a smile, he snarled. "I will be in touch soon." Reyes brushed past me and exited the exam room.

I rubbed my fingers against my forehead to ease the tension headache that started to develop.

Before the headache settled in ultimately, my cell phone buzzed. I pulled the phone out of the pocket of my scrubs and immediately answered when I saw that it was Aiden's school calling.

"Hello?"

"Ms. Greyson, this is Sandy DeLorenzo, the secretary at Bishop Warner Elementary," the woman said.

"Yes, what's wrong? Is Aiden okay?"

"We hope so. We're calling because he didn't show up for school today," she replied. "As you know, our school's policy is that if a student is going to be absent, we must receive notice at the beginning of the day."

"Oh, God." I hung up on the woman without thinking and started dialing Ace's cell phone. He was supposed to drop Aiden off at school. I left him in charge.

His phone went straight to voicemail.

I grabbed my keys and bag from the locker in the employee room in the back. "Reese, there's a situation at Aiden's school. I have to go," I said in a rush as I passed her and the front desk.

"Okay…" I heard her say as I breezed through the door, but I didn't stick around to let her finish.

I was already on edge from Vincent Reyes' visit. What if he'd already done something to Aiden, and he dropped by my job to see what money he could get before I found out?

"No," I said as I drove back to Ace's house. Ace would've called me if there was an emergency with Aiden.

But what if something happened to Ace, too? What if they were injured or lying in a ditch somewhere?

I pressed my foot on the gas harder, surpassing the speed limit on the way back home. I tried redialing Ace's number, but it kept going to voicemail.

When I turned into Ace's subdivision, I sighed a little in relief when I spotted his truck parked out front. I pulled into the driveway behind it and hopped out of my car.

My legs carried me quicker than they ever had to the front door. I burst through the door, my heart beating in my ears. As soon as I stepped over the threshold, Aiden's enthusiastic laughter invaded my awareness.

I let the sound carry me to the living room. I stopped short when I found Aiden and Ace rolling around on the floor, surrounded by what looked like a makeshift fort of pillows and couch cushions.

"What the hell?" I blurted out.

They froze.

"What is this?" I asked, looking between both of them as they remained on the floor.

"We're playing a war game, Mama. Look at this cool fort Mr. Ace built," Aiden said excitedly.

I was too caught off-guard to even respond to Aiden. Instead, I gave Ace a pointed look.

"I tried to call you."

"Shoot," he said as he stood up. He pulled his cell from the pocket of his jeans. "I forgot to take it off of silent. Sorry. Did you need something?"

"Did I need..." I blinked at him like he was half-crazy. "The school called."

"Oh yeah, about that," Ace said as he looked back at Aiden.

"Mr. Ace let me stay home from school today," Aiden said with enthusiasm.

"Did he?" I glared at Ace. "Can I speak to you outside?" I didn't wait for him to answer. I spun on my heels and walked right back out the front door I'd just entered.

I walked far enough away from the front of the house to give myself some breathing room and to hopefully prevent Aiden from hearing me yell. I was livid.

I pinched the bridge of my nose and paced back and forth in an attempt to calm myself down.

Ace came up behind me. Only when I looked up did I realize that I'd walked out to the street.

"What the hell is wrong with you?" I asked with my arms wide, unable to stop myself from raising my voice.

Ace's head whirled backward and he held up his hands. "Look, I know I should've called you and let you know that we played hooky today."

"Should've let me know?" My tone was incredulous. "What do you mean, let me know? You should've never made that decision."

Ace's lips pinched. "It was a little spur of the moment. The kid—"

"Aiden. His name is Aiden," I said, cutting Ace off. "He's not *the kid*. And he's not..." I snapped my mouth shut.

"Not who?"

"He's not AJ," I fumed.

Ace took a step back as if I'd shoved him, but I kept going.

"He's not our son, Ace. Our baby died. Aiden is not a replacement for the son we lost."

Ace stood there, glaring down at me once I finished. The look in his eyes turned cold. I hadn't seen such a stony, icy look in them since I first arrived in Harlington. My stomach churned in anguish.

"That's what you fucking think?" He growled low. "You think I don't know the fucking difference between Aiden and our son?" It was his voice now that turned incredulous.

"You should've taken him to school," I murmured, avoiding his question.

His nostrils flared in anger. "Don't ever worry about it happening again." He charged past me.

I turned and watched him stomp up to the front of the door and pass through without a backward glance.

When I made my way back inside, my entire body felt heavier than it had when I awakened that morning. Not only had I been confronted by the man who threatened to tell Aiden's birth father about him, but I knew I'd hurt Ace's feelings.

"Where did Mr. Ace go?" Aiden asked as I entered the living room. "We weren't finished with our game."

"Help me clean up these pillows," I told Aiden instead of answering his questions. I could hear Ace moving around upstairs and knew I likely wouldn't see him for the rest of the evening.

"Way to go, Savannah," I mumbled to myself.

CHAPTER 15

$\mathcal{A}$ ce Two and a half weeks after that bullshit argument with
Savannah, I pushed through the doors of some dive bar outside of
Vegas. My squadron and I had been in Nevada for specialized
training.

We were due to head back to Texas in two days.

Since the rigorous part of our training passed, and we had the
following day off, all I wanted to do was get shitfaced and forget the
bullshit in my personal life. Work and flying were the only things that
kept my mind off of Savannah and Aiden.

The downtime was the most brutal.

My heart felt like it twisted in my chest just thinking about them.

"Hey, have you been here before?" Josh, more commonly referred
to as Hazard, his call sign, asked.

"Once or twice," I answered as I held up two fingers to the
bartender. A minute later, she slid two ice cold beers down the
wooden bar. I caught both of them with ease in either hand.

"Someone's planning on getting trashed tonight," Blake, another
member of the squadron, said.

"Easy with that shit," Maple commented, patting me on the shoulder. "We have to fly in two days."

I shrugged him off. "I know how to do my job." The last thing a fighter pilot wanted was to be hungover or dehydrated when climbing into the cockpit. It could mean the difference between life and death.

Though I wanted to get plastered, I would cut myself off after two beers to prevent later issues. The beers would give me at least a bit of a buzz.

"That was some flight today," Blake said to Maple as we strolled over to an empty set of tables in the middle of the small bar.

I noticed a few guys already in the bar when we entered, looking us over, but I didn't pay them much attention.

"Yeah, you know, had to make a little show," Maple replied. "Nice of you to keep up."

"What the fuck ever," Blake replied, laughing.

I drowned out much of the back and forth bantering. My heart wasn't in it, even though I loved my squad. We were out to cut loose and relax after two weeks of being on base constantly, with few breaks in between. But my thoughts kept straying back to Harlington.

"What's the long face about, Cannon?"

I peered across the circular wooden table at Will. "Nothing," I said before chugging back the second half of my first beer.

"You've had a bug up your ass since we've been here," Maple chimed in. "Don't tell me Cannon is having women troubles." He laughed.

"No, not Cannon," Will added. "The man who never gets his panties twisted by a woman."

"What's the matter?" Maple asked. "The wife giving you grief?"

"Yeah, speaking of. Where the hell did this wife of yours come from?" Will asked. "We've been flying together for what, five years? And not once did you mention even dating this woman. What's her name?" He turned and asked Maple.

"Savannah," I said with a growl in my voice.

Will blinked his surprise at my tone.

"And keep her name out of your mouth." I tightened my hold around the bottle in my hand.

Maple laughed. "Bingo."

"I thought we were brothers," Will said, looking offended.

I knew it was bullshit. Joking and pulling one another's chains was how we bonded as pilots.

"Anyway—"

"How you are fellas doing tonight?" A deep voice interrupted Blake.

I glanced up to see the group of guys I'd clocked when we first walked into the bar standing over us. The gleam in their eyes implied this wouldn't be a friendly encounter.

Though I knew it wouldn't be a good idea to get into an altercation with these motherfuckers, the pent-up frustration that'd been simmering inside of me since that argument with Savannah itched to get out.

"We're great," Maple said.

I sat silently, observing all three pansies that thought it was a good idea to intrude on our downtime.

"Air Force, right?" the leader of the pack questioned.

"Is it that obvious?" Will joked.

"The haircuts gave it away, didn't they?" Maple stroked his bald head, trying to lower the tension that began building in the room.

"Yeah, they all look like your barber blindfolded himself before he started your haircut," the one in the back said. He was a burly cornfed son of a bitch. But the bigger they are, the harder they fall, and all of that.

"You've been kind of quiet since we were so gracious to come over and talk to you," the leader said as he looked down at me.

Slowly, I rose to my feet and looked him in the eye. "Did I forget to ask you to bend over so I could kiss your ass?" I wasn't in the mood to play niceties or to try to defuse the situation.

A slow, unfriendly smile crossed over his face. "You're the mouthy one of the bunch, huh?"

I heard chairs scrape against the wooden floor, and I knew Maple and Will also rose.

"We're just out on a night off, fellas," Will, ever the peacemaker, said. "We're not looking for trouble."

The big one in the back had the nerve to laugh with his big ass-arms folded across his chest. "We're not looking for trouble," he mimed.

"But we don't fucking run from it, either," I said through gritted teeth with my hands tightening into fists at my sides.

It was stupid.

I knew it was dumb to let these fuckers rile me up with such little provocation, but again, I wasn't in my right frame of mind. Since Savannah had come back into my life, the tight lid I could always keep on my emotions had begun to become pried open.

"I don't fucking like you Air Force bastards," the one in the front said. "You all think you're hotshots when you ain't shit." He stepped closer to me. "If you were that fucking tough, you would've joined the real military like the Marines. Hell, even the Army would've been better than the fucking Air Force."

The guys behind him chuckled until I said, "If you walked in on your wife blowing an Airman, just say that." It was my turn to laugh. "No need to insult our entire branch because your lady left you for one of us."

His face reddened, and I could almost see the steam rising from his head. Their laughter ceased.

A slow, sardonic smile crested on my lips. I knew I'd hit the nail on the head.

"Fuck you," he growled.

I saw the fist coming from a mile away and went to block it and counter, but the follow through never made contact.

Instead, a much larger hand cupped this guy's fist with ease. His face twisted and strained as he tried to break free of the hold.

The air around me stilled and shifted in a way that I was familiar with.

Very few people I knew had that kind of impact on an entire room.

149

Peering up, I saw my cousin, Chael, looming over the prick. He wasn't alone, either.

The bar had filled with about half a dozen other guys with stern faces, wearing leather jackets. It surprised me that I hadn't heard their motorcycles when they pulled up.

"Chael," I said matter-of-factly.

Slowly, Chael turned his head in my direction, a blank expression on his face.

"You've brought the crew, huh?" I asked coolly, glancing around at them.

"We were passing through, little cousin," he said, his voice calm and even, though he still gripped the guy's fist.

I bristled against the reminder that he was the older of the two of us. He was like Micah in that way, constantly reminding me who had seniority.

"Let me go," the fuckface strained to say, interrupting my family reunion.

"Not until you let me know you can keep your hands to yourself," Chael said to the guy.

"Fuck off," he said. "Ow," he howled when Chael effortlessly turned his arm, pivoting the guy's shoulder in a way that required more mobility than he probably had.

"Okay, okay. I promise."

Chael instantly let him go and pushed him away. "It's time for you all to leave," he instructed, with a directive in his voice so sharp, not a soul would question it.

The three guys who hovered over our table damn near broke their ankles, hustling out of the bar.

"The hell?" Will asked behind me.

That was when I realized I should explain this somehow. I glanced over my shoulder. "Will, this is my cousin, Chael." I gestured to the tall Apache standing before me.

"You mean the cousin who always seems to know when you're out west even though you don't tell him beforehand?" Maple asked as he stepped forward.

That wasn't the first time Chael and his crew had shown up out of nowhere when I'd gone out west for flight training. He and Maple met before.

Chael dipped his head at my squad mates. "Welcome." He turned to one of the guys he was with and made a gesture with his head. "This round's on me." He turned his gaze to me. "I need to speak with my cousin."

"Of course you do," I griped.

I left Maple and Will, knowing they would be fine with the rest of Chael's crew.

"You could've called," Chael said as we took one of the booths in the far back of the bar.

"Why?" I questioned. "When you have a sixth sense about these things."

He huffed and his nostrils flared. "You and your brothers are a stubborn lot. I had to find out from your father that Gabriel is getting married."

I nodded even as my chest tightened. I was happy for Gabe and Lena. Really, but fuck if it didn't bother me that both of my brothers were blissed out and in love and shit, and I was…

Fuck, what the hell was I?

"He expects you at the wedding," I told Chael, masking my real feelings.

"We'll be there." He paused, his dark brown eyes burrowing into mine.

I fucking hated when he did that shit. As a kid, it used to creep me out. As an adult, it served to piss me off.

A small, arrogant smile crept over his lips. "You don't like it when I do that."

"Stop trying to read my fucking thoughts," I growled. "Fucking weirdo," I mumbled.

"Brother, I don't need to read your thoughts to see you've got 'messed up' written all over you."

"There's nothing wrong with me," I lied, even though I knew Chael could parse out the truth no matter what I said.

"Full of it." He took a swig of the beer one of his mates had brought over to the table without him asking. "At least Micah had the respect to tell me the truth when I asked if he was falling for his woman."

"I'm not Micah."

"No." He took another drink and swallowed. "Unlike Micah, you were burned by love before. It makes you even more resistant the second time around."

"Who the hell said anything about love?" I held out my arms wide.

Instead of an answer, a deep chuckle fell from Chael's lips.

I rolled my eyes.

"Okay, I'll let you hold onto that lie for as long as you need." He leveled me with another look. "Now you can tell me, specifically, what's your issue."

I thought about telling Chael to screw off. A bar on the outskirts of Las Vegas was the last place I wanted to divulge my feelings on anything, but Chael was family. Distant family, but still family.

"We got into an argument."

"We?"

"Savannah...she's back." He knew the history between Savannah and me. I didn't look him in the face because I sensed that he was smirking.

Once, a long time ago, Chael had told me that she would return. I'd told him to fuck off and that, if she did return, she could screw off as well.

"Do tell," he insisted, taking another pull from his beer.

I told him what happened with Aiden, and me keeping him out of school. Then I went into what Savannah said. Though I didn't admit it aloud, that was what hurt so much—the mention of our son.

"Do you?"

"Do I what?" I asked more defensively than I intended.

"See the son you lost when you look at the boy?"

I ground my teeth but shook my head. "No."

That was the truth. I was logical enough to recognize that Aiden wasn't AJ. Nor was he a second chance at parenting the son that

Savannah and I never had the opportunity to parent together. But I still felt protective over him.

When he cried in my lap over the fear of losing his mother, it gutted me. I kept him out of school, close to me, because I felt he'd needed it that day. I would've told Savannah as much if she hadn't said what she said.

"Then you should tell her that," Chael commented. "And you need to apologize."

I blinked. "The fuck for?"

He frowned and cocked his head sideways. "If someone had promised to drop your child off at school and hours later you got a call from the school saying he wasn't there, how would you feel?"

He answered for me. "You'd be pissed. On top of that, said person had left their cell phone off all day, and you arrived home to find them playing in the living room like nothing happened?"

Again, I squeezed the bottle in my hand. I was surprised it didn't break from the hold I had around it.

I would've been livid if the roles were reversed.

"Exactly," Chael said when I told him as much. "You're lucky she didn't beat the hell out of you."

I would've deserved it if I were being honest.

Chael stood.

"That's what brought you out here?" I asked. "You wanted to talk to me about my wife?"

He shook his head and looked over my shoulder. Something dark entered his eyes, which was saying a lot, considering how dark they already were.

"It's good you're only out here for a short time." He dropped his gaze to mine.

I wasn't nearly as adept at reading my cousin's expressions as he was at mine. However, there was a gravity in his voice that I couldn't miss.

"There's a storm brewing, cousin. Between them and us."

"What the hell is that supposed to mean?" I demanded.

He shook his head. "The less you know, the better."

"Chael."

He held up his hand. "You know I won't say more than I need to." He tapped my shoulder. "Go home to your wife. Work it out. Be grateful you have your mate."

"Here you fucking go," I griped as I stood. "Savannah wasn't my mate back then, and she...." I trailed off because the words *and she isn't now* got stuck in my throat.

Chael's frown deepened. "You full-bloods are ridiculous. Can't even tell when your mate has arrived. "

"Full-bloods" was Chael's term for those of us who were fully human. While I never said anything to many people, Chael was related to me by my mother's side of the family. They were distant relatives of hers, and they were also shapeshifters.

"Whatever," I mumbled.

He paused and placed a hand on my shoulder. Even though I was six-two, he still hovered above at six-foot-six. His hand on my shoulder tightened.

"I'm serious, cousin. Respect the gift you've been given."

His gaze went somewhere over my shoulder. Another one of those far off looks that said he was miles away.

His lips pinched before his jawline tightened. He pushed away from me. "Value what you have found."

"You're not staying?" I asked when he twirled his finger in the air, and all of the men he'd brought with him began filing in the direction of the door.

He glanced back over his shoulder. "My work here is done." He dipped his head. "I'll see you all soon."

I wrinkled my forehead, wondering what that cryptic message meant. He was probably talking about Gabriel's wedding, even though they hadn't set a date yet.

I watched as Chael and his crew exited the bar, leaving only a handful of patrons.

"You have one strange family," Maple said as I approached him at the bar.

"Fucking tell me about it."

"We need to head out too," Maple commented.

I nodded and followed as Will called an Uber to take us back to the base. On the ride back, I thought about what Chael implied.

My cousin was smart, but he wasn't perfect. Thus, he was fallible.

Savannah and my story ended a long time ago. All that was left was to put the final seal on it. In a few months, when I signed those divorce papers, all would be said and done.

But as I solidified that thought in my mind, something felt like it knocked against my stomach in protest.

CHAPTER 16

Savannah

"Mama, can't I stay up until Mr. Ace gets back?" Aiden begged as I followed him up the stairs to his bedroom.

It was almost nine thirty, well after his usual nine o'clock bedtime. I was tired and ready for him to go to sleep for the night–if for no other reason than for him to stop asking about Ace.

Every time he did, guilt bubbled up from my stomach and clogged my throat. I still hated the words I hurled at Ace before he left for his training. I should've never brought up AJ.

But when I'd gotten that call from Aiden's school, I blanked out with fear. My only thought was locating my son. When I realized that Ace and Aiden had been home, playing the entire time, I wanted someone to blame. Even though Ace apologized.

"No," I finally said to Aiden. We entered his bedroom. "We don't know when Ace will get home, and you have school in the morning."

Aiden hopped onto the bed and gave me a look with his bottom lip poked out. "Do you think Mr. Ace is mad at me?"

"What?" I asked, kneeling beside the bed after I pulled back the top covers.

Aiden wore his new navy blue and grey Air Force pajamas he'd begged me to buy when he saw them at the store the other week. We'd gone grocery shopping at the commissary when he'd spotted the PJs. More and more, he talked about becoming a pilot.

I hated to think of the moment when I would move out of Ace's house, and he moved to Germany. I feared it would crush Aiden.

"Why would you think Ace is mad at you?"

He shrugged. "He hasn't called the entire time he was gone. What if he didn't miss us?"

I cupped my stomach with my free hand while the other tightened on the sheets I still held. The thought of Ace not caring about us was a tough pill to swallow, though it shouldn't have been.

"Sweetie, I think Mr. Ace was preoccupied with pilot stuff," I lied. "He probably just got too busy to call."

"Do you think he's okay? What if he got into an accident?"

"H-he's okay," I said, my voice trembling. "The Air Force would've called us if something happened to him." I swallowed, not knowing if that was the truth or not.

Yes, legally, I was Ace's wife, but he'd been in the military so long, and we'd been apart for all of those years. He likely had a different emergency contact and all of that set up.

Would his family have told me if something was wrong with him?

I shook my head to break out of those thoughts. Ace was just out west for training. He was fine. The more likely reason he hadn't called was that I'd bitten his head off before he left.

That, and the fact that we weren't a traditional married couple anyway. We had only a few months before our union was officially dissolved.

The thought should've at least brought me some relief. The divorce meant I could inherit my grandmother's estate and pay off Vincent Reyes. But all it filled me with that night was dread.

"Sweetie." I cupped the side of Aiden's face. "You know that our living with Mr. Ace is temporary, right? We're here for a little while, and then we're moving into a place of our own."

Aiden nodded, his eyes lowered a bit. "But he's my friend." Suddenly, he looked up, his face brightening. "What if he changes his mind and asks us to stay? I think he likes you. He looks at you some-times when you don't see. I think that means he likes you. What if he could be my dad?"

Air whooshed from my lungs.

That question about knocked the wind out of me. Especially since the last words I'd hurled at Ace were akin to telling him that he wasn't Aiden's father.

"What if I read you a bedtime story?" I asked, reaching for one of the books on the nightstand by his bed. I ignored the shake of my hand as I grabbed the book.

"Okay," he said gloomily, lying back against his pillow. "But will you wake me up when Mr. Ace gets home? Please?" he begged.

"No need, kid. I'm right here."

Aiden and I both gasped as he looked toward the door. Ace stood there, taking up most of the entranceway with his arms folded across his chest. My gaze slid down his body, taking in the forest green Henley shirt he wore with dark blue jeans, looking like the embodi-ment of everything masculine and male.

I didn't know who was more excited to see him—me or Aiden.

My son leaped out of bed and ran to him. "Mr. Ace."

Ace easily caught him in his arms as he bent low to grant him a hug. I had to look away because I felt the tears coming. Between what Aiden had just asked about Ace becoming his father and my shame about what I'd last said to Ace, I couldn't look him in the eye.

"How was it? Did you fly a lot?" Aiden bombarded Ace with questions.

I wanted to tell him to let Ace breathe since he'd just gotten in, but words refused to come out of my mouth.

"How about we talk in the morning?" Ace suggested. "It's your bedtime, isn't it?"

"Aw, man," Aiden whined.

Ace laughed. "I'll finish reading you that story. You didn't finish without me, did you?"

Aiden shook his head. My son had given me strict instructions against reading the story about the little boy whose father was a fighter pilot. That was the story only Ace could read to him at bedtime.

"No, we didn't finish last time, remember? Can you read it to me?"

"If it's okay with your mom." Ace gave me a questioning look.

I managed to stand and nod. "I'll wait outside," I stammered out as I made my way to the door.

I didn't even look at Ace as I passed him. I gently closed the door behind me and allowed the two of them to have their private moment.

With my back against the wall, I slid down to the floor and covered my face. I refused to let myself cry, but everything started to feel like it was closing in on me. The week prior, I'd emptied my retirement account and gave every penny minus the taxes to Vicent Reyes.

The son of a bitch had acted like he was doing me a favor by not telling Aiden's birth father about his whereabouts.

Then there was Aiden. He truly was falling for Ace. I knew he needed more of a male role model in his life. And the way he and Ace took to one another should've warmed my heart, but instead, it frightened the hell out of me.

"He knocked out quick." Ace's deep voice startled me out of the emotional spiral I was getting ready to go down.

"Don't," he insisted when I started to stand. He lowered his body to the floor, sitting across from me in the hallway.

"Welcome back," I said with a tight smile on my lips.

He returned the gesture with a nod.

"I'm sorry," I blurted out. I pushed out a deep breath and closed my eyes. "What I said before you left was completely out of line. I didn't mean it." The words came out fast, nearly tripping over one another as they spilled out. "I was just so terrified when his school called and said he hadn't shown up. Then I couldn't get ahold of you."

I opened my eyes and spotted Ace watching me with a curious expression on his face.

"What were you terrified about?" he asked. "I would never let anything happen to him," he promised.

My heart squeezed at his declaration.

I wasn't surprised when my eyes started to water. Briefly, I wondered how he would respond if I told him that I was essentially being blackmailed to keep Aiden safe.

I want to forget everything about you.

Ace's words from when we first moved in came back to mind. This wasn't a permanent situation. He wouldn't remain a long-term part of our lives. I couldn't lay the burden of the mess with Aiden's father in his lap. Not since his main goal was to rid himself of me once and for all.

I had been too much of a burden in his life already.

I pushed down the desire to tell him everything and instead said, "I'm scared I'm letting him down." I turned to look back at Ace. "Every day, I wake up and wonder if I'm doing right by him. And Yvette."

"Yvette?" He cocked his head sideways.

"His birth mom," I told him. "She was my friend, more like a little sister to me. She..." I trailed off. "She was so young when she had him." Yvette had reminded me of myself. She had no family to speak of and wasn't even out of her teens when she got pregnant.

"Most days, I feel like I'm just getting by."

Ace reached out and took my hand in his.

"The problem with being a parent is you don't usually find out until years down the road whether you messed them up or not." I let out a pathetic laugh.

Ace squeezed my hand.

"He's lost so much already," I whispered. "I can't let him lose anything else."

"What would he lose?" His face was a mask of confusion.

I shrugged. "Anything. I just mean, I want to give him the childhood he deserves, and I don't know if I'm doing any of this right."

I let out a sigh, feeling relieved that I'd been able to express my deepest fears to someone besides myself.

"You know, when I first went through pilot training," Ace started, "I was scared shitless. There were so many guys all competing for the same position. And they weren't about to hand it over to me. Most of us dreamt of being pilots since we were young kids."

160

He moved closer, firming the hold he had on my hand.

"For the first time in my life, I started to think, what if I'm not good enough? What if I spent years dreaming of being this, and it was all just that? A fucking dream."

I wrinkled my forehead. "Ace, you're the most competent person I've ever known." From the time I first met him, there wasn't any goal Ace set that he didn't accomplish. He'd graduated at the top of our high school class, with me right behind him at number two.

He gave me a smile that pierced straight through to my heart.

"Those were the words that carried me through flight school." He swallowed and glanced away. "When it got the toughest, and I doubted myself the most, was when I would think about all the times you told me that I could do anything I wanted to. It was your voice that pushed me through those darkest moments."

Of course, the tears I'd attempted to hold back slipped free.

Ace chuckled as he wiped one with his thumb.

"You're the same way with Aiden. I don't know what a perfect childhood is supposed to look like, but from what I can tell, he has a mother who loves and encourages him unconditionally, every day."

He shrugged and looked me in the eye. "Maybe that's what being a good parent is all about."

I dipped my head because the tears wouldn't stop flowing.

Ace moved his hand underneath my chin, raising my gaze to meet his. "That wasn't supposed to upset you even more."

I laughed. "It didn't." I shook my head and wiped the tears. "I just feel like an even bigger ass for saying what I said to you before you left."

"That was an asshole thing to say." He dug the knife in a little deeper.

I slapped his arm and he grinned. "You were a scared mom. And you were right. I shouldn't have kept him out of school. He was just..." He paused and looked up as if considering his following words. "It was fun hanging out with him."

I nodded. "He gave you those puppy dog eyes, didn't he?"

Ace gave me a knowing look. "So that's his thing, huh?"

I laughed but quickly covered my mouth as I nodded. "Yup. I've kept him home from school once or twice when he gave me that look and said he'd much rather spend the day with me. I'm a sucker for that face."

"I think we both are," Ace said.

Our gazes collided. We both stared in silence, letting our eyes drink each other in. The anger-filled tension that had been there before he left dissipated. A new source of tension shrouded us as we sat in that hallway.

It was the kind of strain that came when the air around you crackled with sexual energy.

"I've missed you," I said, just above a whisper.

That was my honest admission. I had come to realize that I didn't like not going to bed without Ace in it. No. Truthfully, I came to that conclusion a long time ago. But over the years, I'd pushed that awareness down. It became covered up, a wound that never fully healed or stopped hurting, but I somehow managed to live with the pain.

Being back in Ace's bed, with him beside me, allowed the wound to resurface in a new way when he wasn't there.

Ace didn't immediately respond. He stood up, and for a nanosecond, I thought he was going to walk away. Like this talk had gotten too personal or something. Instead, he leaned down and extended his hand to help me up.

When I stood, he pulled me into him and wrapped an arm around my waist.

"I was planning on ignoring you." He was so close, his breath brushed against my lips, tickling them.

"What?" I asked, confused.

"I was pissed the entire time I was gone. And I planned to ignore you for the next three months while you were here. But then I walked in on you with Aiden and...." He trailed off and planted his forehead against mine. "I could never fucking ignore you."

I saw the kiss coming before it was delivered. I wanted—no, needed—his lips on mine. There couldn't have been a more painful reality for me than existing in Ace's home and having him completely ignore me.

Him cursing me out every day would've been less hurtful than him not noticing me.

"We should call it a night," he pulled back to say against my lips.

My nipples tightened beneath the bra I had on.

"You're tired." I cupped his face. He'd endured hours of training and had to fly home from out west. He had to be exhausted.

"I'll sleep later."

I gasped as he lifted me and carried me down the hall to his bedroom.

* * *

Ace

I forced back the memories of the last time I'd carried Savannah like this. It was on the night we got married. I'd been so proud to finally make her my wife, despite so many others telling us we were too young.

This night wasn't about renewing that memory. I simply wanted to be inside of Savannah. I fucking needed it like I needed my next breath.

I hadn't lied to her. The truth was that, on the way back from training, I had decided to ignore her until our next three months were up. I knew that would've gotten under her skin more than anything else, but I was weak with her.

And for her son, apparently.

All it took was one walk inside the house and hearing her tuck Aiden into bed while he asked for me. Something dislodged in my chest when I heard him ask if I was okay. And when Savannah turned to me, with uncertainty in her eyes, my anger fizzled out like a wet firecracker.

There was nothing left of my ire when she opened up and admitted her fears of not being an adequate mother.

As I laid Savannah onto the bed, I repressed the memory of Chael's words from the bar the other night. But when Savannah lifted her arms, summoning me to meet her, my world felt more right than it had in a long time.

"I want you on top," I said before pressing a kiss to her soft lips then rolling us over so that she was on top of me.

A slow grin spread across her beautiful face, tugging at my heart-strings. How I could've ever thought that I could be in the same house as this woman and ignore her was beyond my reasoning. I'd have to chalk it up to anger and a bruised ego.

Savannah sat up, straddling my waist, and crossed her arms to lift the short sleeve shirt she wore over her head. She tossed the shirt to the floor and grinned down as she looked at me.

I sat up on my elbows, noting the difference between this encounter and the first time she rode me, all those years ago. She had been so timid and self-conscious then.

This version of my wife stared me in the eyes as she reached around back and undid the clasp of her bra. When her full mounds spilled out of the material that'd held them hostage all day, I reached up and squeezed, one and then the other.

Savannah's head fell backward, and a tiny moan escaped her lips. My dick beat against the front of my jeans in response. It begged to be set free.

I couldn't wait any longer. I reached for the button on her jeans and quickly undid it. She lifted, allowing me to push her pants and panties down over her hips. I regretted that our bodies had to separate even for a short interval as we undressed.

"C'mere," I demanded, pulling her body back to mine once we were naked.

"Wait." She pushed against my chest. "Condom," she panted.

Fuck.

A step I never forgot with any woman. Except for this one.

I swallowed down the desire to feel her unsheathed, even as I wondered if she was on any birth control. Not that she'd need it, and I had been tested for STIs a month before she first came back.

I didn't bother explaining all of that before I yanked open my nightstand and pulled out a box of condoms. When I moved to unwrap one of them, Savannah took it from my hand.

I watched with a cocked eyebrow as she brought the wrapper to her lips. She removed the condom with her teeth and repositioned it between her lips. The gleam in her eye was unmistakable, and I groaned as she pushed her way down the length of my body.

With the condom in her mouth, she covered the tip of my cock, sheathing me with her mouth.

"Shit," I grunted, remembering that I had taught her this particular trick. It was before we'd married when we still used condoms. "You're fucking killing me, babe."

I meant it both figuratively and literally. I wasn't sure how much I could stand.

She sat up and had the nerve to giggle. That sound brought out the beast in me, and I wrapped both hands around her, grabbing her ass and forcing her down onto my rock-hard cock.

She whipped her head back and hissed as if she were in pain. But I knew the sound well because I'd memorized it. I wasn't hurting her.

Especially not when her hips started moving up and down, begging for more.

Though she was on top, this was my fucking show. I held her ass firmly while I bounced up and down, impaling her over and over.

"Ace," she whispered.

"Say it louder," I demanded. I wanted her to shout my damn name from the rooftops.

"Ace...shit," she yelled and then bit her lips.

That move reminded me that we weren't the only ones in the house. I sat up with my hands still connected to her ass, pulling her onto my rod while I brought our lips to kiss.

She couldn't yell the way I wanted her to, but I would pull out every moan and gasp I could and swallow it down as a keepsake.

"You feel so good," she panted against my lips.

"You're mine," spilled out of my lips. I'd had no intention of ever making that declaration to another woman again in my life. But this was Savannah. My fucking wife.

"Mine," I growled again.

"Yours." Her voice was breathless.

Something cracked open inside of me. All bets were off. Fuck a divorce. And double fuck ever letting her go again. This woman was mine to claim. Once and for all.

"Ace." She groaned my name against my mouth and wrapped her arms around my neck. That was all the validation I needed.

I rolled us again so that I covered her with my body. The orgasm rolled through me, and I emptied my seed into the condom.

"This is where you fucking belong," I said to her once I could speak again.

She blinked up at me with confused eyes. We both were tired and consumed inside a passion-filled haze. I would have to hold off on explaining until later, but I made my decision. Just that quickly.

Savannah wasn't going anywhere. Neither was Aiden.

CHAPTER 17

*a*ce A week after returning home from training out west, I felt like I was walking on cloud nine. Savannah and I had fucked like rabbits for half the night of my return.

I had only meant to take her once and then take my ass to sleep. But I couldn't get enough of her. It was the combination of makeup sex, and *I've been gone for two and a half weeks* sex. It was a miracle we hadn't woken Aiden up that night.

I strolled out of the debriefing room with a lift of my chin, feeling myself.

"See ya tomorrow night," Maple said, patting me on the shoulder as he brushed past me. "Gotta date with the wife tonight." He waved back at me with a two-finger salute.

I nodded and chuckled, feeling almost as anxious as he was to get out of there and back home. The only problem was that it was the middle of the day, and Savannah was still working.

Maybe I would stop by the urgent care where she worked and surprise her. Hell, I could offer to pick up Aiden from school, and we could get some ice cream and take it up to Savannah once she got off work.

I shook my head at all the gestures that ran through my mind. Since I decided that she was mine, I wanted to go full steam ahead and convince her to stay.

"Ace," Tricia called right as I passed her desk. "I need to speak with you."

I rolled my eyes skyward. "Not this bullshit again."

I hadn't seen much of her since the night of the Air Force Ball. I still hadn't asked her what she said to my wife that had upset her. And I knew Tricia said something. I could read Savannah's face like a book sometimes.

"I'm busy," I said before pushing through the door to exit the building. I threw my sunglasses over my eyes. It may have been nearing mid-October, but that Texas sun was still piercing and high in the air.

God, the view from the air with the sun at my tail was almost magical. I wanted Aiden to experience it one day. If the kid worked as hard as he asked questions about being a fighter pilot, I knew he would make it.

"Ace," Tricia called again, this time pulling me by the arm.

I halted in my tracks and my ministrations about Aiden and turned to face her.

"Don't touch me," I warned.

Her face balled in anger, and she slammed her hands on her hips. "That's how you're behaving toward me now?" She sounded incredulous.

I inhaled deeply and took a step back. Both of my parents had taught me the importance of being respectful to a woman, but she was pissing me off.

"I need to speak with you," she said again when I didn't answer her.

With a shake of my head, I said, "There's nothing for us to talk about. Unless there's a paperwork issue. Which there isn't, since you could've addressed that matter inside." I turned on my heels and started to head for my bike in the parking lot.

I had more important matters on my mind, like trying to decide if I would get Savannah the Rocky Road ice cream or the vanilla bean.

She loved both, and she wasn't a fan of cones. She preferred her ice cream in a cup.

Aiden, on the other hand, was a mint chocolate chip kinda guy. And he, like me, preferred our two scoops in a delicious waffle cone.

"Ace, this is important," Tricia hissed from behind me. She ran up ahead of me to circle me, getting in my damn way.

"There's nothing of relevance that we need to discuss."

She pushed out a heavy breath through her nose. "Oh, yeah?"

I nodded.

"I'm pregnant," she said in a loud whisper, her eyes darting around the parking lot as if ensuring that no one else overheard her.

I rocked back onto my heels before taking a step backward. Slowly, I panned down the length of her body. I didn't notice anything different about her, but as my gaze reached her abdomen for the first time, I noticed it was a tad more distended than I recalled.

My hands squeezed at my sides into fists. Those two words filled my head, and I heard them over and over.

"How far along are you?" I asked, still staring at her belly.

"Almost sixteen weeks," she declared as if proving something. Sixteen weeks would mean she'd gotten pregnant around a month or so before Savannah returned.

"And why the hell are you telling me?" I cocked my head sideways and glared at her.

Her lips fell apart. "Because." She looked around again and stepped forward.

I stepped back again, maintaining the space between us.

"It's yours."

My mind rushed with the memories of the first time a woman told me she was pregnant with my child. I was eighteen, and that woman was my wife. I remembered the look of fear on Savannah's face.

The way she bit her bottom lip as she handed me the positive pregnancy test.

We were less than a couple of months out of high school, still trying to figure out how to manage going to college and starting our careers as a young married couple. Then we had a pregnancy to contend with.

All of those fears had mounted, but they didn't compare to the joy I'd felt back then. I knew Savannah was my forever and that, eventually, we'd have a family together. Getting pregnant with AJ had been by mistake, but it was no accident, as far as I was concerned.

I wanted him more than anything.

As I peered up into Tricia's face, I felt the exact opposite of what I'd felt with Savannah.

White hot rage consumed me. It took every bit of strength in my being not to step forward and throttle her. To prevent myself from even risking going there, I took another step back and shook my head.

"You're fucking sick," I said through gritted teeth. "Whoever that baby belongs to, you'd better go tell him and stay the fuck away from me."

I brushed past her and started for my motorcycle again. But Tricia pulled me again by the arm.

"Ace, this is your baby."

I snatched it away from her. "Keep your hands to yourself."

Her face reddened and the muscles in her jaw tightened. "You're not getting away with this. You won't leave me to be a single mother while you parade around with that bitch you claim to be your wife."

Tricia's eyes went wide when I got in her face. I didn't touch her, but the scowl on my face gave away my emotion.

"I warned you about disrespecting my wife once. I will fuck up your entire world if you do it again." I moved back because being too close to her started to cause my stomach to turn.

She disgusted me.

"That isn't my baby."

She narrowed her eyes and folded her arms across her chest. "Are you willing to put your career on the line to prove it?"

This chick didn't know when to quit. "You're threatening me? Is that what the fuck you're doing right now?"

I didn't know if it was the force of my voice or the scornful look on my face that made her back up a few steps. Either way, I knew fear when I saw it in her eyes.

"This is your baby, Ace. And I can prove it. I won't let you sweep me under the rug like I'm a whore."

"Your choice of words, not mine."

She had the nerve to look insulted.

"Stay the hell away from me. And do yourself and that baby a favor and go figure out who the real father is. You won't fucking like it if you keep this bullshit lie up. I promise you that."

I glared at her a final time before spinning around and making a beeline for my motorcycle. I was angrier than I had been in a long time. Instead of heading to the ice cream parlor or the urgent care where Savannah worked, I headed home.

There was a punching bag down in my basement with my name on it.

CHAPTER 18

Savannah

I glanced at my wristwatch, noting I only had thirty minutes until the end of my shift here at Brightside. It was over two weeks since Ace had returned from training out west. Though his schedule at times felt all over the place, having him around more was a special comfort.

Every night we could, we had dinner at home. All three of us. That night, I'd planned to make a pot roast, which was why I was anxious to get off work. Aiden was going over to a friend's house after school, and Ace planned to pick him up on his way home from the base.

The ease at which we slipped into a family unit frightened the hell out of me at times. Would Aiden hate me when it ended? Hell, would my heart break wide open, like it had last time?

As much as I didn't want to slip into wishful thinking that, for once in my life, I would get the happily ever after I'd wanted so badly, the hope was still there, taunting me.

I didn't know where it happened, but I'd fallen in love with my husband again. Or maybe the truth was that I'd never stopped loving him. The years and separation had only masked it, making me believe I'd quit. But that wasn't true.

"He's leaving soon," I muttered to myself as I walked down the hall toward the head doctor's office. I forced myself to remember that Ace had orders to go abroad in less than two months. He would be in Germany, halfway around the world, and he hadn't asked for us to go with him.

Why would he? You're asking for a divorce, remember?

My belly sank at that reminder. I needed this divorce, but I started to realize that I didn't want it.

I brushed those thoughts aside and knocked on the open office door. "Hey, Dr. Pierce, you wanted to see me?"

She smiled as she waved me inside. "Yeah, Gwen and I were going over the numbers for the urgent care buy-in."

A week earlier, I'd met with the two owners of Brightside to discuss the possibility of becoming a third owner of the clinic. The buy-in amount was well into the six-figure range. And I would at least need to put down a portion in cash to get a decent business loan.

Yet another thing I wanted that was just out of my grasp. In a perfect world, I could use the money from my grandmother's estate to put toward the investment in Brightside, helping it to expand and aid more patients that couldn't afford appropriate medical care.

"We reworked a couple of things, and Gwen thinks she could slash the buy-in amount by a hundred K or so." She shrugged. "She's the one with the MBA and knows all of that stuff." She rolled her eyes. "I would marry the woman who's an overachiever, being a nurse practitioner and MBA grad."

I gave her a weak smile that I hoped she overlooked. Even with the lowered amount, I didn't have the funds needed.

"I'll have to look it over some more and speak with my financial advisor," I lied. It was the same pitiful excuse I gave the week before.

"Understood," Dr. Pierce said with a wave of her hand. "We're looking at a few different investors. But we've noticed your dedication to our patients since you started working here. We'd love for the investor to be you instead of some corporate investor whose only motive is profit gain."

I sighed, knowing the feeling. Corporations often made healthcare possible, but it didn't always make providing quality care to patients easy.

"I'll see what I can do."

The phone on Dr. Pierce's desk rang. By the sound of the ring, I could tell it was Reese calling from the receptionist area.

"Hey, Reese?" She paused. "Shoot." She glanced up at the clock on the wall. "I have to run over to the hospital to check on a patient, then I have another late appointment over at the other office." She paused. "I hate to send them away."

I gave her a curious look. "What's going on?"

She covered the lower half of the phone. "There's a walk-in, and I don't have time to see them."

"I can take care of them," I said.

"Are you sure?" she asked with a dip in her eyebrows. "I know you're supposed to leave soon, and you have some paperwork to get to."

I waved her off. "Not a problem. I don't have to pick Aiden up from school today. I have some time."

I started for the front of the office. With any hope, this patient's issue wasn't anything serious. I could handle it quickly and get back to completing my paperwork before leaving for the day.

"Let's see what we have," I said as I took the patient chart from Reese's desk. I scanned the form the patient had completed.

The female patient noted that she was experiencing abdominal pains. I scanned a little lower, and my heart rate sped up when I noticed the patient wrote that she was approximately twenty weeks pregnant.

"Okay, Miss…" I paused to look up the patient's name.

"Wallace. Tricia Wallace," a female voice said.

The familiar voice knocked the wind out of me. Looking up from the chart, I came face to face with Ace's ex, or whatever she had been to him.

"Please, follow me," I said as I went around the front desk and pushed open the door that led to the examination rooms. The last thing I needed was to disclose my real feelings in front of Reese.

I gripped the chart in my hand firmly and stood by the door to allow Tricia inside. She breezed past me. I thought I saw a ghost of a grin on her face, but she turned her head too quickly, almost smacking me in the face with her hair.

A queasy feeling developed in my stomach. I shook my head. I was at work, and this woman claimed she was pregnant and in need of assistance.

"Should I sit here?" she asked, her voice sounding innocent as she pointed toward the long chair with stirrups at the end.

"Yes." I shut the door. "So, um, what brings you in today?"

"Isn't it right there?" She directed her nose at the chart in my hand.

I gave her a tight smile. "I'd rather have you explain to me what brought you into Brightside today."

"I've had some stomach pain."

I visually assessed her demeanor. She was sitting up straight, looking me in the eye, and yeah, there was a smirk at play on her lips. She didn't come across as if she were in pain, but that didn't mean she wasn't.

I needed to put my feelings aside.

I sat up on the stool. "And you're twenty weeks pregnant?" It hurt to push those words out.

"Yes," she answered with a flip of her hair. "We're excited for this baby." She cupped her stomach with one hand.

"I would imagine so." I tried to sound cheery. When I questioned her more about her symptoms and whether or not she had tried to make an appointment with her OB-GYN, she cut me off.

"Yes, I knew Ace wanted a little boy for a long time. It was hard, but I decided to wait until it's born to find out whether it's a boy or girl."

I started coughing out of nowhere. With one hand partially covering my mouth, I asked, "Ace?"

Her brown eyes brightened, and her smile grew. That was the moment I knew full well that she did not come into this urgent care, of all places, by accident. Nor was it likely that she was experiencing any abdominal pain.

"Oh, he didn't tell you?" She rubbed her belly. "It must've slipped his mind. You know, between his hectic schedule as a pilot and him spending all of his extra time with me, helping me pick out baby names and deciding on the right furniture for the nursery, he must've forgotten to tell you."

I stood up from the stool so forcefully that it pushed back against the wall, causing a loud *thud*.

"Why the hell are you really here?"

Her mask fell away, and she narrowed her eyes on me. "Because I wanted you to know you're getting in the way of Ace's real family." She hopped off the exam table with more agility than any woman claiming to be in pain should've.

"Whatever history the two of you have is just that. History. We..." She glanced down and rubbed her belly, "are his future."

I shook my head. "You're lying," I insisted. "Probably not even pregnant." I mumbled. I'd heard stories of women faking pregnancies to keep a man around.

Hell, some of those crazy-ass women went so far as to try and steal an actual baby from a new mother. At that point, I didn't put such craziness past the woman standing in front of me.

"Feel for yourself." Without hesitation, she grabbed my hand, pulling me to her and planting it against her belly.

The distinct hardness of a pregnant belly met my palm. This wasn't a pillow stuffed into a pair of jeans for show. And when I felt movement underneath my palm, I pulled my hand away as if it burned me.

Tricia wasn't faking this pregnancy.

"We're going to be very happy," she said, patting her stomach and swaying a little with a smile on her face. "Ace told me so. He said he wants to divorce you. Then we'll join him in Germany. The two of us."

I took a few steps backward and swallowed down the curses I wanted to let fly. She didn't deserve my anger or anything else from me.

Instead of giving her the satisfaction of seeing me riled up, I lifted my

176

chin and looked her in the eye. "Well, obviously, you're feeling better. The pain that brought you into Brightside has seemed to resolve itself. Though, I would advise you to make an appointment with your OB at your earliest convenience, just to make sure you and baby are doing fine."

We had a stare-off for a few seconds before Tricia turned and exited the exam room without another word. Still, she wore that smile that made me want to smack the hell out of her.

As I stood there, staring at the empty doorway, I flexed and tightened my hands into fists. I had no right to be angry. If she was as far along as she said, it was before I'd even come back into town.

Ace and I weren't together and hadn't even seen one another in years until that point. Legally, we were still married, but he'd been free to do whatever or whomever for a long time.

But it did beg the question of whether or not he was still sleeping with her? Was he screwing me and then going to do the same with her in her bed? Did he honestly work those long overnights, or was he going over to Tricia's house and cuddling with her as he rubbed her belly and spoke to the baby in her womb the way he used to do with me?

Bile rose in my throat. I had to turn off those thoughts. I still had paperwork to get through before I could leave.

While working, I made the decision not to confront Ace about it when I got home. Within a few months, our marriage would be over. He'd said he wanted to forget me.

Maybe it was my time to finally learn to forget Ace Townsend the same way he worked so hard to forget me.

* * *

Ace

"Mr. Ace, can we practice playing catch?" Aiden asked as we pulled into my driveway. I'd picked him up from a friend's house on my way home from the base.

From the car in the driveway, I knew Savannah was already home.

She was likely preparing the pot roast I'd seen her put into the crockpot that morning.

"We should probably see if your mom needs any help in the kitchen beforehand," I told him after I put the car into park.

Aiden frowned and groaned. "But we're men. Men shouldn't have to help in the kitchen."

I jutted my head back and stared at the kid in my passenger seat. "Since when did you develop these ideas? You've been helping your mom in the kitchen since you moved in."

He nodded and looked out the windshield. "I don't know. Mike in my class says his mom never makes him or his brothers help in the kitchen. His dad says that type of work is for girls."

I barely kept from rolling my eyes, but I did let out a grunt. "Are you talking about Mike Sheppard?"

"Yeah." He nodded. "How do you know him?"

"I worked with his father." Mike Sheppard Senior was an enlisted Airman. We'd never been in the same squadron, but we crossed paths. The guy was an ass who couldn't keep his dick in his pants. Everyone on base knew it, too. Likely so did his wife.

"Anyway, what works for some households might not work for others. Gender doesn't make a difference in the type of work you should do in the house. My dad and my brothers always helped in the kitchen with my mom when I was coming up."

He narrowed his eyes at me. "Really?"

"Yeah." I chuckled. "Would I lie to you?"

He shook his head. "I don't think so." He gave me a concentrated look, his lips turning up curiously. "I guess if a fighter pilot can help in the kitchen, I can do it."

I let out a laugh. "Hey," I pointed at the kid. "Don't forget, not all fighter pilots are men, either."

Some of the best members of my squadron were women.

He rolled his eyes. "I know."

"Cool. Let's see if your mom needs anything. If not, we can toss the ball around for a while."

"All right."

We climbed out of the car, and I waited for Aiden to circle the front of my truck before I started for the door.

"When am I going to get to meet your dad and brothers?" he asked just as we reached the front door.

I hesitated, realizing that it'd been quite a while since I'd spent any time with my family. Between work and mostly hanging out at home with Savannah and Aiden, I'd avoided my family. I didn't know what to tell them about what was going on between the three of us.

Or, more truthfully, I didn't want to share the little family bubble the three of us had created in the past few months.

I wasn't in the mood to answer questions. Joel and Micah could be like a fucking dog with a bone once they got a whiff of something that seemed strange.

"Soon," I told Aiden before pushing through the door. I couldn't avoid the inevitable, and the more I thought about it, the more I didn't want to evade it.

Savannah and her son were a part of my life. I wanted to share that with my family.

"Mama, we're home," Aiden called as he toed off his sneakers and left them by the door.

I expected the aroma of food cooking coming from the kitchen, but there was none. Instead, Savannah appeared at the top of the stairs.

I stood there and drank in her features as she descended the staircase. The black V-neck and cutoff jeans she wore outlined her silhouette flawlessly. I doubted she meant the outfit to be sexy, but the way the T-shirt dipped to show the skin of her neckline and the cutoffs revealed the curves of her legs and thighs without revealing too much made my mouth water.

My stomach began to burn with need. Not once had I resented Aiden's presence, but shit, if I didn't wish for just one second that he would've stayed the night over his friend's. I wanted to take her right then and there.

"Go change your clothes, Aiden," Savannah said without saying hello to either of us.

My lips dipped to a frown. There was something in her voice. And the way she wouldn't even look at me.

I racked my brain to figure out if I'd done anything that could elicit this type of cold reaction. When we'd each left the house that morning, everything was fine. It had to be something that happened at work, then.

"Mama, do you need help in the kitchen?" Aiden asked.

She shook her head. "We're ordering pizza for dinner."

"Yes!" Aiden cheered. "It's not even Friday." He jumped up and kissed her on the cheek. "Mr. Ace and I are going to play catch outside, then," he said as he started for the stairs that she'd just come down.

Savannah glanced over her shoulder back at him but didn't say anything. The expression on her face was unreadable.

"What happened to the pot roast?" I asked after dropping my bag and gear by the door. I followed her into the kitchen.

She shrugged without turning to face me. "Decided to leave it for tomorrow."

"So, it's pizza Thursday instead of pizza Friday this week?" I asked, trying to lighten the mood.

"I guess."

"Aiden will be disappointed tomorrow to find out he doesn't get pizza two nights in a row."

"He'll get over it." She started doing the few dishes in the sink, with the water turned up way too high and the movement of her hands way too aggressive.

I moved over to the sink and turned the water down. "What's up? Was it something at work?"

She snorted. "Work. Yeah."

Okay. "A case turn bad?" Savannah's patients weren't typically in dire straits when they came to see her, but every once in a while, there would be some emergency, and she'd have to have them transferred to the local ED.

Maybe that's what happened and the patient went downhill. That was the only thing I could come up with.

"Just drop it."

"Can't drop it. Something's bothering you." I never could leave a situation alone if it upset her. It wasn't in my nature to watch her upset and not do something about it.

"I'm fine," she said, turning to me. The problem was, though, her eyes didn't meet mine.

I tucked my finger under her chin and forced her head up so she had nowhere to look but at me.

"Don't start telling me my nostrils are flaring. That's bullshit." She pulled out of my hold. "I'm fine."

"I can't talk about your nostrils? Cool." I stepped back and pulled open one of the cupboards. As I suspected, all the spices and seasonings were in alphabetical order.

I looked from her to the spice cupboard and back to my wife again.

She folded her arms and tucked in her lips, remaining silent.

"How much do you wanna bet that, if I open more cupboards, all of the pots and pans are organized from largest to smallest and color-coordinated?

Savannah rolled her eyes, and I knew I had her.

"You clean when you're upset."

I discovered that tidbit about my wife right after my mother died. She'd been almost as upset as I was, but she held her own emotions back to take care of me.

To channel her grief, Savannah organized the hell out of our kitchen cupboards and living room. She even went so far as to do the same at my parents' ranch when we went over in the days and weeks right after my mother died.

"Whatever," she said with a suck of her teeth.

"Is it work?" I asked, stepping into her personal space.

Her lips pinched.

Again, I reached for her chin, turning her to me. "I'm not letting this drop until you tell me what it is. Was it something at work?"

"You could say that."

Frustration rattled my chest. Whatever was going on, she wasn't going to give it up too easily.

"You can talk to me. You know that, right?"

"I'm all changed," Aiden said as he ran into the kitchen. "Can we go outside now, Mr. Ace?"

I stepped away from Savannah.

"Did you finish your homework?" Savannah asked.

His shoulders slumped. "I only have a little bit left. We can—"

"Uh-uh," Savannah said with a shake of her head.

"We were going to go play catch," Aiden protested

"You can go catch that homework," she said. "Upstairs. Finish it now and then bring it down to me."

Aiden's face dropped but he didn't say anything as he started out of the kitchen with his head lowered. I felt bad for the kid, but homework took priority.

"And you better not turn on that tablet either," Savannah yelled after him.

I let out a smirk at her parenting skills. She was the type of mother I always knew she would be.

When I turned back to face her, she started to wipe down the already spotless countertop.

I stopped her hand with mine again. "Talk to me."

She snatched her hand away and folded her arms across her chest. "I can't talk to you."

"Why the hell not?"

She didn't flinch at the base in my voice. "Because there's a little thing called HIPAA. And if I violate it, I could get fired and worse, sued." She turned away from me. "And that bitch, Tricia, is the type to bring about a lawsuit," she mumbled.

I stiffened. "Who did you say?"

She went motionless as well, likely realizing she'd just said that last comment aloud.

"Tricia," I said for her.

I stepped back and gritted my teeth. It didn't take a fucking genius to figure this shit out.

"She went to your job." It wasn't a question but a statement. "She pretended to be a patient?" I thought I'd squashed that situation with

Tricia weeks ago. She'd left me alone ever since she tried to confront me in the parking lot at the base.

"She told you I was the father of her baby," I surmised aloud.

Savannah's nostrils flared, but this time it wasn't due to her lying. It was anger. "It's none of my business what went on between the two of you."

"How isn't it your business? You're my wife," I said louder than I'd intended.

"Who has been gone for sixteen years," she said back. "Of course, you moved on. You would want a family with…" She trailed off.

I shook my head. "No." Savannah read this all wrong, and I had to do my best to keep my anger from making me say something to make all of this worse.

"That's not my baby," I told her.

"How do you know?"

"It's been months since she and I were together."

"That doesn't mean it's not yours." She waved her hand in the air. "She's more than halfway through her pregnancy, from the looks of it."

"I used protection. Every. Single. Time." I stepped closer. "There's only one woman in my past that I didn't use a rubber with."

For the first time since I'd arrived home, Savannah's gaze met mine. But she soon shook her head and looked away.

"That doesn't mean… Accidents happen," she said, stepping around me.

I grabbed her by the arm to keep her from walking away. "She's not having my fucking kid," I growled, keeping my voice low.

"How can you be so sure, Ace?" She whispered. "How do you know?"

"Because she couldn't be pregnant by me. I can't have kids."

Savannah gasped. "What? How can you say that? We…or…did you get injured in the Air Force?"

I shook my head. "I never wanted another kid. Not after… Not with anyone else. So, I fixed the problem."

She tilted her head sideways and gave me a questioning look.

"I had a vasectomy, Savannah. Right after I became an officer in the Air Force, I got it done."

"You..." Her gaze dropped and then lifted to meet mine. "Why?"

"There was only one person I wanted to mother my children." That feeling had never faded. I have dated since Savannah left. I'd screwed more women than I could count, to be honest. I tried desperately to screw the memory of her out of my body.

But all of those women were temporary, and I knew it. I never wanted to be tied to another woman for life. So, I made sure to prevent something unwanted from happening.

To know that Tricia was still going around accusing me of being the father of her child was bullshit. Knowing that she'd gone to my wife's job to throw around that accusation in her face was a foul I couldn't live with.

And I refused to let that bitch get away with it, either.

"Who are you calling?" Savannah asked as I pulled out my cell phone.

"The best PI in the state of Texas," I told her.

CHAPTER 19

Ace Two weeks after Savannah all but told me Tricia confronted her at Brightside, I watched that liar's car pull into the parking lot of The Rustic.

From my vantage point, I saw Tricia get out and walk toward the entrance. She held her belly with one hand. She'd gotten noticeably bigger over the past few weeks.

I was about to flip her entire world up-fucking-side down. She'd fucked with my wife one too many times. I quietly berated myself for not putting an end to her bullshit sooner.

A memory of the night months earlier when Savannah had walked into The Rustic the night of Lena's celebration swelled around in my mind. I avoided the bar for months since then. Tonight, I was there to end Tricia's bullshit and to move on with my family.

Maybe we could make it work this time.

I silenced that thought, tucking it into the pocket of my mind to discuss with Savannah later.

I got out of my truck and started for the entrance of The Rustic. There was a decent amount of people since it was well after five. Happy hour was in full swing.

I pressed past the bar, giving a nod at Tony while he served drinks. Gabriel was a partial owner of the bar, so I knew much of the staff. I headed toward the back booth I'd reserved for the occasion.

The table was in the far corner, right across from the jukebox. Tricia's back was to me as I rounded the corner of the bar.

Without a word, I slid into the seat across from her.

She plastered on a huge smile. "You know, this isn't the type of place a pregnant woman wants to be caught in." She let out a laugh.

I grinned back at her and leaned in. "Everyone can mind their business. This meeting is about you and me, right?"

Her smile grew even wider. "Right." She inhaled deeply. "I'm so glad you've rethought this whole thing. I know you were hesitant, but seriously, Ace, this baby is a miracle."

She rubbed her belly and looked toward me as if I should've agreed.

I dropped my gaze to her distended abdomen. My stomach muscles squeezed almost painfully. Too many memories of Savannah sitting before me while she gripped her belly, pregnant with my son, assaulted me.

I shook off those memories.

"You know," I started, "bringing a life into this world is a hell of a gift. One you shouldn't take lightly."

"Oh, I agree one hundred percent," Tricia said. "Not a day goes by that I don't think about what's best for this baby's future."

"I'm sure you have." I pulled away.

"Yes. That's why, when you called the other day and said we should meet to discuss our baby, I was thrilled. I knew, given a little bit of time, you would come around."

I lifted an eyebrow. "You threatened me."

Her mouth snapped shut, and she gave me an apologetic look. "Ace, I'm so sorry about that. I should've realized you were just shocked at finding out about the baby. I didn't mean it."

"Didn't mean it," I repeated, at the same time mulling the words over in my mind. "Did you mean to go over to Brightside Urgent Care and confront my wife with this news?"

Her mouth dropped open. But being the actress she was, Tricia quickly recovered. She lifted her chin. "She told you that?"

I shook my head, knowing there was a chance if I said yes, Tricia could have grounds for a lawsuit.

"No, but she didn't have to."

Her eyelids fluttered. "Well, anyway, isn't it better that she knows?" She reached across the wooden table to lay her hand over mine. "Now, you can divorce her, and we can move on with our lives as a family."

I snatched my hands away and scowled at her. "The only person moving on is you," I snarled at her.

She recoiled as if I'd smacked her.

"Well, it sounds like I arrived right on time," Micah interrupted.

Tricia gasped as Micah's imposing figure came to a stop at the edge of our table.

"You're running late," I said to Micah as I glared across the table at Tricia.

"Traffic," Micah spat out.

"Wh-who are you?" Tricia questioned, staring up at my eldest brother.

"Me?" Micah pressed a hand to his chest. He gave her a sideways grin. "I'm that child's uncle, apparently." He pointed at her belly.

Her eyes widened before she blinked. "Oh, he's one of your brothers?" She glanced at me.

"He won't be for too much longer if he keeps bullshitting me." I finally peered up at Micah. "Do you have the package?"

"Am I not the best for a reason?" He slapped my shoulder with the back of his hand. "Scoot over."

I moved in so that he could sit.

Micah looked across at Tricia. "I'm sure our other guest will want the seat next to you."

"Is your other brother coming?" she asked with a wrinkle between her eyebrows.

"Gabriel?" I asked. "Fuck no. I wouldn't have any of my family within ten feet of your ass if it weren't necessary."

"Ace," Tricia gasped.

187

"We can nix the offended face and all of that shit." I waved her off with my hand. I pointed at her. "I told you not to fuck with my wife, didn't I say that? I told you to keep her name out of your damn mouth, and what did your ass decide to do?"

I didn't give her a chance to respond.

"You take your scheming ass up to her job and lie to her face."

Tricia shook her head as her eyes watered. "I-I'm not lying."

"Quit it." I swiped my hand across my throat. "I'm sick of your fucking voice. It's making me want to hurl right now. Just being this close to you."

"Daaamn," Micah said under his breath.

"Here's what you're going to do. You're going to resign from your job at the base. Effective immediately. No one will miss you. Then you're going to find a place far away from Harlington. I'm talking outside of the fucking state of Texas. Alaska might be far enough. Settle down there, with your kid and the *real* father of that baby, if he'll have you."

"Tricia?" Another voice interrupted us.

"Speaking of the devil," Micah said, standing. He placed a hand on the guy's shoulder. At six-foot-three, Micah towered over the man, who couldn't have been taller than five-seven.

"Charles?" Tricia asked. "What are you doing here?"

"Did you think I wouldn't find out?" I asked before he could say anything. "Did you think I was dumb enough to take your word that that was my kid without asking questions?"

Tricia, like most people, didn't know that I'd purposefully prevented my ability to have another child. Micah was the only one who knew, since he was the personal contact I'd had pick me up after the surgery.

Savannah was the second person to know, outside of my doctors and healthcare team.

"Ace, this baby is yours," she said, looking desperately between the real father of her child and me.

"Tricia, how could you say that?" Charles asked, taking the seat next to her. "We've been together for years. And we don't use protection. I thought you wanted children with me." He sounded as desperate as she did.

I looked away, unable to watch him grovel pitifully over this woman. Once I found out that Tricia had gone to confront Savannah, I called Micah. And just like he always did, he came through quickly.

He'd found out that Tricia had years' long, off-and-on relationship with Charles McGee. McGee had been an enlisted Airman but had done his original term and decided not to re-up.

Two days earlier, when the three of us sat in Micah's office, he told us that the two of them had been together for the past year, but over the past few months, she'd all but ghosted him.

Charles worked up in Alaska and was away at sea for months, which was why it was easy for her to act single. Not that any of it made a difference to me, but I would've advised Charles to do his damnedest to get full custody of his kid and get the hell away from Tricia.

But he was in love.

"No, no, no. You're messing everything up," Tricia yelled so loudly, a few of the customers from around the bar turned our way.

I nudged Micah with my elbow. "That's our cue to head out."

Micah stood, and I moved to stand.

"Ace, wait." She reached for me from across the table, but I moved out of her reach. "Hand in your resignation letter first thing in the morning," I said with a tone that was hard as stone. "Your landlord has already been told that you're breaking your lease to move away. Go with your kid's father and have a nice life. Or don't. Either way, this is the nicest I'm ever going to be to you again.

"You don't want to see me any more pissed off than this. Trust me." I gave her one last glare before turning and following Micah out of the bar.

"You were mean as hell in there," Micah said with a chuckle in his voice as we entered the parking lot.

I frowned. "No more than she deserved."

He shrugged. "That might be true. She might not have tried that bullshit if you would've told her from the beginning that you went and got yourself fixed."

I shot him a middle finger. He'd been calling it that ever since I got it done.

"Anyway, I hear those things are reversible."

I stared at my brother. "What the hell are you doing looking up information on vasectomies?"

Micah was happily married and had just had his first child with his wife, Jodi, nine months earlier. I wouldn't be surprised if he were working on baby number two already.

"I wasn't," he replied. "A client of mine had one and then got it reversed years later. His wife got pregnant with twins soon after."

I rolled my eyes. "Thanks for the information." Like it wasn't anything I didn't already know.

"Welcome."

We stopped at my truck, next to which Micah had parked.

"I figured any man willing to go to that length over his wife isn't ready for a divorce." He peered at me expectantly. "Speaking of, I gave you some time to think about it. Are you certain you want me to dive into your wife's financial records?"

I swallowed.

I'd made the request months ago, when Savannah told me she wanted the divorce for her grandmother's inheritance. Until then, Micah hadn't done a deep dive into her accounts. I thought about what giving Micah the greenlight on his question would mean.

Did I trust Savannah?

"Yeah," I answered. "Don't fucking look at me like that," I said after Micah peered at me out of the corner of his eyes.

He chuckled. "Whatever. Also, don't you think it's about time you brought Savannah and your stepson around the rest of us?"

My chest swelled at the mentioning of Aiden as my stepson. I supposed technically, he was, but no one had ever said it out loud.

"He asked to meet you all," I said, recalling the day I picked him up from his friend's house. "It's probably time for that to happen, formally."

Aiden had technically met them that night at The Rustic, but he'd been half-asleep. He barely even remembered that night.

"How about this weekend? Gabe and Lena will be back in town for wedding planning. We'll grill out in the backyard."

I nodded, agreeing. One of the best things about my home state was that, even though it was early November, the weather was still perfect in the afternoons for outdoor activities.

In my military career, I'd lived or was stationed in countries worldwide, but nothing beat the Lone Star State, in my *least* humble opinion.

"We'll be there," I said, knowing Savannah had weekends off. "But not until afternoon. Aiden plays in a soccer tournament this Saturday morning."

Micah gave me a look. "Did I say stepson?" He shook his head. "That's more like, dad shit. See ya Saturday." He climbed behind the wheel of his truck.

Dad.

The word vibrated around my brain while I drove back home. I hadn't experienced the feeling that one word elicited in years. It was a combination of pride, joy, and fear.

A lump worked its way up my throat. Maybe it was time to talk to Savannah about staying for the long haul. And therefore, making me Aiden's father, legally.

Aside from when I was in the cockpit, nothing felt more right than that thought.

CHAPTER 20

$\mathcal{A}$^{ce} "And you said Joel isn't going to be there, right?" Savannah asked as she came down the stairs from changing.

It was a few days after the confrontation with Tricia had gone down, and I was finally taking Savannah and Aiden over to Micah's for an afternoon with the family.

I wrinkled my forehead. "That's the third time you've asked me the same question." I'd told Savannah that my father was in Houston for the weekend, handling some ranch business.

It would only be Gabriel, his fiancée Lena, Micah's family, and us.

I stared at Savannah. She sucked in her bottom lip and glanced around the living room behind me, as if avoiding eye contact.

"Hey," I said, taking her hand into mine. "I know Joel wasn't the most welcoming back then when he thought we were too young. But he's not all that bad. Honestly." I shook her hand a little, trying to garner a smile.

Savannah didn't respond. Instead, she glanced over her shoulder. "Aiden left this place a mess. I need to make him clean it up."

There were pillows thrown all over and a few of his toys strewn on the floor.

She started to turn for the stairs, but I grabbed her by the arm.

"Leave the kid alone," I told her. "He scored three goals in the championship game today. He's earned to let his mess sit for a little while."

She snorted.

"Besides, I'm the one who helped him make the mess." I grinned, remembering the fort we'd built out of the pillows that morning before we left for his soccer games.

"That's because you're a bad influence." She pointed at me and stuck out her opposite hip. A move that forced me to drop my gaze, noting the way the floral wrap dress rested over her curves.

My cock stirred in my jeans, and briefly, I contemplated calling Micah to pick up Aiden and take him over to his place while I took Savannah back upstairs.

"I'm ready," Aiden yelled as he charged down the stairs, interrupting my thoughts of what I wanted to do to his mother.

When I peered into Savannah's eyes while a smile played on her lips, I knew she read my thoughts.

"*Later*," I mouthed to her right before Aiden came running into the living room.

"The gang's all set," I said.

"Let's bug out," Aiden said.

I laughed at him using my military lingo, directing us to head out. "You're learning," I said as I ruffled the top of his hair from behind him.

He glanced back and gave me a proud smile that punched me directly in the solar plexus.

"I almost forgot the potato salad," Savannah said, right before we got in the car.

I directed Aiden to run in and get the massive bowl of salad that Savannah had left in the refrigerator.

A few minutes later, we were off. Micah and Jodi's place wasn't far from mine. I'd bought my home within weeks of getting my orders to relocate back at the base outside of Harlington. That was almost four years ago.

Though I should've been doing everything to close out my life in Harlington, I dragged my feet. The Air Force scheduled me to head out to Germany in less than two months, and for the first time in my career, I found myself begrudging a move.

For years, the constant moving and being out of town that my career required didn't bother me. At times, what agitated me the most was being in one place for too long. The loneliness would settle in.

But the past four years had spoiled me. Being so close to my family was something I hadn't even realized I'd missed, until I had it again.

Though, I had to admit, as I looked over into the passenger seat at my wife, that the lonely feeling I carried for so long had begun to ebb. I wasn't in a rush to pick up and move as I had been for so many years.

"We're here," I said as I pulled up in front of Micah's home. Gabriel had parked his huge-ass truck right in the middle of the driveway.

"Aiden, stop running," Savannah called when he hopped out of the SUV and darted for the door. "Come grab the potato salad," she instructed.

She turned to me as I rounded the front of my truck to come beside her. "You'd think as much as he ran around this morning, he would've burned some of that energy off."

I chuckled. "Wishful thinking on your part."

She groaned. "Don't I know it."

Before we even knocked, Jodi, Micah's wife, pulled the door open. Her smile was wide and there was a sparkle in her eyes.

My stomach turned.

"Well, well, well, if it isn't Ace's secret wife," Jodi said as casually as if she were reporting the weather.

"Micah, come get your wife," I yelled above Jodi's head into the house. A second later, I heard Micah's heavy footsteps.

"Secret wife?" Aiden said, turning to face Savannah and me.

I glared at my sister-in-law. It was no secret Jodi wasn't the type to mince words, which at first I'd found endearing. But right then, I wished she had more restraint.

"Guilty as charged," Savannah said at the same time Micah arrived behind his wife. He held their son, Lonzie, short for Alonzo, in one arm.

"And you must be Micah's less-secret but beautiful wife, Jodi," Savannah said as she held out her hand for Jodi to shake.

Jodi cocked her head to the side and her eyes narrowed. She nodded. "Okay. I might like you." She shook her hand and then moved aside. "Come in."

"This is my son, Aiden," Savannah introduced.

"Hi," Aiden waved. "Is that your son?" he asked, pointing at the baby who was doing his best to stuff his entire fist into his mouth.

"He is," Micah said before lowering to introduce Aiden and Lonzie.

Aiden groaned when Lonzie reached out with a slobber-filled hand and caressed his face. All of the adults laughed.

"I hear laughing and we're not invited?" My youngest brother's voice beckoned from the back of the house. A heartbeat later, he and Lena appeared in the doorway.

"Nice meeting you under better circumstances this time," Lena said to Savannah.

"Yeah, well, I don't currently have a flat tire with a sleeping nine-year-old in the backseat," she joked before handing the potato salad over to Jodi.

We took the party outside. Micah had purchased the property years earlier and built the house to his specifications.

The expansive backyard allowed one to see out to the hills that lay around the Texas Hill Country. It was well into the fall season, which meant the absence of wildflowers in the distance. But the green and rocky, rolling hills held a certain appeal, even without the diverse colors that the wildflowers provided.

"Hope you've brought your appetites," Micah said over his shoulder. "We've got burgers, chicken, fish, corn on the cob, grilled vegetables, and salad."

"And potato salad," I added, mentioning Savannah's dish.

"I'll have to be the judge of that," Jodi said. "You know you can't eat everybody's."

Savannah laughed instead of taking offense. "My mama used to say the same thing."

"'I assume she's a smart woman," Jodi replied.

"She was," Savannah responded and cleared her throat.

"Mama makes perfect potato salad," Aiden said, sticking up for his mother. "Everything she cooks is great. Right, Mr. Ace?"

I smiled down at the kid, liking the defensiveness in his voice. "Affirmative."

Savannah waved us off as we sat around the glass patio table on the large white brick deck.

"I think Jodi and Micah thought they were assigned to feed an army," Lena said.

I grunted.

"Cin, please. No Army talk in the presence of an Airman," Gabriel said, using his pet name for Lena while rolling his eyes at me.

The entire table laughed.

"My bad," Lena said, holding up her hands as she looked at me from across the table.

"As long as you don't let it happen again," I teased.

"Don't listen to him," Savannah interjected, glancing between Lena and me. "This guy has respect for all branches. So much so, he briefly contemplated being a fighter pilot in the Navy instead of the Air Force."

"I didn't know that," Micah said, turning to me.

I shrugged. Few people knew that I'd considered going into the Navy. I'd still wanted to fly fighter jets, but some of the benefits of flying for the Navy appealed to me.

I'd talked with Savannah about the different options when we were together. One of the reasons I'd chosen the Air Force was because of the number of bases it had in this area of Texas, where we both had wanted to remain or retire.

In the end, I went with the right branch for me.

We all talked and laughed for the next hour while we ate. Micah then pulled out his huge, standing Connect Four game. It became a competition between Aiden and me against him and Lonzie.

Savannah and Jodi cheered for their families, while Gabe and Lena declared themselves Switzerland, cheering for both teams.

Later, Micah showed Gabe and me around the area where he and Jodi decided they would build an in-ground pool the following year. Lena, Savannah, and Jodi went off to the living room to discuss the details of Gabriel and Lena's wedding that would happen next spring.

Jodi took a sleeping Lonzie with them while a drowsy Aiden tried his best to hang with the three of us. Eventually, he wandered into the house and fell asleep beside his mother.

As I entered the living room and found Aiden's head propped on his mother's lap as he slept, I ate my words. As it turned out, the kid didn't have endless energy.

"So much for getting him to take a bath before bed tonight," Savannah said when I came to sit next to them.

"That'll be a losing battle," I commented.

She chuckled. "Tell me something I don't know." She glanced down at him and stroked his hair. "He had a good day." Her eyes met mine. "Thank you." Her voice was low, loud enough for only me to hear.

It was a tiny, shared moment between the two of us, even though we were in a room full of the rest of my family.

"Hey Ace, weren't you out west last month?" Gabriel asked, breaking our eye contact.

"For training." I nodded. "Yeah."

"I bet you had a visitor," Micah added.

I grunted. "Hell, yeah. Chael and his crew showed up, per usual, without my telling him where the hell I was."

"You didn't tell me that," Savannah said.

"Chael?" Lena asked.

"He's one of our cousins from out west," Gabe told her. "You'll meet him soon," he said.

"Be careful when she does meet him." Micah pointed at Gabriel. "That fucker damn near tried to steal my wife when he first met her."

Jodi laughed out loud. "That's hardly true. All I said was how fine that man is. And this guy," she gestured to Micah with her thumb, "got all jealous and possessive."

"I mean, you weren't lying," Savannah spoke up.

"What?" I demanded.

She peered at me with an innocent expression. "I'm sorry, babe, but your cousin is hot."

I narrowed my eyes and glared at her. "Now I have to kill my cousin."

She leaned in and pressed a kiss to my lips. "He's got nothing on you, though. Shapeshifter or not," she whispered that last part so that only I could hear.

Savannah, having met Chael long ago, knew the secret about that side of our family.

"Hm, so you've been keeping this cousin of yours away from me?" Lena asked Gabriel.

"Fuck yeah," he answered.

We all laughed, unfortunately forgetting that there were sleeping children in the room.

While Aiden stirred, he readjusted himself so that he lay on the edge of the couch instead of in Savannah's lap. However, baby Lonzie decided to make his disapproval of our disturbance known.

He awakened on a scream.

"He's got a powerful set of lungs," Savannah said. "Can I?" She held out her arms and looked over at Jodi.

Jodi hesitated. "He doesn't normally take to new people. Especially when he's ornery like this."

"Just like his mama," Micah said.

Jodi glared at Micah but handed Lonzie to Savannah.

"Hey there," she cooed. She rose to her feet. "Are we pesky adults being too loud for you?" She stroked the side of his face and bounced him on her hip. "Or is somebody teething?"

Lonzie, though not completely pacified, began to quiet.

"We've got teething rings in the freezer." Jodi started to stand, but Savannah held her hand out.

"I'll get it."

I watched as she carried Lonzie in the direction of the kitchen. A beat later, I heard her opening the door of the freezer.

"That's what you wanted, huh?" She continued to talk to him in a soothing voice while she held the cold teething ring to his mouth.

He'd completely mellowed out. Savannah swayed from side to side, comforting the baby, and soon, he began dozing off again.

Though the scene before me was a sweet one, it caused my chest to hurt. A pain I believed I'd successfully suppressed over the years resurfaced.

I sat there and watched my wife cradling a baby in her arms. She cooed and held him close, creating a safe environment for him. Secure enough that she lulled him to sleep without breaking stride, unperturbed by his earlier screams.

Memories of white walls, sterilized rooms, and the sound of Savannah's cries assaulted me. I felt battered by the reminder of the son that we never got to hear cry or scream from teething.

I stood abruptly and ignored the three heads in the room that shot my way. I needed air. I felt suffocated by the memories firing off in my head.

The memories were too much, and I needed some space. Before I knew it, I was at the first door I could find and exiting the house. I ended up on the front porch of the house.

Only after a long while of pacing back and forth in front of Micah's home did I finally start to breathe regularly again.

My body felt like someone ripped it inside out.

I heard a noise behind me but didn't turn around. When Savannah began stroking my back, some of the hurt in my chest began to ease.

She didn't say anything for a long while. I knew I should've explained what the hell that was all about, but I didn't have the words.

"You know, it took me years before I could even stand the sight of babies." Her voice was soft, consoling. "Especially mothers holding their babies or playing with them."

Finally, I turned to face her. "How did you get over it?" I asked, grateful I didn't need to explain myself.

"Work." She gave me a tight smile. "I had to work with all kinds of patients when I started in healthcare. I'd successfully avoided young children and babies up until then. But then I couldn't. So, I had a decision to make. I could either put my pain above their needs, or I could push through and be the healthcare provider they deserved."

She shrugged.

"And I didn't have anything left." She looked me in the eyes. "I no longer had you, or our baby, a family. Even my dream of going to medical school, I gave up on. I decided that eventually becoming a PA was one more thing I didn't want to lose. So, I sucked it up."

I stood to my full height and peered down at her.

"You no longer had me?" I asked, my voice tight. "You always fucking had me. Always. All you had to do was come back."

There was the truth.

I was hurt, pissed, and brokenhearted when she left. But all she would've had to do was walk through my door, and all would've been forgiven.

I tried but couldn't ignore the tear that fell from her eye.

"Why did you leave?" I had to know, finally. "You tore a fucking hole in my chest when you walked away. Why?" I demanded.

She looked away from me, staring at the ground.

"Look at me, Savannah. Why the fuck did you walk away?"

She pushed out a heavy breath. "You deserved better. More."

"How can you even say that?" I shook my head, not understanding.

"I couldn't..."

"Couldn't what?" I yelled, louder than I intended.

But Savannah didn't shrink away.

"I couldn't be the one to cause you any more pain. If it weren't for me, you wouldn't hurt so much. After AJ died, I knew you did your best to be there for me, but it hurt to see the pain in your eyes. For what we both lost. I knew it was my fault that pain was there."

Her shoulders dropped.

"And then after what Joel said to me, I knew..."

"What do you mean it was your fault? What did my father say to you?"

Her eyes widened, and she shook her head. "Nothing."

"Don't tell me nothing. I've been waiting sixteen years for an explanation. You owe me that."

She rubbed her hands up and down her eyes as she closed her eyes. "That was the worst time of my life." She opened her eyes and started to tell me what had happened sixteen years ago.

CHAPTER 21

hen
Savannah

"Hey, Savannah, can you take these boxes upstairs?" Jerry, the store manager, asked as soon as I stepped from behind the retail counter to take my lunch.

My stomach had been growling for the past thirty minutes, and I was anxious to use the bathroom. No one told me that, once I reached the six-month mark of pregnancy, I'd have to pee every five freaking minutes.

I peered at the cardboard box that sat on one of the rolling racks we used to transport clothes from one side of the store to the other.

"I'm kinda in a rush. Does it need to be taken right away?" I asked, shifting from one foot to the other, trying desperately to hold in the current contents of my bladder.

"Come on," he insisted. "Look, it's not that heavy." He held up the box with one hand. "And once you drop it off in the storage room, you can take your break." He said it as if he were doing me a favor.

"Okay." I sighed but grabbed the box, knowing one of the other employees could've carried it upstairs.

But whatever.

On my way to the stairs, I made a mental list of the positives of my job.

One: I got paid every week.

Since Ace's job paid him bimonthly, my weekly paycheck was what helped keep us afloat until his next check came in.

Two: I liked most of my co-workers.

Three: The customers were friendly.

"Ah," I yelped after tripping on one of the stairs and landing awkwardly on my side. "Shit."

I dropped the box in my hands and immediately grasped for my belly. My first concern was for my baby.

"Are you okay in there?" I asked AJ, as I'd come to call him affectionately. It was short for Ace Junior, but his dad was still on the fence about naming his son after him.

He wanted him to have his own identity, he'd told me. But I loved the idea of having a junior and senior in the family. It probably stemmed from my lack of family throughout my life.

"Okay," I said, relieved when I felt AJ kick in my womb. I paused, trying to feel if there was any pain.

My butt was a little sore from where I fell, but it wasn't too bad. As I lifted myself up again, I winced. I'd likely have a bruise on my ass. Indeed, I'd have to explain that one to Ace.

He wouldn't be happy about it.

He'd wanted me to quit my job almost as soon as we found out that I was pregnant. He hated that I stood on my feet for eight hours a day while carrying our child. But we needed the money.

I felt okay as I went up the stairs. By the time I got to the top, my bladder screamed to be emptied.

Eventually, as time passed that day, I forgot about the fall. I assumed that both AJ and I were all right. For a brief moment, I considered calling the clinic where I went for my prenatal care to make an appointment, but knew that would cost a considerable amount of money we couldn't afford at that time.

Hours later, when I got off and walked back home to our apartment, I started to feel a twinge of pain in my lower back.

I knew back pain was yet another symptom of many pregnancies because of the expanding belly area. But when the pain grew stronger over the next few hours, I started to worry.

That was when I made the first call to the clinic.

"No, there's no spotting," I told the woman on the other end of the phone.

"Hang on," she said before I could get in another word.

I paced back and forth, breathing heavily, trying to will the pain to go away. It did stop by the time the woman came back on the line.

"Yeah, it might be nothing since there's no spotting. But you can make an appointment if you'd like. What insurance are you with?"

My heart sank. I hated that question. Our insurance sucked, and very few healthcare providers in the area accepted it.

"Hold on again," the receptionist said again.

I blew out a deep breath. Feeling defeated, I chose not to wait for her to come back to the line. The pain had stopped, and I was just probably overreacting. First-time mom jitters and all.

These were likely Braxton Hicks contractions, I reasoned. I'd felt them for the past two months.

I told myself to chill out and started to make dinner. Ace would be home from his shift in the next hour. All we had was some leftover ground meat that I'd taken out of the freezer that morning and a box of Hamburger Helper. We did have some fresh vegetables that I'd bought the day before, so I could prepare a salad to go with it.

At least part of our dinner would be something healthy.

My lower abdomen started to cramp up again as I began chopping the vegetables. I did my best to hum, sing, and even dance a little through the pain. I managed to get the hamburger meat cooked through and poured in the seasoning packet and noodles from the box.

However, when I went back to the counter to toss the salad, searing pain ripped through my lower belly. I instantly fell to my knees and cried out in agony.

My belly burned and my vision blurred from the tears it caused.

"Ow." I had one hand on my belly and one clutching to the edge of the counter.

"Baby," Ace's panicked voice broke through the haze of fire in my stomach. "What's wrong?"

"I don't know," I panted out in between breaths, gasping for air. It hurt so badly I could barely breathe.

"I'm calling the doctor."

"No." I shook my head. "They—they said since I'm not spotting, it's okay."

"Fuck that," Ace growled. "You're hurting."

He kneeled on the floor next to me and dialed 9-11. The pain refused to subside, and instead of clutching to the counter, I held onto the front of Ace's shirt.

"The baby," I whimpered. "Please, let him be okay."

Everything felt like it moved in slow motion. I couldn't recall how long it took the ambulance to arrive or even when they loaded me onto the stretcher. All I remembered was Ace squeezing my hand tightly as he sat next to me in the back of that ambulance.

"It's okay," he said over and over, in between kissing my hand.

I tried to focus on one breath at a time. The pain in my stomach and back persisted while the paramedics wheeled me through the doors of the emergency department.

A curtain separated the room where they took me and then left. No one told us anything.

"What the fuck?" Ace growled after we waited for what seemed like forever but was likely only ten minutes or so.

"It—it's all right," I told him, squeezing his hand.

"The fuck it is. You're in pain." He barged through the curtain, turning his head this way and that, then disappeared.

Before I knew it, I heard him yelling at someone.

"My wife is in pain. She's six months pregnant. What is going on?" he growled.

I wanted to yell for him to calm down, but the truth was that I was in too much pain to reel him in. I needed someone to tell me what was happening.

His temper worked in our favor that time because, minutes later, a doctor and nurse came through the curtain. Ace was right behind them, grilling them with his gaze as they wheeled in an ultrasound machine.

They asked several questions I felt like I either answered already or was in too much discomfort to even think of an answer to.

Once they conducted an ultrasound, all my hopes were dashed. Ever since my knees first hit the old, wooden floors of our kitchen, I'd silently prayed that our son was okay. I begged and pleaded to spare his life.

But then the words "Placental abruption" came out of the doctor's mouth. Something about bleeding behind the placenta being the reason why I wasn't spotting.

"There's nothing we can do." It was the ultimate crushing blow to what remained left of my heart.

I tried to fight. I attempted to get up from the bed and tell the hospital staff that they were wrong. My baby was still alive.

I almost fell, but Ace's strong arms held me close. He whispered in my ear that everything would be okay.

I yelled at him too. How could everything be okay? Our baby was dead, and they told me that I still had to give birth to him.

Somehow, they got me calm enough to move ahead with the treatment that would force my body to go into labor. The staff told us it could take days for the delivery to start. Meanwhile, we could go home and wait for my body to respond to the medication.

Everything hurt. It was as if the pain in my heart engulfed my entire being, causing it to be one sore pile of bone and tissue, walking around—bone and tissue with a dead baby inside of it.

It took less than twenty-four hours for the medication they gave me to kick in, and Ace and I returned to the hospital to have him.

A stillbirth.

I thought I hurt before, but it wasn't until the moment of AJ's birth that some small piece of me had managed to hold out hope. A faith that maybe the doctors were wrong, and my little guy's heart was still beating.

Yet, after he was born, and the nurses wrapped him up in a blanket and handed him to me, I knew they were right. Outwardly, he looked like he could've been asleep. But as I held him, he was motionless.

Too still.

No up and down movement of his chest to indicate breathing.

No flickering of his eyelids.

"I'm so sorry," I whispered to him before kissing his forehead. I knew this was my fault. If I had listened to Ace and quit my job sooner, maybe I wouldn't have fallen, and AJ would still be alive.

I concluded that my fall at work had to be responsible for what happened to him.

When I passed our son over to Ace to hold, I burst into tears. It was my fault. I was responsible for the pained expression on his face as he held his dead son.

I turned over in the bed and wept like I never had before.

A FEW WEEKS LATER...

There was a knock on the door. "Ace, someone's at the door," I called out from my fetal position in our bed.

I didn't feel like I had the strength to get up and answer it. I hadn't had the energy to do much aside from lying in bed and stare at the wall with the TV on.

I'd tried to go back to work a week earlier, and that turned into a disaster.

"Ace," I yelled again, then remembered he wasn't home. And whoever was on the other end of the door wasn't getting the message.

I sat up and slowly stood. I took my time getting to the door even though our apartment was tiny. Physically, I was better, though not fully healed. It was mentally that continued to wear on me and slow me down.

"Mr. Joel," I said as I pulled the door open.

Ace's father hated to be called Mr. Townsend for some reason and insisted on everyone calling him by his first name. Even his sons. Yet, I never felt comfortable calling someone much older than me by their first name.

Joel's lips tightened. "Is my son home?" he asked without any type of greeting.

"No." I bit my tongue to keep from adding 'sir.' The man hated those types of formalities. "He's at work but should be home in a few hours." Ace had taken on extra hours to make up for my loss of pay. And the additional medical bills.

"And what are you doing at home?"

I swallowed, not liking the bite in his voice. Joel hadn't ever been overly friendly with me. I always got the sense that he disliked me. Or at least, he didn't think I was good enough for his son.

Probably because I was from the other side of the bridge. That's what I concluded, at least.

Ace's mother, on the other hand, had always been loving and kind to me. Up until the day she died.

"I was resting," I lied. I couldn't rest. Every time I closed my eyes, I either saw Ace Junior in that hospital blanket, or I would experience phantom kicks in my belly. Only to discover, when I opened my eyes, that they weren't real.

It was like reliving over and over, every morning, that my son died.

Joel snorted and took a step back.

"You can come in, if you'd like," I offered, even though I wasn't in the position to be good company to anyone. I tried to be as nice to my father-in-law as possible. I knew he hadn't responded well when Ace told him that we had gotten married. Though, he never told me word for word what Joel said.

"No, thanks," he said, still staring at me. His expression wasn't angry. It was more like distant and unfeeling.

Then he said the words that would effectively end my marriage as I knew it.

"This is all your fault. You know that, right?"

I bulged my eyes and shook my head. It was the same sentence I told myself repeatedly. But this time, they were coming from an outside source.

"He's in so much pain because of you," he hurled the words at me, and they impacted my heart like an arrow. "I knew you were too young for all of this. Now look, you couldn't even take care of your baby, and my son's heartbroken because of it."

I stood there frozen, unable to speak.

Joel had just confirmed all of the doubts and fears that swelled in my mind and heart ever since AJ died.

I was the source of Ace's pain. I was the reason he was living in this tiny apartment, hurting, instead of away at the Air Force Academy, studying to become a pilot.

I was holding him back in life. In the same way, I'd held back my mother's life when she got pregnant with me.

I had fooled myself into believing that Ace and I could overcome everything together. But I was the ball and chain around his neck.

Joel took one final look at me then turned on his heel, walking away.

My entire body trembled. I couldn't deny it anymore. If Ace was to accomplish everything he was meant to in his life, I had to leave him.

I couldn't let myself be the source of his pain any longer.

As I stood in that doorway, my body shaking, tears running down my face, I decided to leave my husband.

CHAPTER 22

Ace

My mind whirled as I sat on the edge of my bed with my head in my hands. Savannah's revelation had knocked me over.

We were home from Micah's, and I still couldn't wrap my mind around all that she'd told me. Especially about Joel and what he'd fucking said to her.

My own father.

I stood up and patted my pockets to search for my keys. I was going to confront his ass before the night was over. Face to face.

"Aiden's out for the night," Savannah said as she entered the bedroom. She'd gone to check on Aiden after I carried him up to his bedroom and put him in bed.

She paused. "What are you doing?"

"Looking for my keys," I answered while opening the drawer of my nightstand.

"Your keys are downstairs on the hook where you always leave them."

I started for the bedroom door, but Savannah blocked me. "Why are you searching for your keys?"

I looked over her shoulder. "I need to make a run."

"Where?"

I didn't answer.

"Where?"

Finally, I dropped my gaze to meet hers. "To see Joel."

She folded her arms and lifted an eyebrow. "Joel is away in Houston, remember?"

"Then I'm driving to Houston."

"Ace, that's almost a four-hour drive."

"What's your point?" I clenched my jaw, the words he said to her replaying in my head.

"I should've never told you what he said."

"No," I snarled, peering down at her. "What you should've done is told me that same day. I would've told you it was all bullshit." My voice rose with each word I said.

"Shh." She pushed me with her hand flat against my chest, forcing me back into the bedroom as she shut the door behind her.

"It's almost midnight. You can't drive to Houston to confront your father. You're too angry, and you'll regret whatever you say to him."

I shook my head. "The only regrets will be his. I promise you that." I couldn't believe he dared to say such horrible things to my wife. Right after our son died, no less.

Who the hell did that?

"No, Ace," Savannah said, wrapping her arms around my waist.

I felt my resolve growing weaker, and I lifted my arms to hold her to me.

"Stay with me tonight." She rose on her tiptoes and softly pressed her lips against mine.

It was like ice water to the flame of my anger. I lowered my hands to cup her ass and walked her back against the wall by the bed.

"You should've fucking told me what he said," I said against her lips.

She shook her head. "It wouldn't have made a difference." She panted as I dipped my head and kissed her neck. "I blamed myself anyway."

I found the vein in her neck that pulsed whenever she got aroused and licked it to the space just behind her ear. Her entire body trembled.

I nipped at her earlobe and squeezed her ass. My cock thumped against the zipper of my jeans, seeking freedom.

With a few flicks of my wrist, I undid the string holding Savannah's dress together. She found the bottom of my shirt and lifted it. I assisted her by raising my arms so she could remove my shirt.

We undressed each other, caressing here and kissing there. Everything felt new, somehow.

Although this wasn't the first time Savannah and I had made love since she'd come back, this time felt rawer. I finally knew the reason she'd left.

She'd always had a hang up about holding me back. She believed she was the reason her mother hadn't accomplished more in her life before she died. Savannah blamed herself for her own mother's death. I knew that.

I should've fucking realized that she would blame herself for AJ's death. And for my pain.

Add to that the bullshit my father spewed at her when she was in such a vulnerable state; no wonder she believed leaving was in my best interest.

Fucking Joel.

"Hey," Savannah said, cupping my face to look at her. "Are you here? With me?"

I looked down into her brown irises and planted a kiss on her lips. "Affirmative." My voice came out hoarse.

"Fuck," I growled when she reached down and gripped my cock, rubbing her thumb against the top.

"Good." She grinned.

I walked her back to the bed and pressed her back against it. When she was in the position I wanted, I eased down her naked body, stopping to press a kiss to her belly before moving lower. I parted her legs even more with my palms, opening her center to me.

I dipped my head and licked down her slit.

Savannah hissed loudly and I acquainted my tastebuds with the flavor of her pussy, devouring it.

In seconds, her body rewarded me with a gushing of liquid from her orgasm. Nothing felt better than making her entire body tremble for me. And I fucking flew fighter jets for a living.

When I sat up, Savannah immediately lifted as well and circled her arms around my neck, bringing our lips to a searing kiss. She moaned against my mouth, and I felt my entire body warm with a burning need only one woman had ever inspired in my lifetime.

"I don't want to use a condom," I said as I pulled back.

She paused, then nodded. "Okay."

I pushed her back against the bed and wrapped her legs around my waist. She felt so good as I eased inside of her without a barrier for the first time in sixteen years that it stole my breath.

Savannah didn't move, either. For an undetermined amount of time, we lay facing one another, our eyes burning into one another's.

Right then, I had one regret in this world.

The fact that this coupling wouldn't result in a pregnancy. The only time in the years since I'd gotten my vasectomy that I wanted to reverse my decision.

"Ace," she whispered, a plea in her voice.

"I know," I said, then pressed a kiss to her lips. I began moving my hips, and she held tighter onto my neck.

We moved with the familiarity that came only from knowing another so profoundly that our souls were intertwined.

When Savannah squeezed her eyes tightly and arched her back, I let myself watch the orgasm take over her entire body. I reveled in it.

And when her pussy muscles clamped around my rod, I couldn't hold back any longer, either. Another time, I could make this last a while, but not that night.

I shot my load off in her, blanketing internal canal with my bodily fluid. Again, sorrow filled me knowing that even without the barrier of a condom, the chance of us having created a baby that night was practically zero.

I leaned in and kissed her after pushing away the regret. "I love you," I whispered to my wife for the first time in sixteen years.

"I love you, too," she said back.

I fell against the bed a satisfied man that night. I cupped her body to mine and held on tight. For the first time in a very long time, it felt like everything might be all right.

That possibly, somehow, the promises I'd made to her in that ambulance when we were rushed to the hospital weren't in vain.

But first, I needed to speak with my father.

CHAPTER 23

ce
A week had passed since I'd found out the truth of what my father had said to Savannah.

It'd taken another few days of Savannah talking me out of driving over to Houston. It was only my promise to her, and the fact I had to work, that kept me off of my father's ass for this long.

But it couldn't wait any longer. I headed over on my motorcycle, let myself in with the key under the mat, and took up a seat at his dining room table.

"I know you're in here," Joel's deep voice boomed through the house as soon as he stepped over the threshold. "I saw your bike outside."

Heavy footsteps padded from the front door to the kitchen and over to the dining room.

"I parked it right out front. You should've seen it," I affirmed, glaring at Joel as he came into my line of sight.

I didn't rise from my seat.

"I knew once she came back that this would be inevitable." He ran his hand through his dark brown hair that was greying on the sides.

My father stood around six-two, same height as me. Even in his late fifties, he was broad as hell.

"Never thought I'd see the day when one of my grown sons would look at me with disdain in his eyes." He almost sounded sincere, regretful even.

Fuck him. He'd known what he'd done for years and never said anything.

"I never thought I'd see the day when my wife would tell me what the fuck you said to her."

Heat flushed through my body while I rose to my feet. I did my best to remember this was the man that raised me. It was for that reason alone I hadn't struck out already.

Not many other people walking this Earth could say what he'd said to my wife and get away with it.

"How the hell could you?" I demanded.

Joel dipped his head and stared at the kitchen floor before peering back up at me. "What do you want me to say?"

"Something. Say fucking something that would make it okay for you to go to my wife six weeks after she had to hold our dead son in her arms and tell her it was her fault."

I got in his face, poking at his chest. "Tell me anything that would make it okay for you to tell the woman I love beyond reason that she was the cause of all the pain in my life."

Joel's body went rigid, and he sucked in his cheeks. He didn't say anything for a long, drawn-out minute. When he did speak, his response proved insufficient.

"There are few men who've ever talked to me like that or put their hands on me and lived to tell the tale."

I spread my arms wide. "And?" It strained against my very instincts to protect what was mine. My wife. The same instincts he'd instilled in me.

"A woman is to be sheltered, cared for, loved. Isn't that what you told me?" I seethed through gritted teeth. "Aren't those the very same fucking words you said to me when I came to you after Savannah and I got married?"

I remembered it like it was yesterday. He told me I was too young, too immature to take care of a wife and family the way I needed to.

"You were full of shit," I spat out. I could barely look at my father. He'd raised me, loved me, but for the past sixteen years, he'd been a source of my deepest pain, and I never fucking knew it.

He knew it, though, and had looked me in the eye all these years and never said a word.

My father took a step back and shook his head. He turned and went over to the refrigerator, pulling it open.

I watched as he pulled out two bottles of water. He tossed me one. I caught it before slamming it on the kitchen island.

"Drink the water. It'll calm your ass down."

"Fuck your water. I need an explanation."

The tension between us was at the highest it'd ever been. I was two seconds from doing something I never believed I could do to my father. Amid my anger, I wanted him to say something, anything that would make this better. There had to be some explanation.

"Your mama had died, Ace," he finally said after a long silence.

I reared back. "What does that have to do with it?"

He recapped his bottle and sauntered over to the kitchen island. "Your mother was—is—the love of my life. She was my entire world. I fell apart when she died."

I thought back to the painful period of my mother's death. I knew Joel hadn't handled it well. The night after her funeral, I remember Joel had gone upstairs while Gabe, Micah, Savannah, and I remained downstairs.

We could hear Joel's cries from up there. Hours later, when he finally emerged from the bedroom they shared, he was stone-faced. There was a blank look in his eyes as if someone had turned off a switch.

Joel inhaled deeply. "All I saw was that she was gone. I was angry, pissed as hell. At everyone and everything. Except for you three." He paused and studied my expression. "I've done a lot of shameful things in my life, but there's not much of it that I'm ashamed of. What I said to Savannah is one of them. I'm sorry."

My hands tightened into fists at my sides. Joel's gaze dipped to my hands, and his shoulders dropped.

"I'm sorry for what I said to her that day. If I had it to do over again, I would—"

"You can't do it over again. Isn't that what you always taught us? No use in regretting anything since you can't go back in time and change it?"

That was one of the mottos he taught us coming up. Live with no regrets.

"I have regrets, Ace. The way I treated Savannah is one of 'em."

"Then why the hell didn't you ever tell me?" I yelled, my anger boiling over. He'd apologized like that was somehow supposed to make it better. "You stole sixteen years from us with your bullshit words."

If he had been anyone else, he would've been flat on his ass. I couldn't stand there for another second, looking at him. My father had been my hero my entire life. There were many others I respected and even wanted to emulate when it came to my career.

But Joel?

I'd revered my father. The love he had for my mother was always evident. Even when he was a hard ass, the soft spot he had for her was apparent to anyone in their presence. When I met my wife at sixteen years old, all I knew was that Savannah was the one I wanted to pour all of my love into.

Because my father showed all three of us how to do it.

Up until the day my mother died.

To know he was the impetus that made her leave was something I couldn't live with.

"You lost your wife," I started. "And within a year, I lost my mother, my son, and then *my* wife." I paused, hating the way my throat clogged with emotion.

"You weren't the only one who lost something. The death of my mother and my son, I couldn't prevent those. But you," I jabbed a finger into his chest again. "You caused that final loss, and it almost broke me."

I shook my head and swallowed. He didn't deserve to see me so emotional after what he'd done.

"Ace," he called as I brushed past him.

I pulled away from him when he caught me by the arm.

"Can you forgive me?"

I gritted my teeth and stepped closer. "If someone had said to my mother what you said to *my wife,* would you have forgiven them?"

It was his turn to step back. His eyebrows rose and then dropped. He remained silent.

"I didn't think so." I moved back a few steps. "Take your apology and shove it up your ass."

With that, I walked out of Joel's house, intending never to return.

CHAPTER 24

Savannah

"Ace," I called as Aiden and I walked through the front door. It was Saturday mid-morning, two weeks after Micah's barbeque.

Aiden and I didn't have any plans for the rest of the day, so I thought since Ace was finally off, he might want to do a lunch picnic at the river. The weather was great and still hovering around the eighties, even though we were approaching mid-November.

The weather is one thing I missed so much about living in the South. At times the summers could seem unbearable, but fall weather that hovered between mid-sixties and eighties was okay with me.

"Mr. Ace," Aiden yelled as he toed off his sneakers and kicked them to the side of the door where we tended to keep our outside shoes.

"Hey," Ace said as he came up through the basement door, dressed in only a pair of workout shorts. Sweat ran down his bronzed chest. Heat rushed through me at the unexpected sight of him sweaty and with his skin slightly red from exertion.

Ace had always kept in great shape. I had to keep my eyes from trailing down to the V-cut of his tapered waist.

"Were you working out?" Aiden asked, allowing me to remember he was still in the room.

Ace grinned and winked at me before turning his attention to Aiden.

Sexy bastard.

I dipped my head, feeling slightly scandalous for thinking about sex while my son stood right in front of me.

"Sure was," he answered Aiden.

"I thought you were sleeping in," I said. He'd had a night flight the evening before, which usually meant that he slept in late the next day. Thankfully, though, he was off for the remainder of the weekend.

"I tried to sleep in but couldn't since you two weren't here, so I decided to do a quick workout."

I could barely smother the smile that passed through my lips.

"Mama and I want you to come on a picnic with us," Aiden said before I could.

"Thanks for speaking for me." I stared down at him with my hands on my hips.

He shrugged and turned back to Ace. "Wanna come?"

More and more each day, it was apparent that Ace had become Aiden's hero. He could do no wrong in my son's eyes.

"A picnic?" Ace looked up at me. "You know your mom was the first woman I ever took on a picnic?"

"Really?" Aiden looked between the two of us.

"She's the only woman I've taken on a picnic," he added with a laugh.

My belly flip-flopped.

"Aiden, go upstairs and change your clothes. Then you can help me pack up the food to take with us."

Aiden was on the run before I could even finish my sentence.

I gasped when Ace snatched me by the waist as soon as Aiden was out of sight.

"You smell good," Ace murmured into my neck.

"And you smell like sweat." I squirmed out of his hold, pushing him away. "You're not going anywhere with me smelling like that."

He tossed his head back and laughed. "You can join me in the shower."

"Hell no," I whispered. "Aiden is here."

"Turn his tablet on. He won't know the difference."

I pushed him in the direction of the stairs. "Go. I need to make some sandwiches and pack up the food."

It took about thirty minutes for Ace to shower, Aiden to change, and for me to prepare the food I bought the day before. Instead of making sandwiches, I packed bread, cheese, and turkey, along with a few condiments and silverware to make them once we sat out.

"All set?" Ace asked Aiden as he came down the stairs.

"Affirmative," Aiden answered. He'd taken to using as much Air Force terminology as he could learn. He'd even gone so far as to start practicing his military time. Lately, I found myself having to do the mental calculations in my head from military to pedestrian time, since it didn't come naturally to me.

"Thank you," I told Ace as he held the door open for me.

"I'll take this," he said, taking the wicker basket out of my hands.

"Here you go, Mama," Aiden said, holding the door of Ace's truck open for me.

"Since when do you hold my door for me?" I asked with a lifted eyebrow.

He glanced over at Ace, who'd started in the direction of the truck after locking up the house. "A man's job is to be courteous to the woman of the house."

I cocked my head to the side, surprised. "Did you tell him that?" I asked Ace once we all got in the truck.

"What?"

"To hold my door open for me?" It was something Ace had always done when we were a young married couple. Even before then, honestly. And he'd recently started doing it again.

Over the past month, it felt like we fell in stride with the couple we used to be. The couple to whom things came easily and naturally.

Ace shrugged. "Respect the queen of the home. Right, kid?" He peered into the rearview mirror to look at Aiden.

"Right."

I rolled my eyes. Aiden would've agreed if Ace had said the sky was fluorescent green. But honestly, there were worse lessons he could pick up on.

The drive to the park where we were picnicking was only about twenty-five minutes from Ace's house. We reached the park a little after one o'clock, and surprisingly there weren't too many people there.

A few families were scattered throughout, but we had plenty of room to spread our blanket and belongings on the grassy partition, a few feet from the Gaines River.

Along the river bank sat various shades of grey, pewter, and ash-colored stones. The smooth edges of the rocks made them perfect for sitting or walking on without getting uncomfortable.

I took a seat on the blanket and watched Ace follow Aiden out to the water. Ace helped Aiden roll up the edge of his jeans to his knees before doing the same for himself. He took his hand as they waded mid-calf into the crystal-clear river.

Ace pointed at the cliff on the far side of the river and told him something I was too far away to hear.

A sigh fell from my lips. In front of me was the dream for which I'd so often wished over the past sixteen years. I had asked myself over and over, what if I had never left? Or, what would happen if I went back to Ace?

I had convinced myself that he hated me. That, in the time I'd been gone, he'd wizened up and recognized that I had been the cause of his pain.

Much as I regretted hurting Ace, I couldn't say I wouldn't do it again, in all honesty. Because if I had remained in Texas, then I never would've met Yvette, who'd entrusted me with the greatest gift of her life, when she found out she was dying. I wouldn't have Aiden.

Thoughts about Aiden forced me to recall that I still had the threat to his safety hanging over my head.

"Mama, Mr. Ace is teaching me how to skip rocks," Aiden said as he ran up to me.

I'd gotten so wrapped up in my thoughts, I didn't even realize they'd come out of the river back over to the blanket. There was a glimmer of laughter and delight in his eyes. I always wanted to keep that shine in his gaze.

"He's good at that." I smiled and watched as Ace trailed behind Aiden up from the river.

"I'm going to practice some more." Aiden started to turn back in the direction he came.

"Uh-uh, not before you eat," I scolded.

"Aw, man," he whined as he dropped to his knees on the blanket.

"Don't sound so down, kid," Ace cut in. "The river isn't going anywhere. Besides, the food is the best part about picnics. That and..." Ace's words broke off, and his eyes trailed over to meet mine.

We both paused and stared at one another. When I saw the smile on his lips, I knew the same memory came to mind.

I'd lost my virginity to him on our first picnic. Every picnic after that ended up with me flat on my back.

I looked away.

"And what?" Aiden asked, hanging on to Ace's every word.

"That other part, I'll tell you about when you're older," he said.

My heart leaped in my chest. The way he talked as if he would be around for a long time.

God, I want that so much.

"Besides," I said, trying to make myself think about the here and now and not the future. "You haven't eaten since your practice, and you need the food for energy if you're going to work on your stone-skipping today."

Aiden made his sandwich while Ace helped him. Their budding relationship was one of the highlights of my days. My heart ached at how much I wanted to see it continue to grow.

"I need to give you something," Ace said.

I peered up and realized that Aiden had finished his food and was back at the river trying to skip stones.

"What?"

Ace stood and dug into his pocket. He pulled out a small, black velvet bag.

"This." He loosened the drawstring on the bag and poured the contents into his free hand.

I inhaled sharply, noticing the beautiful sparkle chain. Slowly Ace undid the chain and held the necklace up. Hanging from the white gold necklace was a heart shaped locket.

My locket.

The one I hadn't seen since the night of that fight.

"I got it fixed," he said as he undid the clasp.

Wordlessly, he stepped forward and placed the chain around my neck before securing it at the back.

He opened the locket and stared at the pictures inside. "Now, you can always keep them close."

I was too moved to speak. I brushed my fingers over the locket, turning it upside down to see the image of my mother on one side and our son on the other.

I held the locket and closed my eyes. My body warmed from the sensation of his lips on my forehead when he kissed it.

"Thank you."

"I'm sorry," he said. "For even thinking you would've used that picture to manipulate me." He brushed his lips across my knuckles.

I swallowed and lifted my chin. "You know what would really say *I'm sorry?*" I asked with a raised eyebrow.

He looked at me out of the corner of his eyes. "What?"

"Dance with me," I said. I grabbed my phone and turned on my favorite playlist, a mix of hip hop and pop songs.

I held out my hand out to Ace when Taylor Swift's "Shake It Off" came on.

Ace lifted an eyebrow and smirked, but he took my hand. He held up our clasped hands and I spun around before tossing my free hand in the air and moving my hips to the music.

I clapped in time with the music and laughed when Ace gave me that *you're crazy* expression.

I sang the part about haters hating, in his face, making him laugh out loud. I loved the resounding ripple that his laughter caused in my stomach. I danced all the more harder as a result of it. When Taylor sang about having the music in her mind that kept her going, I raised my hands in the air and shimmied my hips.

I let my hips whip back and forth and imagined myself on stage. By the end of the song, I didn't even realize that I'd gotten my foot a little twisted up in the blanket. I went to take a step and stumbled right into the arms of my husband.

"Caught ya," he declared, his lips only a few inches from mine.

"Just like you always do." My voice was breathless. "You think Lena Clarkson would be willing to give me some lessons on performing?" I joked.

He shook his head. "You don't need any."

By then, Taylor Swift gave way to Sam Smith's "Make It to Me." Without asking, Ace held me as our bodies swayed.

I lifted my arms to his shoulders.

"Now singing, I don't even think Lena could help you there, babe."

I punched his shoulder playfully. "Thanks a lot."

He shrugged. "Just telling the truth."

I stared into his shimmering grey eyes and ran my hand over the side of his face.

"You want me to sing, don't you?" he asked about halfway through the song.

I nodded with a huge grin on my face.

He chuckled and shook his head. "I haven't sung in years. And I don't plan on it today." He kissed the tip of my nose.

I rolled my eyes.

He kissed my forehead. While he didn't sing, he did hum a little bit of the song.

"You always loved the sappy songs," he said.

"Don't pretend like you didn't, either."

"I only listened to them for you."

I snorted. "If you say so. It's okay, tough guy." I patted his chest. "I won't tell anyone the hotshot fighter pilot is into sappy love songs." I pulled back. "I bet you know the entirety of Lena's new album."

"She's my soon-to-be sister-in-law," he defended. "I have to support her."

I laughed almost hysterically. "Babe, I've seen your playlist."

He shrugged. "Fine. But it's your fault. You left your imprint on my taste in music, just like every other area of my life." His voice suddenly became much deeper and more serious.

The air between us came to a standstill.

"Every area?" I asked.

We continued to sway even though the music changed from Sam Smith to Lizzo.

He nodded.

"What about the area that has to do with your father?"

He narrowed his eyes. "What about him?"

I shook his shoulders a little, hating the anger I felt in his body. "He's your father, Ace. You love him."

"And?"

I sighed, happy that at least he didn't deny that he still loved Joel.

"And you need to forgive him."

He rolled his eyes. "That word is thrown around too much."

I squeezed his shoulders as I tried to figure out how I could make him understand that he couldn't hold onto his grudge against Joel.

"Family is the most important. Remember you told me that when you asked me to marry you?"

Family was what mattered most in this world. I couldn't bear to be the person that came between Ace and his father.

"You're my family," he said so vehemently that I felt its force throughout my body. He looked over toward the river.

I followed his gaze with mine and found Aiden standing at the water's edge, still attempting to skip stones. It appeared he'd managed to make friends with a few other boys who were there with their families.

We turned back to each other at the same time. "And Aiden. You're both my family, Savannah."

"What are you saying?"

"I don't want a divorce." His voice was thick with emotion. "I never did, which was why I never filed. I could've found you all those years ago. All it would've taken was one call to Micah or another PI. But I wanted you to come back on your own."

He inclined his head.

"When the Air Force assigned me to the base here, the place where you and I first met, I knew, deep down, it'd be where we came together again. Don't ask me to sign those papers."

I had to close my eyes to stop the tears from falling. Try as I might, a few managed to escape. He'd just said the words I longed for, for so many years. I wanted to scream out the word *Yes* more than anything.

This was so much better than a proposal. He was asking me to stay. To continue being his wife.

But I couldn't say yes.

My son's well-being rested on me doing the right thing for him.

"I—"

"Mama, Mr. Ace, look," Aiden yelled, interrupting my response.

Ace and I looked over at him.

"I did it. I skipped a stone across the entire river. Come look." He waved us over.

Ace gave me another look, but I was speechless. There was too much left unsaid that I wanted desperately to tell him. But how could I bring him into this situation?

We were so close to getting the happily ever after we both wanted. How was I going to burst his bubble again?

I dropped my hands from his shoulders and stepped out of his hold. The space between his eyebrows wrinkled, but when Aiden called us both over again, we turned toward the river.

I would have to figure this out, and soon.

CHAPTER 25

Savannah

I sighed as I stepped out of the shower and started to dry off. Ace had taken Aiden to school that morning before heading over to the base. I only had to work a half-day, thankfully, since I was dragging.

A few days had passed since Ace, Aiden, and I had spent the day at the river. While Ace hadn't brought up the divorce again, there was an apparent strain between us.

I went back and forth on whether or not to tell him about the situation with Aiden's birth father and Vincent Reyes. Would he even believe me? It sounded insane even to me. If I didn't have the very distinct memory of Reyes coming to my apartment door in Philadelphia with a gun to tell me that he was assigned to kill my son, I wouldn't have believed it myself.

Maybe it was time I shared the truth with Ace. Keeping things from him had never worked out well in the past.

"Who is it?" I yelled when the doorbell sounded. Then I rolled my eyes at my ridiculousness. Whoever was at the door probably couldn't hear me from upstairs, anyway.

Instead of yelling out again, I grabbed my phone off the nightstand

and checked the app connected to Ace's security system. I did a double-take when I spotted a figure that looked suspiciously like Ace's father standing at the front door.

My heart pounded as I quickly finished dressing into my work scrubs and headed down the stairs. The doorbell rang again just as my foot touched the bottom step.

"Thought you were ignoring me," Joel said when I pulled the door open.

I didn't know quite how to respond to that. This was the first time I was seeing him in over sixteen years. I hadn't thought much about what I would say to him if I ever saw him again.

"Given what I did the last time we were in this position, I wouldn't blame ya if you were," he said, his Texas twang making an appearance.

"Mr. Tow—Joel," I corrected.

He stood a little taller and removed the cowboy hat he wore. He slapped the hat against his thigh, almost as if he was nervous. It was hard to picture a man like Joel Townsend as anxious or uncertain.

"May I come in?"

"Um." I cleared my throat. "Ace isn't here," I said, assuming he didn't already know.

He nodded. "It's you I came to speak with."

"Sure." I stepped aside.

He came inside and glanced around as if seeing the house for the first time.

"A shame he's got orders to leave soon." Joel turned to face me. "This is a fine house. We'll miss him."

That ache in my heart started again. That was the other issue hanging over our heads. Ace's eventual move to Germany. He'd all but asked Aiden and me to go with him, but I hadn't given him an answer.

Joel looked me up and down. "Do you need to leave for work soon?"

I shook my head. "I have some time. Would you like something to drink?" I pointed over my shoulder toward the kitchen.

He waved his cowboy hat as he shook his head. "Nah."

An awkward silence fell between us. I'd always felt uneasy around Joel.

"I'm going to tell you something I've told very few people in my life," he finally said.

I remained quiet, waiting.

"I'm sorry." He shook his head, regretful. "I never should've said what I said to you. If I hadn't had my head stuck so far up my ass, I would've told you the truth."

"What's the truth?" I braced myself for his answer.

"You weren't the cause of Ace's pain. To the contrary, you saved him."

I jutted my head backward, totally not expecting that response.

"He's a hothead. He gets that from me. And some of it from his mama." He pointed at me with the hat in his hand. "Most people don't know it, but my wife could lose her temper now and again. Especially when someone she loved was threatened."

He smiled as if a memory he chose to keep to himself came to mind.

"I knew all of the trouble he started getting into when we found out her condition was terminal. The skipping school and getting into those stupid races. But I was too wrapped up in my grief to help him."

I slowed my breathing as I listened to Joel. It felt as if something deep inside me needed to hear these words as badly as he needed to say them.

"You were the rock he needed. To cut that stupid shit out and be the man he needed to be then. It was you that helped him do that."

"You don't have to…" I trailed off.

"I'm not just saying it," he said forcefully. "I mean it. I knew it back then. If I hadn't been so clouded by my grief and jealousy, I would've said it back then."

"Jealousy?" Grief, I understood. It made us act in uncharacteristic ways. But I didn't get the jealousy.

He gave me a half smile that reminded me of Ace. "My wife was my first and only love. The first day I met her, I knew she was the woman I was going to marry. When Ace met you, I remember he came home from the river that day and told me, *Joel, I met the girl I'm gonna marry.* I knew he wasn't shittin' me."

I had no idea Ace told his father that the day we met.

"It was selfish as hell of me, but to watch my boy falling in love for the first time and getting married and starting a family, while it felt like my entire world was coming apart, filled me with envy."

He held his arms wide.

"I hate myself for it, but I was envious that your story was just beginning while mine had come to an end."

You could've knocked me over with a feather. Never, in all of those years, would I have thought I'd hear those words from Joel Townsend.

"I always thought you didn't think I was good enough for your son."

He looked surprise. "Why?"

"Because I'm from the other side of the bridge."

He tutted and shook his head. "I'm not like one of those uppity fuckers. Hell, *I'm* from the other side of the bridge."

"You are?"

He nodded. "Not from Harlington, but up North. Anyway, I know what it's like to be the black sheep. Trust me. That was never my issue with you. Truthfully, I never had an issue with you. It was my own bullshit.

"You saved Ace, Savannah. That's what I should've said that day. And I'm fucking sorry I didn't."

Before the last word was out of his mouth, I threw my hands around his neck and pulled him in for a hug.

"You have no idea how much I needed to hear that," I mumbled, still holding onto him.

After a few moments, I felt his arms circle around my back.

"I think I needed to say it even more than you needed to hear it."

I continued to hold onto him simply because it felt right.

"So, you're a hugger, huh?"

I finally released him and laughed as I wiped my tears away.

"Yeah, he said you were a crier, too."

That made me laugh harder. "Ace is always teasing me about how much I cry."

"Don't let that boy of mine talk shit. You feel those emotions." He squeezed my arm.

"He doesn't mean it," I said, knowing that, although Ace teased me, he wasn't bothered by my tears.

"Hey," Joel commented. "I hear you have a son now."

My smile widened as I nodded. "His name's Aiden." Without even thinking, I pulled out my phone and brought up a photo of Aiden. It was the most recent one in my phone's gallery and happened to be from the previous weekend when we were all at Gaines River. Ace was standing beside him, smiling down as Aiden waved at me.

"He'll be ten in February."

"Good-looking kid." Joel sobered. He looked up at me. "I'm sorry I wasn't there at the hospital."

The muscles in my throat tightened.

"That I didn't get a chance to meet my first grandson. I don't even know what he looked like."

I ran my hand over the locket that lay against my chest.

"Hang on a sec." I held up my finger and then spun around and headed up the stairs.

When I reached the bedroom, I took down one of the bags of personal belongings that I kept in the closet. I pulled out a photo that I'd kept for years.

A minute later, I was downstairs in front of Joel.

"This is him," I said as I handed him the full-sized photograph of AJ. "One of the nurses took the picture. She mailed it to our apartment a few weeks later. I couldn't look at it for years."

Joel stuffed his cowboy hat under his arm and took the picture, staring at it. He traced AJ's little face with his free hand.

"He looked just like him." His eyes met mine.

I nodded, which was what had made the picture so damn painful to look at. AJ was indeed Ace's junior.

"Thanks," he said, handing me the photo.

"No." I pushed his hand back to him. "Keep it. I have a copy. He's always right here." I pressed my palm to my chest, covering the locket.

"I see why my boy fell in love with you."

I started to say thank you, but my cell phone rang. I hesitated when I saw that it was an unknown number. The number had a Washington, D.C. area code. I knew who it was immediately.

"I-I have to take this," I told Joel.

He peered at me after looking at the phone in my hand. "Work?"

I was grateful for the out. "Yeah." I nodded. "They probably need me to come in a little earlier than expected."

He nodded. "I'll let you get to it."

I walked him to the door and made sure to wave brightly, seeing him off, before answering.

"What the hell took you so long?" Reyes barked into the phone as soon as I said hello.

"I was busy."

"Too busy to save your kid?"

I squeezed the phone in my hand, wishing I could punch him in the face.

"There's been a change of plans. I need the money sooner than later."

"What are you talking about?" I screeched. "We still have another month. You said so."

"Fuck that. I could always tell your son's father where he is," Reyes threatened.

"I don't have it."

"Well, you better fucking figure it out. I'll be in Texas by the end of the week."

With that, he hung up the phone on me.

"What the hell am I going to do?" I murmured, looking around the empty house. I would have to swallow my pride and fear and finally tell Ace the truth.

* * *

234

Ace

I lifted my head from my desk. I had a mountain of paperwork that I was trying to work through. My goal was to spend as much of the evening with Savannah and Aiden as I could before I had to get to sleep early.

How much my life had changed in the span of a few months. Work had always been my priority. Ever since Savannah left, I made being a pilot and the Air Force my entire identity.

Even after moving back to Harlington, I spent time with my brothers and Joel, but my job remained number one in my life. That was because the family of my own I'd envisioned always had my wife attached to it. With her gone, no matter how much I achieved in my career, something inside of me felt empty.

That was all different now.

Though, maybe I hadn't convinced her of that yet. Possibly, that was what made her hesitant to call off the divorce. Being the spouse of an officer in the military was not an easy job.

We were often gone for long periods, had odd hours, and moved from one place to another every few years.

Maybe Savannah took one look at my life as it was now and decided it wasn't for her. Or Aiden.

I ran my hand through my hair, trying to figure out how to convince her that with me was where they both belonged.

"Captain Townsend?"

I shook loose my previous thoughts and peered up at the new office administrator who'd replaced Tricia.

"Yes?" I asked.

"Commander Caldwell needs to speak with you, sir."

I stood and wondered what this was about. I nodded and thanked the new guy. I was still surprised they'd found someone to replace the witch so quickly.

The last thing I heard about Tricia from Micah was that she had packed up her shit and moved to Alaska with her child's father.

Good riddance.

"Sir," I said as I entered my Commander's office. I saluted him. "You needed to speak with me?"

"Yes, close the door."

For the next twenty minutes, Commander Caldwell gave me the news that I'd secretly been wishing to hear. He granted me new orders. I wouldn't be shipping out to Germany after all.

"How's your wife doing, sir?" I asked.

My Commander let out a grateful smile and nodded. "She's doing very well." He nodded. "She's doing some rehab and we're constantly monitoring her but her doctor thinks she's on the road to a full recovery."

I pushed out a sigh of relief. "Great news, Sir."

"Please thank your wife for me, again. The doctors in the ER said because of the information she relayed to the 9-11 operator, they were able to be ready for her as soon as the ambulance arrived. It allowed them to treat her that much faster."

"I will let Savannah know, Sir." She had asked about the condition of Commander Caldwell's wife since the night of the ball. I was glad to report to her that the woman was doing well.

When I emerged from his office, there was only one person I wanted to tell. But I had to finish out my workday.

The news traveled quickly. Many of the guys in my squadron came up to me to pat me on the back. Though this meant I wouldn't be leaving with them, it did mean that I got the assignment I'd wanted. They were happy for me.

At the end of the day, as I exited the building that housed my office, I pulled out my phone to call Savannah, but it rang with a different number instead.

"Micah, what's up?"

"Hey, are you busy?"

"Just getting out of work. Got some good news and was headed home to tell Savannah. I'm not transferring overseas, after all."

"That's great," he said, but there was something in his voice that told me all wasn't well.

"Look, I probably shouldn't tell you this over the line," said Miach

"The base isn't too far from my office...can you stop by on your way home?"

"Yeah. I'll be there in fifteen."

"See ya soon."

I didn't bother figuring out what Micah had to tell me that he couldn't or wouldn't say over the phone. I'd be at his office, LS Investigations, within the next few minutes. I did know whatever it was had to be serious.

I tried to focus on my good news as I drove.

I pulled into the parking lot of Micah's offices a little after five thirty. The door was left unlocked.

"Hey, Ace," Jodi greeted as I breezed through the door. She waved her head toward the back. "He's waiting for you."

"Thanks."

"I'm heading home. Have a good night," she called. "And don't keep my husband for too long."

"Will do, sis."

I started for Micah's office and knocked on his door before entering.

"Hey," he stood from his desk.

"What's up?" I asked, wanting to skip the formalities.

"You asked me to continue monitoring your wife's financial accounts and whatnot, right?"

I nodded, remembering that he'd asked me if that was what I wanted after the confrontation with Tricia.

"Yeah." As I answered, a sinking feeling started in my stomach.

Micah gave me a pensive look. "This might not mean anything."

"Just tell me what the hell it is. Don't bullshit around."

He sighed and pulled a manila folder off of the top of his desk. He leaned back against the desk, crossed his legs at the ankles, and opened it.

When he pulled out a piece of paper and leaned forward, handing it to me, I snatched the paper. I scanned it, noting the name of a well-known financial institution at the top. The account holder was Savannah.

"That was a retirement account she had with her former employer. A few months ago, the account had a little over fifty thousand dollars in it. A few weeks ago, she made a withdrawal."

I glanced up at my brother. "For how much?"

"Everything," he answered and inclined his head at the paper in my hands.

I looked toward the bottom and saw the account balance now read zero. I shook my head. "She could've done a rollover."

She worked for a new company and was laid off from her last job months earlier. People did rollovers of their retirement accounts all the time when they changed jobs.

"Thought so, too," Micah started. "But we haven't found any new retirement information for her. She hasn't opened a new account with her current employer. There aren't any private accounts for her, either. In fact…"

He sighed.

"While one of my guys was looking, he found that she deposited the check into her account and then withdrew the complete amount in cash."

I bulged my eyes. What the hell did Savannah need fifty thousand dollars in cash for?

"Money," I said out loud as I stared at the paper. That was why she'd wanted the divorce. She told me when I asked why she'd come back to have me sign the papers. Her grandmother had left her an inheritance, and the will insisted that she get a divorce to receive it.

I had pushed the thought aside when she first told me because I was still full of anger and bitterness. But months later, it was apparent she still wanted money.

That day in the park, when I asked her to forget about the divorce, she hesitated. I blamed myself, my lifestyle, and my career for why she didn't say yes. But that was a fucking lie.

Savannah was still after money.

"I need to go home."

"Ace," Micah called.

"What?" I asked, still heading toward the door with Micah behind me.

"Don't get all hotheaded. There might be a perfectly reasonable explanation for this."

"Yeah?" I asked, turning to face him. "And in your career, have you ever come across a good reason that someone is withdrawing that kind of cash?"

He frowned. "No."

"That's what I thought."

I yanked the door open, feeling a wave of anger I thought had been quelled. For months, I thought that Savannah and I were rebuilding what we had lost. And there she was, keeping secrets from me.

Not any fucking more.

CHAPTER 26

avannah
    I hadn't heard from Vincent Reyes since he called me earlier. But I made my decision. As soon as I got home and put Aiden to bed, I was going to tell Ace the truth. Come clean.

It made me sick to my stomach to think of keeping something from him, considering how far we had come in the past few months. Besides that, maybe we could talk to Micah, who was a PI and had connections from his time in law enforcement.

Perhaps there was something that we could come up with to keep Aiden safe from Reyes.

I snapped off my blue latex gloves and tossed them in the hazardous material wastebasket before entering the examination room.

"I'm calling it quits for the day, Reese," I told her.

She lifted her head and smiled. "Sounds good. Hey," she called, "you know we're open the morning of Thanksgiving, right?"

I smiled. "Dr. Pierce informed us at the last staff meeting. I'll be here."

She nodded. "Me too. Not like I have any other plans," she mumbled.

"Why don't you come over?" I suggested. Ace and I hadn't discussed our Thanksgiving Day plans at all, but I hated the forlorn note in Reese's voice.

She waved me off. "I couldn't impose on your family like that."

"You can." I laughed. "Wait. What I mean is, it's not an imposition. Ace and Aiden will probably have their faces stuck in front of a football game all day, anyway. I'll need the company."

"Aiden likes football?" she asked with her brown eyes going wide.

I shook my head. "*Ace* loves football. Aiden loves whatever Ace does. He's like his mini-shadow."

"That's so adorable," she swooned, then sighed.

A longing expression covered her face.

"Say you'll come," I urged.

She nodded. "I'll be there."

"Great." I waved to her and left for the day. I didn't need to pick Aiden up since it was a Friday, and I let him go to a friend's house after school. I would pick him up after dinner. His friend's parents all but begged me to let him have dinner over there.

I pushed out a sigh. Aiden had grown since we'd moved to Harlington. This move started to look like the best thing for my son. He gained several friends in his fifth-grade class, a father figure in Ace, and he hadn't had a nightmare in months.

I called Ace's cell phone on my way home but didn't get an answer. He was probably on his way home from base.

My suspicions were confirmed when I reached the house and found his truck parked in the driveway. A piece of me felt nervous but almost lighter since I decided to tell him what was going on with Vincent Reyes.

"Ace?" I called when I entered the house and hung up my keys on the wall mount by the door.

He didn't answer, but I heard stirring in the kitchen. I followed the sound and found him seated at the far end of the table, facing the entryway, as if he was waiting for me.

"Hey." I entered the kitchen. "How long have you been home?"

He lifted his head, and his eyes met mine. Immediately, I knew something was off. The look in his eyes was cold. It hearkened back to months ago when I first returned to town. The angry and closed- off way he would look at me.

"What's wrong?"

Because it was evident from the stiff way he held his position at the end of the table, something was the matter.

"I got some news today." He slowly came to his feet. He still wore his ABUs.

"What kind of news?" I asked.

"The good kind."

I slumped my shoulders. "Oh, then why are you being cryptic? What was it?"

His jaw ticked. His expression didn't slacken, and I knew that couldn't be the end of the story.

"Then I got more news. From Micah."

I tilted my head to the side.

"I had him monitoring your financial accounts," he continued.

"You what?" I blurted out.

He didn't even look a tiny bit ashamed.

"You heard me. Is there anything you want to tell me?"

I folded my arms across my chest and narrowed my eyes on him. "Yeah, like, that is a complete invasion of my privacy."

He rolled his eyes. "Save the holier than thou act, Savannah. You withdrew over fifty thousand dollars from your retirement account, and it wasn't to open another one. You're planning on skipping town again, aren't you? That's why you hesitated when I asked you to forget about signing the divorce papers. Because you want the money from your grandmother's estate so you can leave, free and clear this time," he accused with venom in his voice.

I hated the betrayal I heard in his tone. It was the visceral kind, the type of anger that only came from pain.

"You have it all wrong."

"Which part?" he demanded. "The part about you taking your entire life savings out, or the part about you using the money to ditch me without a word again?"

He didn't give me time to answer either question.

"Because that was the plan, right? Maybe you thought I wouldn't sign the papers, so why not take what money you had and leave me again without so much as fuck you." He seethed.

"That's not what I'm doing," I yelled, pissed off at him and the situation.

"Then tell me, for once, Savannah. Fucking look me in my face and tell me the damned truth."

"He's threatening Aiden," I yelled.

Ace's eyes ballooned. "Who?"

"Almost six months ago, this guy, Vincent Reyes, appeared on my doorstep and told me that Aiden's biological father sent him." I swallowed.

"Why?" Ace asked.

"Because Aiden's real father is a Florida senator. Who's been married for over twenty years."

Ace's forehead wrinkled. "Which one? Flores?"

I nodded. "Yvette was only sixteen when she got pregnant with Aiden. She had him at seventeen."

I paused and inhaled, trying to stop myself from crying. Talking about Yvette always broke my heart. She'd been taken advantage of so young, abused and threatened.

"She was trafficked at a young age." I shook my head as I revealed the story of the pieces of her life that she'd shared with me. "Somehow, when she got pregnant, she managed to run away and made it to Philadelphia. That was where we met. She never told me the name of Aiden's birth father, but she said he was a powerful man. Well-connected.

"I saw fear in her eyes whenever she talked about him. When she was diagnosed with cancer, and her condition turned terminal, she begged me to keep Aiden safe. I thought he was, until a few months ago, when Vincent Reyes showed up at my door."

I pressed my palm to my forehead. I'd kept this secret for months, and it felt relieving but damn tiring to say it all out loud.

I sunk into one of the chairs at the table. Ace took a seat next to me, his demeanor noticeably different now.

"He told me that Flores wanted him to *get rid of the little problem* he had. Can you believe that?" I peered over at Ace. "He called my son a fucking problem?"

I tightened and flexed my hands.

"But Reyes said he would make a deal with me. At first, he demanded one hundred and twenty-five thousand dollars to go away. He said he would make up a lie to Flores and tell him that he'd handled it. Then he doubled the amount."

"This was all before you came back to Harlington?" Ace asked.

"Yeah." I sighed. "I had just been laid off from my last job and had no means to raise that kind of money quickly. But a letter I received from my grandmother's attorney six months earlier got me thinking. I went to the lawyer, and he told me about the inheritance. It was what I needed, but the condition was…"

"You have to divorce me."

I swallowed and nodded.

"A few months ago, Reyes showed up at Brightside." I peered up at Ace. His face tensed.

"He was here? In Texas?"

"He insisted that I pay him a portion of the money. All I had was my old retirement account, so I withdrew it. Reyes was silent for a while, then he called today and said there was a change of plans and he needed all of the money sooner."

I pushed out a breath.

"Ace, I was coming home to tell you the truth today. I swear I was."

He reached across the table, covering my hands with his much larger and stronger ones. When he squeezed them, I almost lost it.

"I'm sorry I didn't tell you from the beginning, but you were so angry when I first came back. We were barely speaking, and I didn't feel like I could burden you with my mess. And then, we got back to *us*."

Our eyes met, and the coldness that had been in his when I first got home was gone.

"I don't want a divorce. I never did. But, I...I can't lose Aiden. I wouldn't survive the loss of another child." My voice cracked.

The loud scraping of Ace's chair was the next sound I heard as he rose to his feet. He lifted me and pulled me into his arms. I cried at the fear I held in my heart for months, the terror at the possibility that Flores would find out the truth about where Aiden was, and use someone to take him from me.

"That's never going to happen," Ace said with steel lacing his voice. "I promise you, no one is taking Aiden away from us or going to hurt him." He pulled back and cupped my face.

"You believe me, right?" I asked. "I wouldn't make any of this up. I can show you the calls Reyes made to my phone."

"I trust you, baby." He kissed my forehead. "I'm sorry for flying off the handle again."

I squeezed him back. "I get it." With the way I left last time, and the way I responded the day at the river when he'd asked me to drop the divorce, I understood.

Although I didn't want to, I pulled back from his embrace. "I'm sorry for laying all of this on you."

He frowned. "Are you out of your mind? This is the type of shit you're supposed to lay on me. Anything this big that affects our family is never to be handled by yourself. You don't have to take on anything alone, Savannah."

My body relaxed in relief, but only so much.

"What are we going to do? Reyes still knows about Aiden, and Flores could find out about him."

"We're going to get the best damn PI in the state of Texas to help us."

He kissed my forehead again.

"Nothing will happen to you or Aiden. You have my word on that."

CHAPTER 27

Savannah

"Do you need any help in the kitchen today, Mama?" Aiden asked as he came down the stairs.

It was early afternoon, the day of Thanksgiving. I'd just gotten off work and planned to finish cooking the numerous dishes I'd started preparing the night before.

"Yeah, we're here to help," Ace said as he came down behind Aiden, placing his hands on his shoulders.

I grinned at the matching Air Force pajamas they both wore. I'd left them that morning, sleeping in bed after Aiden had crawled in to show Ace something on his tablet.

"No." I waved them off. "Besides, I see both of your eyes roving over toward the television anyway. I know the game is on," I teased.

"Thank God," Ace said in relief. "Come on, kid." He pushed Aiden by the shoulders in the direction of the living room.

I laughed and started for the kitchen.

"Hey?"

I turned back to face Ace. He wrapped his arm around my waist and pulled me into his body for a kiss.

"Seriously, do you need any help?" His eyes traveled over my face.

"No." I slid my arms around his shoulders. "Really, I'm good. You two would just be in my way."

His smile grew.

"All I ask is that you both shower before our guests arrive. They'll be here around four," I reminded him.

"Not a problem." He squeezed my behind and kissed me again before releasing me.

I watched him head to the living room and lift Aiden, tickling him before tossing him around on the couch. I had the urge to tell them both to be careful, but bit my tongue.

I knew Ace wouldn't hurt Aiden. He loved him as much as I did. That I knew from the bottom of my heart.

I turned on my Christmas playlist and started cooking. I danced and poorly sang along with all the songs on my playlist as I did my best to push out the fears that still hung over our heads.

While I prepared the food, hours went by in a blur. I vaguely remember Ace and Aiden heading up the stairs to shower and change. It wasn't until around three thirty that Ace came into the kitchen and insisted that he and Aiden do the table settings while I got cleaned up.

I happily let them take over the rest of the work. By four o'clock, the first couple to arrive were Gabriel and Lena.

At times, I still couldn't believe that Gabriel was engaged to Lena Clarkson. I was a big fan of all of her music. But her latest album, *All of Me*, was by far my favorite. Being in a room with the two of them for all of five minutes, anyone with a pulse could sense the love they shared. She'd obviously written her album about Gabriel.

Next to show up was Reese with a dish of her special sausage stuffing.

"It smells delicious," I said, taking it from her. "Come on." I led her to the dining area.

The long wooden table with matching chairs on either side sat in front of the bay window. It gave a picture-perfect view of the back-yard and the surrounding wooded area that lined the community.

"Is there anything you need help with?" Reese asked.

I shook my head. "No way would I invite you over and then put you to work." I brought her to the living room. "Let me introduce you to everyone." By then, Micah and Jodi had arrived with Lonzie.

Joel wasn't too far behind them. When he walked through the door, Ace glared at him and then across the room at me. I shook my head, warning him not to make a scene.

He hadn't spoken to Joel in weeks. Every time I brought it up, he would change the subject.

"Oh my," Reese said, almost breathless, with a hand pressed to her chest. "I saw your husband that day when he came into the office. I hope this doesn't sound too disrespectful, but I instantly thought he was *fine*. A little scary, but fine."

I laughed awkwardly. "We, uh, were working through some things then," I told her of the day he'd stormed into Brightside.

"And he has two brothers and a father who are all as gorgeous as he is," she whispered.

I tossed my head back and laughed. "You get used to it after a while."

She shook her head. "It's not like I could get anyone who looks like them to look twice at me, anyway." She waved her hand in the air. "But I can admire from a distance."

"Don't say that." I frowned. "You're beautiful, Reese."

"I know. I know. You're supposed to say that because we're friends. It's okay. I know my lane."

I started to ask why she felt that way, but Jodi called my name and I got distracted. Reese went into the living room and started playing with Lonzie and Aiden.

A few young, enlisted Airmen from the base squadron came over, since they didn't have any family in the area and couldn't travel home for the holiday. It was a full house, and it wasn't until Ace made the first cut into the turkey and we all started passing dishes around the table that I realized how much I longed for this.

As a kid, it was mostly just my mom and me for the holidays. We rarely had money to travel back to Texas where my grandparents lived. After my grandfather died, my grandma would sometimes visit.

When my mother died and I moved in with my grandmother, she

occasionally had a few friends of hers over for the holidays, but she was someone who mostly kept to herself.

Holidays with her always felt cold and stiff. The few times I remember enjoying Thanksgiving as a teen were when Ace and I started dating, and he invited me over to spend it with his family. I always arrived late, though, because I didn't want to leave my grandmother by herself for too long.

Even when Ace told me his mother said my grandmother could come, she refused to go with me. She continued to believe that Ace was using me for a good time and that, she said, she would not be a part of it.

Those people don't want us, she'd told me over and over.

After dinner, a few people left, but most of the family remained. I headed into the kitchen with a few plates to throw away to find Joel in there, standing at the sink.

"You are not in here washing dishes," I said, going over and turning the water off.

"These dishes need to soak if you have any hope of getting all that grease and shit off," he said, going to turn on the water again.

"Aht." I swatted his hand.

He gave me a skeptical look and I laughed. "Leave it," I insisted. "We have a dishwasher for that, and if it needs to be handwashed, there's tomorrow." I glanced back over my shoulder.

"Did you talk to Ace?" I asked.

He wagged his head. "No, and I'm not about to force myself on him. There are laws against that sort of thing, you know."

I chuckled, enjoying Joel's sense of humor even when he was upset about Ace's lack of communication.

"Let me talk to him." I went to leave the kitchen, but Joel caught me by the arm.

"Leave it alone, doll," he said. "He'll come around when the time comes." The resignation in his voice saddened me, but I supposed he was right.

"Do you want some pie? I baked sweet potato and apple pie."

"Trying to grow my waistline, huh?" He patted his flat stomach. "I see you're still pissed with me, too."

"No, nothing like that," I said in horror.

He let out a deep laugh. "I'm messing with you. I'll take a slice of both to go. I got to head out. Early morning."

I cut Joel a slice of each kind of pie and a piece of the strawberry cake that Jodi had brought over. I watched as he said his goodbyes to Gabriel and Micah and their families before rustling Aiden's hair, making him laugh.

I glanced over at Ace to find him looking between Joel and me. I gestured with my head to the back deck.

He met me outside. I pulled out my phone and started playing my Slow Jams playlist. Ace didn't wait for me to ask as he wrapped his arms around my waist. We slow-danced to one of Lena's songs that came up.

"You need to forgive him, you know," I said after a long silence.

"The stars look beautiful tonight," he said, glancing up.

I sucked my teeth and punched his shoulder.

"That kinda hurt," he joked.

"Good. My husband taught me how to throw a punch a long time ago."

"He's a hell of a teacher." He spun me around to the sounds of Ed Sheeran's "Thinking Out Loud."

"He's the best," I said when he held me in his arms again. "A little stubborn, though."

His smile grew. "But you still put up with him."

I laid my head against his chest. My eyelids slowly closed as I listened to the sound of his heartbeat.

"I want to adopt Aiden."

I pulled back. "Are you serious?" I searched his eyes and didn't find a hint of laughter in them. I knew he wouldn't joke about something as serious as this.

"I love him like he is my own. If something happens to me, I want him to receive all of the benefits from my service that he should be entitled to."

I looked up into his face and had no idea how I got so lucky at sixteen to meet the love of my life.

"What about Reyes and his biological father?" I hated to ask, but it was a relevant question that we couldn't avoid.

"Guess it's my turn to interrupt," Micah said behind me.

I turned to face my brother-in-law. "Have you heard anything?" I'd wanted to ask ever since he arrived hours earlier, but I pushed my questions aside to focus on family and the holiday.

Micah looked between Ace and me, his face remaining neutral. Though his expression didn't change much, I got the sense he wasn't bearing good news.

"You haven't found Reyes yet." My shoulders slumped.

"No," he said flatly.

"Maybe he decided to leave Aiden and me alone?" I offered, looking between Ace and Micah.

That day Reyes called me, when Joel was over at the house, he said he would contact me later. But he never did. I hadn't heard anything from him since that day. He hadn't shown up at my office again, either. I hoped that was a good sign.

But as I read my husband's and his brother's faces, my hopes were dashed.

"People like Reyes don't just go away out of the goodness of their hearts," Ace said, staring over my head at Micah.

"I figured," I mumbled.

"We've tracked some of his movements out West," Micah told us. "But the trail ran cold. We'll find him," he assured

"And what about Flores?" I asked, whispering because I didn't want any chance of anyone still inside overhearing me mention his name. "Even if Reyes goes away, Aiden's biological father could send someone else to hurt him."

"We'll never let that happen," Ace said, squeezing my shoulder for comfort.

"We have to take things one step at a time." Micah sighed. "This might go deeper than any of us knows." I didn't like the tone in his voice. It was heavy and coated with something dark.

A sense of dread filled the inside of my belly. I peered inside through the sliding glass doors at Aiden, who was wrestling with Gabriel. He was none the wiser about what was happening, and I wanted to keep it that way. He was just an innocent child.

"I'll keep you both in the loop. Make sure all of your security codes are updated," Micah said.

"They are," Ace assured.

"He came to your job, you said, right?" Micah asked.

I nodded. "Months ago." I glanced inside again. Reese was standing, evidently preparing to leave. "You don't think he could be a threat to any of my co-workers, do you?"

Micah shook his head. "Probably not. He's more focused on you, but since he knows where you work, you should be extra careful."

"Hey," Reese called, sliding open the door. "Sorry to interrupt, but I'm heading out. Thank you for inviting me."

"I'll walk you out." I stepped around Micah and ushered Reese back inside. After insisting that she take more leftovers than a slice of pie, I accompanied her to her car.

"See you on Monday," she said before driving off with a wave.

A chill ran through me even though the temperature wasn't all that cold. I rubbed my hands up and down my arms as I swept my gaze around the street.

"We're safe here," Ace said, coming up behind me and wrapping his arms around me. "It's a gated community. No one gets in or out without the code."

"I know. I just hate that there's still this threat out there." I turned to face him.

"Yeah, I was thinking that maybe until this is all over, you should take some time off from work."

I shook my head before he could finish. "I can't take off work. I'll leave them short-staffed, and we're already scrambling trying to get as much done as we can while we take days off through the holidays."

Ace sighed. "Fine, but no night shifts."

That would be easy enough. I worked mainly the day shift, anyway. I'd been doing some overtime during evenings, but I could cut that out. I didn't love the idea of leaving some patients hanging, but I understood Ace was concerned for my safety.

"I can do that."

His frown deepened. "As much as the kid is going to hate it, I don't think he should have any more sleepovers or go over to his friends' places after school." He paused. "At least until we find Reyes."

I disliked hearing it, but I knew he was right. "We'll have to talk with him. Tomorrow, not tonight, though."

Ace nodded.

I lifted on my tiptoes and wrapped my arms around him. "We're going to be okay, right?"

His lips spread as he smiled down at me. "The three of us are going to be more than okay. We're going to be happy. We'll find that bastard, take care of Flores, and make Aiden legally mine. Just as it should be."

I hugged him tightly, needing the reassurance. I trusted Ace with everything inside of me. But even as I held onto my husband, I still couldn't get thoughts of Reyes being out there somewhere, out of my head.

CHAPTER 28

Savannah

"Are you leaving work now?" Ace asked through the phone.

"Yes," I assured him. "And going to pick up Aiden from school."

Two weeks after Thanksgiving, it had become routine for me to call or text Ace when I was leaving from work, and then call or text again once I arrived home safely. I swore the man was one step away from hiring one of Micah's PIs to be my bodyguard or something.

When I joked about that the other week, his facial expression turned pensive, as if genuinely considering it. I was able to get him to drop the idea, thankfully.

Truthfully, I did look over my shoulder and always carried a can of mace whenever I was going to or from the car.

Micah still hadn't located Vincent Reyes, but he could pinpoint some activity on his accounts in the Philadelphia area. Which meant he wasn't in Texas. At least, not at the time they traced the movement. He could be anywhere by now, though. So, I kept vigilant.

"And then you're both headed home, right?" Ace asked.

"Yes," I told him as I pulled out of my job's parking lot. A small smile creased my lips at the protective edge in Ace's voice.

The day after Thanksgiving, we'd told Aiden that he wouldn't be able to go over his friends' houses after school for a while. We told him it was because of a family matter. He asked many questions, but I insisted on withholding the whole truth from him.

His curiosity was only satisfied when we changed the subject to Ace adopting him. Aiden turned to me and asked if that meant Mr. Ace would become his dad like I became his mom.

I nodded, too choked up to answer him. He didn't respond with words, either. Instead, he jumped into Ace's arms, hugging him and asking him if it was too soon to call him Daddy.

Even my stoic fighter-pilot husband got choked up when he told Aiden the choice was his but that he would love to be called Dad.

"All right," Ace said. "I leave at five, and I'll be on my way home then. Love you. Kiss the kid for me."

"Will do. Love you."

I made it over to Aiden's school about fifteen minutes later. The pickup line was long as usual. Aiden poured himself into the backseat.

"You look beat, kid." I smiled through the rearview mirror. I'd taken to using Ace's nickname for him.

"I'm tired and hungry." He sat up with his eyes going wide, and I knew he was about to ask for something.

"Can we get ice cream?" he asked as I pulled out of the line and started for the long driveway out to the road.

"Hmm." I peered down at the clock on my dashboard. It was close to three thirty. "Did you eat all of your lunch today?"

He nodded.

"What'd you have?"

"They served turkey and mashed potatoes with gravy, but it wasn't as good as yours. So, I asked if I could switch out for a PB&J. I had that with chocolate milk and an apple."

"That's a lot of sugar if we add ice cream on top of that."

He groaned. "Please, Mama? We'll get any flavor you want. And some for Mr. Ace, too. I mean for Dad," he quickly corrected with a smile.

The inside of my chest warmed as I looked back at the smile in the mirror. I was pretty confident this kid knew he had me wrapped around his finger.

"All right, but I'm only letting you eat a few spoonsful before dinner. The rest is for dessert. And you better eat all of the peas I put on your plate."

"Cross my heart and hope to die." He made an X across his chest with his finger.

"Don't say die." I tightened my grip around the steering wheel.

"Sorry," he mumbled. Then he stood up and pushed his head in between the driver's and passenger seat to kiss my cheek. "Thanks."

I gestured with my head toward the backseat. "Sit down and put your seatbelt on."

I sent Ace a text to let him know that Aiden and I decided to make an ice cream run and then would be on our way home.

"What kind does Dad want?" Aiden asked once we parked in the small lot behind the parlor.

It made my heart stutter a little hearing Aiden call Ace *Dad*.

"Chocolate with fudge swirls," I told him, knowing Ace's favorite flavor by heart.

"That's right." Aiden snapped his fingers and turned to me after we passed through the door of the ice cream parlor.

Another benefit of living in Texas was that, even though it was nearing mid-December, ice cream shops were still open and serving. That was not the case back in Philadelphia.

"I want to try the chocolate with the fudge swirls, too. On a cone," Aiden added.

With a roll of my eyes, I laughed. Aiden typically went for mint chocolate chip. "How did I know you'd want the same flavor as Ace?" I asked as we entered the ice cream shop.

Aiden shrugged and turned to get a glimpse of the tubs of ice cream in the freezer bins behind the glass counter.

"What flavor are you getting, little guy?"

The male voice chilled me to the bone. I looked up from my purse in which I'd been fumbling around, searching for my wallet, to see Vincent Reyes standing right next to Aiden.

To my horror, he cut his gaze in my direction, and his lips parted in a devious smirk. He stooped down low.

"My favorite type of ice cream is strawberry. What's yours?"

"I'm not supposed to talk to strangers," Aiden said before looking up at me. He moved closer to me. "Right, Mama?"

I grabbed Aiden by the arm and pulled him behind me. "Right."

"It's all right, little man," Reyes said, rising to his full height. He stared me in the eye. "Your mom knows who I am. Don't you, Savannah?"

With my hand still partially in my purse, I discreetly dug around for the cell phone I'd carelessly tossed inside. Just my luck, it somehow managed to weasel its way to the bottom of my damn bag.

"What are you doing here?" I swung my gaze side to side, trying to see if I could capture the attention of anyone around us. There were about five other customers and two employees behind the counter.

"Uh-uh," Reyes warned with a stern shake of his head. "Don't try any funny shit," he said in a low, gravelly voice.

He stepped closer and grabbed hold of my arm. With his free hand, he partially opened the side of his jacket, revealing the butt of a gun that stood out from his waistband.

I knew as soon as I heard his voice that Aiden and I were in trouble, but seeing the gun nearly caused my heart to stop beating.

I couldn't fall apart. I had to keep my head on straight to get us out of this.

"Mama, it's our turn in line," Aiden said, trying to push ahead toward the counter.

"Change of plans, little guy," Reyes said.

"Don't talk to him," I hissed.

His hold on my arm tightened to the point of pain. "You want to be careful how you speak to me. We're leaving, and I would advise you to keep the kid quiet. I have no problem killing both of you right here and now."

His threat echoed in my mind, and all I could picture was watching my son be shot right in front of me. That was a thought that I couldn't bear.

Luckily, my hand managed to find and grab my cell phone at the bottom of my bag.

"Tell him," Reyes demanded.

I stuttered a little before saying, "Aiden, um, we're going to have to come back to get the ice cream a little later."

I looked to Reyes, who gestured with his head to the door.

"But why?" Aiden whined.

"Come on," I said, ushering him to the door. In my heart of hearts, I knew this was the wrong move.

Never be taken to the second location, my mind whispered. The advice was from a self-defense special I'd watched on television years earlier. That was the one piece of information that always stuck with me.

"Where are we going?" I asked Reyes when he yanked my arm in the direction of the tiny parking lot behind the parlor where my car was.

Panic struck me when I realized that only my car and a dark blue minivan sat in the parking lot. Most of the other patrons had parked out on the more highly trafficked street.

I managed to pull my phone out of my bag and slip it inside of Aiden's jacket pocket.

Aiden peered up at me, but I shook my head and pressed a finger to my lips, signaling him to keep quiet.

"We're going for a little ride," Reyes said, his voice ominous.

"I don't want to go with him," Aiden complained, pulling away from the van.

"Shut up, boy," Reyes said, his voice dropping all of the fake politeness it held while we were in the ice cream shop.

Aiden gasped when he saw Reyes pull out his gun.

"Don't point that at my son," I growled when he aimed it. I yanked Aiden behind me.

Reyes' smile grew even more devious. "Look at you, all protective. If only you had that same energy when it came to getting my damn money. Get in the fucking van." He pulled the driver's side door open. "You're driving."

He pushed me toward the driver's seat.

"No," I yelled when he yanked Aiden from my hold.

"Get in the car," he growled, aiming the gun at Aiden's head.

"Don't hurt him." My voice trembled. I ached with the fear I saw in my son's face. His brown eyes begged for me to do something. To save him.

"D-do what he says, Mama."

I choked out, "Okay, okay." I held up my hands and climbed behind the steering wheel.

Reyes didn't say anything as he slid open the back door and forced Aiden to get in before climbing in behind him.

"We're going on a trip." Reyes turned to Aiden. "Doesn't that sound fun?"

"I want to go home," Aiden said.

Reyes rolled his eyes. "Yeah, I'll send you home, all right." He turned to me. "Close the door and start the damn van. We're leaving."

"Where am I driving to?" I asked as I started the van.

"First, you're going to get my damn money. There's an ATM not too far from here. Make a left out of the parking lot."

I gave Aiden a look in the rearview mirror. He looked back at me with wide, frightful eyes.

"It's going to be okay," I promised, not knowing if that was true.

"Put your seatbelt on, boy. You don't have a death wish, do you? Safety first." Reyes fucking chortled.

Bastard.

"At this red light, you're going to make a right to merge onto the highway," Reyes instructed.

"I thought you said this ATM was close," I told him.

He leaned forward and pointed his gun to the side of my face. "Is there a problem?"

I gritted my teeth and shook my head.

"Didn't think so. Take the next exit."

I took the off-ramp that took us to a side road. A minute later, I noticed one of my bank's branches. Unfortunately, Reyes was right.

Though the bank wasn't too far off the main highway, there wasn't much around it. Just a few businesses that didn't look as if they received much foot traffic.

"The ATM is around back."

Of course, it was.

"I don't have much in my account," I told him.

"Really?" he asked. "Didn't you just get paid? That should be a few thousand. We'll work with that for now."

I pulled up next to the ATM. Reyes sat back and raised the hood of his jacket over his head, covering most of his face. I knew he was shielding his identity from the camera.

"Take out the money," he murmured from the back seat.

I inserted my card, and all of those stupid tips about codes to punch into the ATM pad to alert the bank that you're in trouble ran through my mind. I knew none of that would work with him watching me.

So, I withdrew the limit that my bank would allow. I turned to Reyes. "It only allows me to take out three thousand."

I swung back around after he took the money, purposefully hitting the unlock button with my elbow.

Reyes heard the sound of the unlock button go off while he stuffed the cash into the pocket of his jeans. But I turned fully in my seat and lunged at him, capturing the hand that held the gun.

"Aiden, run!"

"Bitch," Reyes grunted when I clawed at his face with my nails.

"Get out. Run!" I yelled at my son.

He hesitated but then yanked the door closest to him open and was able to hop out of the back of the van. When Reyes attempted to reach for him, I threw a palm strike against his cheek.

The force of the hit was enough to stun him, giving Aiden time to escape.

"Mama," Aiden screamed for me.

"Go, now," I insisted, praying he followed directions. "Oof," I gasped when Reyes clobbered me with his backhand.

The bastard followed that smack with a fist slammed into the side of my face. It was either his fist or the butt of his gun. A searing pain exploded on the right side of my face. I felt my entire body weaken from the beating.

I tried desperately to keep fighting, to maintain Reyes' attention, instead of letting him get to Aiden.

"Stupid bitch," Reyes insulted before punching me again.

I doubled over as much as I could in the front seat, with the steering wheel in my way. With my head tucked, I tried to protect my ribs from another one of Reyes' hits.

Soon, though, he stopped and got out of the van.

I was dazed and out of it from the brief but vicious beating. The inside of my mouth tasted like pennies.

When I looked up again, all I saw was the opened backdoor of the van. Aiden was nowhere in sight.

Despite the pain emanating throughout my body, I exhaled, relieved that my son had managed to escape.

Reyes circled the front of the vehicle.

"Move over," he demanded when he yanked the driver's side door open. "Get in the passenger seat." He pushed me into the seat, painfully forcing me over the center console.

"You try to escape again and I will put a fucking bullet in your head," Reyes seethed with the barrel of his weapon at my temple.

If I weren't in so much pain, I would've told him that I hadn't tried to escape. My only objective was to get Aiden as far out of his reach as possible.

"If you try to jump out of this fucking van, I swear to God, I will run you over and shoot you right where you lay. Is that clear?" he yelled, jutting the P365 into the side of my head.

"Y-yes," I croaked out.

"Fuck." He slammed his hand against the steering wheel. "The little shit's gone."

I closed my eyes in silent joy that Aiden was nowhere in sight.

"You just cost me a lot of money," Reyes seethed. He continued to hold one hand on the steering wheel and the other on the gun, directed at me. "We're going to find that little bastard of yours. His father wants his head on a platter, and I need that fucking money."

He glared at me. "I need to regroup. Then, I'll come up with a plan to get that little shithead of yours. And once that's done, I'll personally take care of the both of you," he promised.

The evil glint in his eyes was horrifying. When Reyes turned out of the bank's parking lot, I realized that he never had any intention of letting Aiden and I go off to live our lives in peace.

I was so stupid to think he would've taken the money and left us alone. My only hope at that point was that Aiden was able to find someone safe to notify or to use the phone I'd managed to stuff into his pocket.

CHAPTER 29

Ace

I took a deep breath as I exited the building that housed my office. It was Friday and I had the weekend off. Although I wouldn't be moving to Germany, I still needed to head out to another training with my squadron before the end of the month.

That one would be for three weeks, which meant that I'd be apart from Aiden and Savannah for that long. While it had been pushed back until after Christmas, I hated the idea of leaving them when that fucker Reyes was still on the loose.

I ran my hand through my hair and pulled out my cell phone with my free hand. Scrolling through my texts, I smiled at the message from Savannah telling me that she and Aiden were stopping for ice cream.

I bet he'd suckered her into it on the way home from school. She tried to play it tough, but she was just as much a sucker for his puppy face as I was.

While there was nothing strange about her first few texts, the last one was odd.

It read "He".

That was it. As if she had sent it by accident...or hadn't gotten the opportunity to finish whatever she was trying to say.

As I strolled in the direction of my bike, unease filled my chest. I started to text Savannah back, but my phone rang as I made it to my motorcycle.

"Savannah?" I answered.

"Dad!" Aiden's high-pitched voice pushed through the phone.

The hairs on the back of my neck stood up.

"Son, what's wrong? Where's your mom?"

"I-I don't know."

Three words that almost stopped my heart beating. Savannah would've never left Aiden alone, whatever the reason.

"We-we were getting ice cream, and this man came up to me, and then he was pushing us out the door. He had a gun."

"Slow down," I told Aiden, trying to calm my nerves as well as his. My heart beat so loud that it thundered in my ears. "Tell me where you are."

"I don't know."

"Okay, look around you. What do you see?"

"Um, I see a street sign," he said.

"Good. Tell me what it says."

He ran off the name of the street he was near with a few other landmarks. While Aiden tried to tell me where he was, I texted Micah everything he said.

I sent Micah Aiden's location once I pulled it up on my phone. LS Investigations turned out to be only a few minutes from where Aiden was.

"Thank God." I sighed, relieved when Micah told me he and his team were on the way.

"I'm scared, Dad," Aiden said into the phone.

"I know. I'm on my way to you. Your Uncle Micah will be there soon. Stay on the phone with me," I told him as I pulled out of my parking spot.

I revved the throttle of my bike and sped onto the onramp of the highway.

It would take about fifteen minutes to get from the base to the bank.

Every minute that passed felt like an eternity. I knew my brother was on his way and he would keep Aiden safe, but that didn't stop my heart from racing. Thoughts of Aiden alone and helpless collided with images of a terrified Savannah calling out for help.

From the description Aiden gave me, I knew the person who took them had to be Reyes. I'd seen a picture from the information Micah was able to gather on him. I was ready to rip that motherfucker, Reyes, from limb to limb.

"Move it," I growled at the cars in my way.

I ignored the blare of horns honking at me as I cut them off. The speed limit, the possibility of getting pulled over for speeding, or even the threat of an accident weren't my concerns at that point.

"He's here," Aiden said. "Uncle Micah's here. I see him."

"Okay, that's good." A beat later, I heard Micah's voice through the phone.

"Ace?"

"I'll be there soon."

I revved my bike and sped up, not caring about the speed limit. Any officer who tried to pull me over would catch a windshield of my dust. Consequences be damned.

My tires squealed as I turned into the parking lot of the bank. I hit the brakes and parked, hopping off my bike so quickly that the damn thing almost fell over when I barely lowered the kickstand.

"Dad." Aiden ran into my open arms.

I hugged him so tightly to me that I feared I was suffocating him. I released him after a long minute.

"I shouldn't have left her," he said with tears running down his face. "She yelled at me to run. I didn't want to leave. But she kept yelling for me to," he explained. "I'm sorry." He cried into my shoulder.

I lifted him and rubbed his back. "No, son. You did the right thing. Your mama wanted to save you." I had to stop talking because I choked up.

265

I knew Savannah would put Aiden's life before her own, as I would have. If Reyes kidnapped them both, he had no intention of leaving either one of them alive. She'd acted on her motherly instincts.

"We're going to get her back," I told him, because it was what we both needed to hear.

When Aiden's body stopped shuddering as much, I lowered him to his feet. I looked up to see Micah flanked by two of his guys. All three wore grim expressions.

"There's no trace of them around here. We found tire tracks out the back way. It looks like he took her east." Micah pointed.

"I have Bass already working on the bank's security system."

I clenched my jaw. While I loved Micah and knew he would move heaven and Earth to help bring Savannah home, I needed someone a little more savage for this job.

"We need to get back to the office," Micah said.

"Take Aiden with you," I ordered. "Don't let him out of your sight."

Micah paused, giving me a curious look. "Where are you going?"

I didn't answer him. Instead, I stooped low to get eye level with Aiden.

I cupped his face, my heart cracking at the tears and fear in his eyes. He tried to put on a brave face, holding the tears back.

"I'm going to find your mama and bring her back to us." I clenched my teeth, hoping that I wasn't lying to him. "I need you to go with Uncle Micah, okay?"

"Where are you going? Maybe I can help." A tear slipped down his cheek.

After wiping it away with my thumb, I kissed his forehead. "You've already helped. You're safe, and I know your mom will be relieved when I let her know you're okay."

I stood and pushed Aiden into Micah's arms when he wouldn't budge. I looked into my brother's eyes.

"I'm going to visit our father. Let him know I'm on the way."

He nodded, and I spun on my heels and hopped back on my bike.

Micah was a hell of a PI, but he started his career in law enforcement. He approached everything through the lens of the law.

Though he often bent the law here and there when obtaining information, he rarely went off the rails. I needed someone who wouldn't ask questions or try to hold me back when helping me with this.

In less than thirty minutes, I pulled into my father's driveway and hopped off my bike. I raced up to his doorway and pounded on the door. I knew that, by the time I arrived, Micah would've called and told Joel what had happened.

While my father focused now on his ranching business, he had spent years working as a henchman of sorts, for his father's company, Townsend Industries. He was the illegitimate son that no one new about, which allowed him to engage in all sort of criminal activity to benefit the father and the company that refused to acknowledge him publicly.

Though, he walked away from that lifestyle, years ago, he still had all sorts of connections to it. I would need those to get my wife back.

Joel yanked open the door.

"I need you to find this motherfucker. And then I need some alone time with him." I paused, looking my father square in the eye. "Not a soul can know about this, either."

A muscle in his jaw ticked, and he nodded. "Your brother already sent me everything he had. I placed a few calls," Joel said, his voice stern.

I nodded. "Let's go."

CHAPTER 30

a *ce* It didn't take much after that, and we found out where Vincent Reyes had been staying for the past few days. It was a hotel on the outskirts of Harlington. He was listed under an alias.

"You should let me bring him to the safe house," Joel said for the fifth time from the passenger seat. I was behind the wheel of a dark SUV with blacked-out windows.

I shook my head without taking my gaze off the road. We were five minutes out from the hotel. One of Joel's contacts found out Reyes' room number and would wait for us outside the back of the hotel with a keycard.

The contact informed us that he arrived not long ago with a distraught-looking woman.

The description fit Savannah.

"I need to see her first." I needed to lay eyes on my wife. I would get my alone time with Reyes, but first, I needed to make sure she was okay.

"Pull around back," Joel instructed while I was already pulling to the back of the hotel.

I parked in a space and Joel hopped out. I followed and lifted the hood to my black hoodie overhead.

A hotel employee was already waiting for us. He passed Joel a keycard.

"Room one fifty-one," the employee confirmed.

I followed my father. There were more guys from Joel's connections with us, but they were scattered throughout the hotel and parking lot in case Reyes tried to make a run for it.

As far as we knew, he was alone, but that didn't necessarily mean shit.

The closer we got to the room, the more anxious I grew to wrap my hands around this motherfucker's throat.

Joel quickly slipped the keycard into the lock and pulled it out before bursting through the door. I was right behind him, pushing forward.

I zeroed in on Reyes standing in the corner. He stood over a low-sitting chair, where Savannah sat.

I took off running across the room.

"Shit," Reyes yelled.

He darted from the corner, just out of Joel's grasp.

"Get my wife," I barked out to my father.

I went for Reyes, grabbing the back of his shoulders before he made it to the balcony door. With a yank around his arms, he stumbled backward and tripped. I landed on top of him, sending my fist to his jaw.

The instant cracking sound sent a rush of adrenaline and a need for more.

"Ace," Savannah shrieked.

That stopped me from doling out the punishment I so badly desired to give this son of a bitch. I needed to tend to Savannah first. She was my priority.

"I got him," Joel said, coming over to wrestle Reyes onto the floor.

I turned to Savannah and my stomach tightened at the sight of her swollen face. *I'm going to rip him apart.* That was all I could think, but I needed to make sure she was okay first.

"He-he…" Savannah panted. "Aiden."

"Aiden's safe with Micah." I brought her wrists up for my inspection, and again boiled in my veins when I spotted rope burns there.

"Thank God," she said and threw her arms around my neck. She quickly pulled back. "Are you sure Aiden's okay? He…"

"Shh," I shushed. "He's fine. Micah has him. Let's get you checked out."

I peered over my shoulder at Joel. He gave me a nod and I led my wife out of the dingy hotel room. We took the back exit, knowing there weren't any cameras in that location.

Savanna winced as I helped her into the back of the SUV. "You need a doctor," I said.

"I'm okay," she lied.

She was trying to be strong for me, but she couldn't hide her grimace. Nor could she hide the bruises that had already formed underneath her right eye. I could barely see straight, I was so pissed.

I peered over one of the other cars and watched as Joel and another man led Reyes into the back seat. I knew where they were taking him.

We left the hotel, my SUV turning left while Joel turned right. I dropped Savannah off at LS Private Investigations with Micah and Jodi. They had a doctor already on standby to look her over. Aiden was safely with them.

"Mama!" Aiden yelled and ran to her as soon as we entered Micah's office.

Savannah let out a strangled cry and fell to her knees, wrapping Aiden up in her embrace.

"Are you okay?" I asked, pulling away and holding him out for inspection.

Aiden nodded with tears running down his cheeks. "Your face." He cupped the side of her face that was swollen.

Another lump formed in my throat as I moved to the both of them.

"I-I'm fine," Savannah told him.

But she couldn't hide her swollen eye and bloodied lip. I hated to see her like that and worse, that Aiden had to see her like that.

I kneeled down beside Aiden. "I have to go handle something." I stroked his back. "The doctor's going to treat your mom. You take care of her while I'm gone," I told him before leaving. "I'll be back soon, okay?"

He nodded. His face turned serious. "I'll protect her."

I planted another kiss on his forehead and to Savannah's before handing her over to the doctor. I gave Micah one final nod and then departed to finish Reyes.

* * *

AN HOUR LATER, I arrived at the safe house, as Joel called it. It was little more than a tattered wooden ranch out in the middle of nowhere.

I inserted my hands into a pair of black leather gloves as I strolled up the stairs to the door. Not bothering to knock, I barged in to find my father and another guy sitting on a few stacks of hay.

Joel looked up at me and silently waved his head toward one of the back stalls. I brushed past them and found Reyes on the floor, hogtied with tape over his mouth.

I stepped inside the stall, a sick thrill filling my stomach at the terror in his eyes.

I pulled my tactical bowie knife out of my back pocket and slid it out of its leather case. The horror in Reyes' face intensified, but that wasn't enough for me.

I moved closer and stooped low. He tried to scoot away as best he could while tied up. Strangled cries came from his mouth. I supposed they were cries for help, but it was tricky with the tape over his mouth and a broken jaw.

"Let me help with that," I encouraged before leaning over and cutting the electrical tape from his mouth. "There." I moved back. "This way, I get to hear every scream. Every cry that's about to result from what I'm going to do to you."

"F-fuck you," he slurred. "I don't beg."

I paused and gave him a look. "Is that right?"

271

"Fuck yes. That bitch should've given me the money when I told her to," he managed to say through clenched teeth.

"That bitch?" I rose to my full height.

He howled when the bottom of my steel-toe boot came crashing down against his face. A waterfall of blood gushed from his nose.

"A broken nose to go with that jaw."

Reyes groaned in agony before spitting out a couple of his front teeth.

"What was all of that about not crying or whatever?" I kicked him again, that time in the ribs. The same side that he'd hit Savannah.

She'd told me how he'd beaten her after she helped Aiden escape.

He was going to get what he'd given her and so much more.

I held the second, smaller knife I brought with me and bent low to cut through the ties holding his arms behind his back.

Reyes shrieked when I stuck the second knife directly through his palm into the wooden floor beneath it, trapping him in place.

"You blackmailed my wife for months." I held up his hand. "You were sent by a fucking U.S. senator to kill a child, and instead of going to the police or hiding Savannah, you opted to blackmail her."

I pulled his pinky finger out, away from the rest of his fingers. "You had a choice. To save a child, or to do what you did."

Reyes' bellowing bounced off the surrounding walls when I sliced clean through his pinky, separating it from the rest of his hand.

The blood that splattered across my face, hands, and shirt didn't stop me.

"For what?" I demanded. "For fucking money?"

Micah hadn't been able to find anything on Vincent Reyes aside from the fact that he was a former police officer. There were no gambling debts or anything of note that would make him hungry enough for money to hunt down a child.

"Th—" he slurred. "They killed..." He trailed off, unable to speak through his broken and swollen jaw.

"Answer me," I yelled in his face, grabbing him by his shirt.

He glared at me. "Just," he heaved, "just kill me."

"As you wish."

The son of a bitch. I sliced through another one of his digits before stuffing it into his mouth. I blacked out in a rage as I thought about the harm he'd done, and intended to do, to Savannah and Aiden. Even if she had given him all of her money, he probably still would've killed them.

That was a thought worse than my own death. And I made damn sure Reyes knew it as I ripped the rest of his fingers from his body and forced them down his throat. My feet moved on their own while I kicked the hell out of him.

At some point, he passed out or died. I didn't know which.

Not until Joel and the other guy came in and pulled me away from Reyes' body did I come out of the dark stupor into which I'd fallen.

My breathing was out of control and I was covered in all types of bodily fluids, not my own.

"That's enough, son," Joel murmured in my ear from behind me, holding me back. "He's dead as a doorknob. Go with Anatoli to get cleaned up."

I followed my father's instructions and started to follow the other man.

"Knife." Joel held out his hand.

I placed the knife, sticky with drying blood and flesh, in his hand.

There happened to be an outhouse not far from the ranch with a shower that I used to clean off. Joel had a fresh set of clothes waiting for me back at the barn.

"I need to get back to my wife," I told him.

He handed me the keys to a new car that I hadn't seen when I pulled into the driveway.

"Go be with your family," he said. "There's a pig farm with this bastard's name written all over it."

I nodded, knowing all about the pig farm that Joel kept for occasions like this. My father had lived much of his life on the opposite side of the law. For once, I was thankful that he never completely severed ties with that part of his life. I knew he would dispose of Reyes' body and all the other evidence that went along with it.

It took me an hour to get back to LS Investigations. When I arrived, I expected to see my wife and son, but they weren't there.

"Chael?" I asked when I walked in and spotted my cousin, along with one of his brothers. "Chance? What are you doing here? Where are Savannah and Aiden?" I looked over at Micah, who stood beside them.

"They're back home. A few of my guys are with them."

"I need to see them." I turned to head out the door, no longer concerned about my cousins.

"Ace, wait," Micah called. "Savannah and Aiden are safe. But you need to hear this." Micah circled me, stopping me from exiting.

"What?"

"I told you I would see you again soon, cousin," Chael spoke.

"Is this about Reyes?" I looked between the three of them.

"Did he say anything to you?" Chael asked, ignoring my question.

"Hard to speak with a broken jaw." I folded my arms across my chest.

Chael's face turned grim.

"What the hell is going on?" I demanded. "Was Reyes into something?"

Micah shook his head. "Remember when I said this might go deeper than any of us knew?"

I nodded.

"This isn't about Reyes," Chael said. "He was low-hanging fruit in a very complex and deeply rooted tree."

I narrowed my eyes. "Flores?" Aiden's biological father.

"The Senator," Chael said to Chance.

Chance's facial expression remained impassive, but his hazel eyes darkened.

"He's Aiden's biological father," I said. "We need to handle him so he doesn't come after my son again."

Chael stepped forward. "Leave this to us, cousin."

"He's my son."

"You have my word. Senator Flores will not so much as touch a hair on Aiden's head. But you can't be involved." Chael peered over at Micah. "Neither of you can. This goes beyond the world you know."

His words sucked all of the air out of the room. A cold, dreadful warning filled his statement.

"We will speak with your father." Chael placed a hand on my shoulder. "Go home to your family. We'll take it from here."

The reminder of my family waiting for me at the house doused the embers of my mounting curiosity. Chael often held us at arm's length to protect his family's secrets from the world.

I didn't understand it entirely, but knew that there were layers to it.

"You will tell me if there's anything I need to know."

Chael and Chance exchanged a look.

"This is my fucking family," I growled.

"They are safe," Chael said. "And they'll remain that way."

I nodded and turned to leave. While I had more questions, they would have to wait for another time. Reyes was dead, which was satisfying enough, for now. I needed to check on my wife and son.

CHAPTER 31

our months later
        Savannah

"Where are you going?" Ace asked, his arm circling my waist from behind.

On instinct, I snuggled into his warmth in our bed. He'd just returned from a two-week training and I'd missed him like crazy.

Still, I needed to get up. "To the lawyer," I answered. "Remember?"

"It's Saturday," he groaned.

"I know, but he said he would make a special trip to the office for me today." I was meeting with Jason Wolcott, my grandmother's lawyer. I hadn't spoken to him since our initial meeting.

Months earlier, when Ace and I decided to call off the divorce, I didn't bother calling the attorney. Then, in the aftermath of being kidnapped, Ace starting his new position in San Antonio, and then leaving for training, I didn't even think about the lawyer.

Until he called me.

"I have to go." I sighed as I forced myself to pull away from him.

"Where's the kid?" Ace asked, sitting up also.

I took a moment to admire his bare chest and the bedhead he sported. He looked utterly delectable. If we hadn't been up half the night getting reacquainted, I might've been tempted to stay in this bed all day.

"You took him back in his bed last night, remember?" I said.

After the kidnapping he had admitted that the nightmares he'd been having for over a year were from his fear of me dying like his first mom. Even my reassuring him that I was fine, didn't completely stop the dreams. He took to sleeping in our bed, especially when Ace was away for training. Only recently, had we gotten him down to sleeping with us only one or two nights a week.

Though, at times it required walking him back to his room in the middle of the night.

"Oh yeah, because his mama couldn't keep her hands off of me. The kid didn't need exposure to all of that." He whipped the covers off, completely naked.

It took all of my strength not to acknowledge his massive erection, directing itself my way.

I rolled my eyes. "Whatever, Captain Townsend. From what I recall, that was *you* who couldn't keep your hands to yourself."

"Was that me?" He pressed a hand to his chest. "My memory's a little fuzzy. You should come back to bed and remind me."

I giggled and pushed him away when he tried to tug me back into the bed. It was difficult, but I summoned the strength to break free of my husband and jump into the shower.

Within thirty minutes of waking, I was showered, changed, and headed out the door. I gave Ace and Aiden a kiss as I left them making breakfast in the kitchen.

I arrived five minutes before nine to meet with Jason Wolcott, my grandmother's attorney. He ended up pulling in a minute later and parked right next to me.

"Ms. Greyson," he greeted.

"Mrs. Townsend," I corrected. I'd started to go by my married name. I'd hyphenated my last name when Ace and I first got married. Though, legally I would put Townsend, I had everyone refer to me as Greyson.

His bushy eyebrows lifted, but then his face resumed a neutral expression. He ushered me inside.

"Mr. Wolcott," I started once I was seated in his office. "Like I tried to tell you over the phone, I don't think this meeting is necessary. I'm sorry to have wasted your time."

"Why is that?" he asked, arms folded across his desk.

"My husband and I have decided to stay together." I kept my head held high. "We're not getting a divorce, so that leaves me ineligible to receive my grandmother's inheritance."

I had come to terms with that. I wasn't interested in the money beyond what it could've done for me when I was being blackmailed.

Jason Wolcott sat back in his chair and smiled. It was surprising, only because it appeared genuine, as if he'd been waiting for me to say that.

"That's great news."

I wrinkled my brows. "Yes, it is. For Ace and me, but I thought you would be disappointed."

"Why would that disappoint me?"

"Well, your job was to carry out my grandmother's wishes, and she wanted me to divorce Ace."

Carlton shook his head. He pushed out a breath. "Your grandmother," he paused and looked at something over my shoulder before his gaze returned to mine. "She told me I have permission to tell you what I'm about to say. So, I'm not violating attorney-client privilege."

"Okay," I said with hesitation.

"Your grandmother had a contingency in her inheritance that she asked me to carry out. It was that, even if you didn't divorce, you would still receive the money in her trust."

"I don't understand. You told me the stipulations to receive the money were that I had to divorce Ace."

He nodded. "Yes, it's confusing. I know." He sighed. "I told your grandmother there were better ways to do this, but she was adamant."

I snorted. "Stubborn is more like it."

He chuckled. "That, she was. Anyway, she asked me to give you the stipulation if and when you came to me, but said that if you went through with the divorce, the money was yours free and clear."

"Okay," I drew out the word, not comprehending what was happening.

"Your grandmother wanted you to have the money either way," he continued. "In fact, she insisted that, if you didn't return, to reach out to you again to make sure you get the money."

I shook my head. "Why would she do that?"

"I thought you might have difficulty understanding her intentions. She thought you might, as well." He opened a drawer from his desk and pulled out an envelope. "She left this for you to read."

I reached across and took the envelope. I looked from the paper in my hand to Wolcott as I opened it. It was a handwritten letter.

To Savannah,

I'm sorry if this whole mess with the lawyer and the inheritance has confused you. I've tried and failed to talk to you, call, e-mail, or visit you a hundred different times to explain myself. Alas, this letter will have to suffice.

The reason I made the divorce a stipulation of your inheritance was that I hoped it would force you to contact Ace again. You see, it had taken me a long time to realize the mistakes I made when you came to live with me. I was grieving the loss of my daughter, your mother, and I took it out on you.

I looked at Ace as one of "those people" from across the bridge. The same type of people who talked about us like we were dogs while I cleaned their houses and washed their clothes. The kind of person that would impregnate a girl from over the bridge and leave her to fend for herself. Like your father did to your mother.

I didn't care for you as I should've, nor was I there for your mother when she became pregnant with you.

I know you think that I blamed you for her life turning out the way it did. I said those things out of grief. They were not the truth. Your mother was barely seventeen when she became pregnant. She had been out of control, skipping school, partying, and all manner of trouble. Once she found out about you, she turned her life around.

By then, I was too angry with her to be the help she needed. But she proved that she didn't need me. She picked you up and moved you both to

Georgia to create a better life for herself. She worked hard to be the mother to you that I fell short in being to her.

You, my dear, saved her from that destructive path she was headed down.

That I made you feel anything less than perfect is my most profound regret.

If you are reading this letter, that means you have decided to forego the divorce, and you and Ace are still together. I genuinely hope that is the case. I wouldn't allow myself to understand it back then, but what you two have was real then, and it is real now. My prayer is that you both continue to grow in love.

I am ashamed of how I treated you, not only when you and Ace were dating and got married, but after your son died. It would be too selfish of me to ask for your forgiveness, so I won't.

But please know that those words came from a place of fear and pain. I wish you and Ace a lifetime of happiness. Please take this inheritance and do whatever it is you would like to do with it.

Love,

Grandma

I STARED AT THE LETTER, barely able to make out the words because they were so blurred from the tears in my eyes. Before I could ruin the letter with my tears, I folded it back up and placed it inside the envelope.

Wolcott pushed a box of tissues across his desk.

"Thank you." I blew my nose into a tissue. "I, um, I don't know what to say."

He stood up and nodded. "Not much to say. Take some time and decide how you want the money disbursed to you. Provide me with the adequate information, and I will make sure you get it."

I opened and closed my mouth as I stood. "A college fund," I blurted out. It was one of the first things that came to mind. "I need to start one of those for my son."

He nodded.

"Oh," I said, an idea suddenly overtaking me. But I didn't finish my thought out loud. If the money was mine, I could use the rest to invest in Brightside to become a partial owner of the medical office and clinic.

"I have to go," I told him. I was anxious to get back home and tell Ace. The night before, he'd all but written me a check when I told him that the owners of Brightside were looking for a partner and wanted me to buy in.

"Thank you, Mr. Wolcott." I threw my arms around him and pulled him in for a hug.

He chuckled. "I didn't do much, but you're welcome."

I waved and exited his office to start for home.

* * *

I DROVE HOME IN A RUSH, anxious to share my good news with Ace. A thousand thoughts ran through my mind. I stared up at the brilliant blue sky above and smiled, recalling the first day Ace and I met.

To think those two idealistic kids from opposite sides of the bridge somehow made it baffled me.

When I arrived home, I was surprised to see Micah's truck in the driveway.

"Hey?" I said with a wrinkle in my eyebrow when I walked into the house to find a smiling Micah. Aiden stood by his side.

"Hi, Mama."

"Someone want to tell me what's going on?"

Micah and Aiden exchanged a look.

"It's a surprise," my son said.

"Orchestrated by your husband," Micah added.

"Are you hungry?" Aiden questioned.

"Why?" I asked.

"Because it's after ten, and Ace didn't think you'd eaten breakfast yet," Micah answered. "Luckily, we have you covered."

Micah stepped aside and extended his arm. Aiden fell in step with me and escorted me to the kitchen. There, a beautiful breakfast spread sat on the table.

"Scrambled eggs with cheddar, sausage, and a Belgian waffle," Aiden pointed out. "Oh." He snapped his fingers.

I watched him head over to the counter and grab the glass pitcher.

"Fresh-squeezed orange juice." He smiled as he set it down in front of the plate.

"Eat up," they both said.

My stomach growled.

"Enjoy."

"Wait, you two aren't staying?" I asked when they started for the door.

"We have to help—" Micah quickly slapped a hand over Aiden's mouth.

A smile cracked my lips. It looked as if my son almost spilled the beans.

"We'll catch up with you later. Just know you have a long day ahead of you," Micah said.

"A great day, though," Aiden added.

I nodded.

"Don't read that until after breakfast." Micah inclined his head toward a small envelope next to the plate.

"Oh." Aiden ran over to me and pulled something out of his pocket. "Dad said you'll need these." He handed me an unopened packet of Kleenex.

When I held up the tissues with a question on my face, Aiden shook his head and ran his fingers across his mouth, making the sealed lips gesture.

"Don't you dare clean the dishes," Micah said from the front door. A second later, they left.

I shrugged and sat to eat what turned out to be a spectacular meal. After finishing, I opened the letter.

Breakfast is done. Now it is time to let the day begin.

On your next stop, you will be treated like the queen you are.

Beneath those two lines was an address with which I wasn't familiar. When I plugged it into my GPS app, I discovered that Ace was sending me to a day spa.

There, I met Jodi, Lena, and Reese. The three women refused to tell me what Ace was up to or what he had in store for the rest of the day. However, we all indulged in prepaid massages, facials, and a manicure and pedicure.

It was nearing four o'clock when we all emerged from the spa, but I felt completely rejuvenated.

"This belongs to you," Jodi said as she handed me another envelope.

I greedily accepted it, peeling it open.

I hope your spa day was as magical as you are.

Your next destination will be at the spot where we first met.

A lump in my throat formed. I didn't have to think or try to remember back to that first time we met by the river, not far from Tucker Bridge.

The other three women and I parted ways. I drove across town to the spot where I met my husband almost seventeen years ago. The entire time I thought about all the ups and downs I'd endured since then.

There'd been so much pain, but it started to feel like I was on the verge of something so special that I couldn't put into words.

That feeling only grew when I drove as close as I could to the spot by the river. I had to walk a little way, but I found Joel standing there with a grin on his face.

At his feet lay a checkered blanket with a wicker picnic basket. Surrounding the basket was another spread, including crackers, assorted cheeses, meats, and olives.

As soon as he was in arm's length, I pulled him in for a hug. He laughed and hugged me back. "Still a hugger."

He'd become used to my customary greeting anytime I saw him. I was a hugger, yes, but I always felt like Joel needed one. There was a pain in his eyes that no matter how hard he tried, he couldn't hide. I wondered if it was from losing the love of his life so long ago.

"This is where it all started, huh?" Joel asked, glancing around the area. He held out his hand to help me to sit.

"It was a little more crowded in the summer." I gasped and remembered. "Today is May ninth."

I turned to Joel. "It's Ace's and my…"

He nodded. "I couldn't make the first wedding, but I damn sure am making this one."

So that was what was happening? Ace and I were renewing our vows on our wedding anniversary?

"He's a romantic. That boy." Joel shook his head and smirked. "Live long and prosper, huh?" Joel commented.

I smiled at him. "That was all it took. Our mutual love of *Star Trek*. And he taught me to skip stones that day. Right before he told me he was going to be a pilot."

"He was trying to impress you," Joel said.

We both laughed.

"Probably. But I believed him. I knew Ace could be anything he wanted to be."

Joel and I sat there, talking and eating for the next thirty minutes. I suspected that this experience with my father-in-law was a gift. To somehow make up for the lost time.

Ace knew that I'd gained a soft spot in my heart for Joel. I suspected Joel had one for me and Aiden, as well.

"It's time for me to get you to your next appointment."

"Where's that?" I asked, retaking his hand to stand.

"You'll see."

We started for the parking lot.

"Leave your car. Micah is sending someone to pick it up. This ride's on me, doll."

Ten minutes later, Joel held open the door of a dress shop. I walked in to be welcomed by the smiling owner.

"Mrs. Townsend?"

I nodded.

Her eyes lit up. "It's a pleasure to meet you finally."

I looked over at Joel.

He nodded at the woman. "She's all yours, for now. Bring her back in one piece or my middle son will have my ass."

The woman laughed, but I suspected Joel wasn't joking.

I followed her to the back of the store. We entered a sizeable dressing room. On the far wall hung a stunning white silk slip dress.

"Your husband chose this one for your special day."

Before I put on the dress, another woman entered the dressing room. She did my makeup to perfection and styled my hair into big barrel curls that were pinned up, with a few hanging down loosely. They both helped me to get dressed.

The white dress against my skin looked heavenly. I ran my hand over the silver locket that the V-neck cut of the dress perfectly displayed.

"One final thing."

I turned to find the owner holding a sunflower crown. She placed it around my head, and I found myself searching for the tissues Aiden had given me earlier.

"He warned us to make sure your makeup was waterproof."

I laughed as I blotted away the tears with one of the Kleenex Aiden had given me earlier.

I met Joel in the central area to find him dressed in a black and white tuxedo.

"Rarely do I wear one of these things." He looked me up and down. "But you kids are worth it."

I took his arm and he escorted me back to the car. I knew what our next stop was.

The car ride was silent as we drove to where Ace and I first became husband and wife. I thought about riding in that cab with Ace's mother, feeling nervous and uncertain. This time around, there was no fear.

When we arrived at the parking lot, I could see the gazebo where Ace and I said our "I do"s.

Most of our family and friends now surrounded it.

Ace stood in the center.

Thankfully, Joel was there to wrap his arm around mine and help guide me toward my husband.

"I wasn't there for this part the first time around," Joel said. "Glad I am for this one."

He walked me to the pavilion. In my periphery, I spotted Micah, Gabriel, their wives, Jodi and Lena, and Reese with my other co-workers.

Ace turned to face me, beaming. He looked dapper in his dress blues.

He nodded before pulling his father into a hug. My heart squeezed, happy to know they'd finally mended the rift in their relationship.

"I would only do this for you," Ace murmured in my ear.

I assumed he meant all the extravagance, but when he told me to stay put, and went over and retrieved a microphone from a table set up behind the gazebo, the waterworks started.

The opening chords of a song started. When the guitar strings began playing, I recognized Ed Sheeran's "Perfect."

Ace parted his lips and the sound that came out caused my knees to buckle. He looked me directly in the eyes as he sang about finding a love, beautiful and sweet. He slowly approached while singing about refusing to give me up.

The words felt like they were written just for us.

After the first chorus ended, Ace turned and handed the microphone to Lena Clarkson, now Lena Clarkson-Townsend. I realized this was the duet version of "Perfect" that Ed Sheeran did with Beyoncé.

Ace took me into his arms and we danced as Lena sang. I stared into my husband's eyes and mouthed the words to the song, feeling as if they came directly from my own heart.

The song was the perfect description of our relationship. I wept like a baby as Lena finished singing.

"Thank you," I whispered to Ace.

He leaned down and softly kissed my lips. "Anything for you."

He dug into his pocket and pulled out a ring box.

I covered my mouth when he opened it.

"Years ago, I told you that I would buy you the type of ring you deserved once I could afford it." He held the beautiful square-cut diamond in a white gold setting out to me. "It's about time I made good on that promise."

He wiped another tear that ran down my cheek. "You ran out of tissues, didn't you?"

I nodded.

He laughed and slipped the ring onto my finger.

"Let's get married," he said. "Again."

"Okay." I could barely speak.

Ace turned and waved his hand. A second later, Aiden popped in between the two of us.

"I've got the rings," he whispered loudly.

Out came the same pastor that married us seventeen years earlier. When Ace and I turned to face each other, holding onto each other's hands, this felt like the fresh start we needed. The one we deserved.

I vaguely heard the pastor mention the bridge that was the backdrop of our wedding, and just as before, that love is the bridge to one another's hearts. We recited our vows and promised always to be true to one another.

"Captain Townsend, you may now kiss your bride. Again," he declared.

I heard the applause from our friends and family and Aiden cheering, but mostly, my senses were overloaded when Ace cupped my face and pulled me in for a deep kiss.

"My forever," he whispered as his lips brushed against mine.

"Forever."

"Yay," Aiden cheered, causing all of us to laugh out loud.

The rest of the day was a whirlwind. We ended up at The Rustic for our reception. We danced, partied, and celebrated our second chance at love.

By the end of the night, everyone was exhausted. Micah and Jodi volunteered to take Aiden home with them overnight, so Ace and I could have the night to ourselves.

Aiden didn't hesitate. He loved spending time with his baby cousin, Lonzie, and his Uncle Micah. When Gabriel promised to take him to the gym the following day and then take him over to Grandpa

Joel's to feed and ride the horse, Aiden acted as if he barely knew Ace and me.

The way Ace's family had taken in Aiden warmed my entire heart.

As for Aiden's birth father, soon after the kidnapping, news broke that Senator Flores was involved in a sex trafficking ring. He was in a boatload of trouble and looking at federal charges.

Flores was no longer a threat to Aiden, given that all of his ties had dried up, and he sat in a federal prison awaiting trial.

Not long after that, Ace started the process to adopt Aiden formally.

"I have an appointment next week," Ace said as we slow-danced again to one of Lena's songs from her last album. We were the final two people in the bar.

"For what?"

His grin widened. "Vasectomy reversal."

I stilled. "Really?"

We'd talked about it briefly, but I didn't want to pressure him into doing something he didn't want.

"There was always only one woman who was going to be the mother of my children," he said. "Now that she's back, nothing is stopping us from making more babies. Aiden will need at least a few more siblings."

I leaned up on my tiptoes and brushed my lips across his. "I think we should go home and practice."

"I love the way you think."

EPILOGUE

Twelve months later
Savannah

"Mm," I hummed as I paced back and forth in the hospital room, with one hand gripping onto the pole holding my IV fluids.

"How're you doing, baby?" Ace asked as he rubbed my back in the circular motion that he'd learned in the birthing class we took.

"Well," I paused to inhale deeply. "I'm considering never having sex with you again." I blew out a shuddering breath as another contraction gripped the lower half of my body.

"Okay," Ace said, slowly drawing out the word.

"Keep rubbing." I swatted at his hand on my back to spur him into action. The massaging didn't help much, but it possibly was a psychosocial element of knowing he was trying to comfort me through this birthing process that helped.

"Just remember, you say that now, but in six weeks..."

I groaned.

"Okay, maybe eight," he corrected. "In eight weeks, you'll forget all about this discomfort and..."

"Shut up." I lifted one of the pillows from my bed and hit him with it. "Maybe you should get another vasectomy."

He shook his head. "Negative."

I grunted. Another contraction was coming. When I bellowed out in pain, Ace ceased all joking and called the doctors and nursing staff into the room.

Minutes later, the doctor determined that it was finally time for me to push. After ten hours of labor, I was exhausted but ready to meet the little girl who'd given me heartburn over the past nine months.

Obviously, Ace's vasectomy reversal was a success. I prepared myself for it to take a while for his body's ability to produce sperm at a regular rate. I expected it to take at least a year before I would get pregnant, and that was if everything went well.

But, not even three months after Ace's reversal, I found myself staring at a positive pregnancy test.

"We're almost home, baby," Ace encouraged, squeezing my hand at the side of the bed as I pushed.

The previous nine months had been a mix of fear, joy, excitement, and more terror. Painful reminders of how our first son died gripped me unexpectedly. Ace would calm my worries and remind me that we were living our second chance.

I did the same for him, even when he didn't want to admit he was afraid.

It took another two hours, but finally, our baby girl, Parker Elise Townsend, was born. Her middle name was for my mother. When I heard her cry for the first time, I burst into tears of my own. I didn't know whose cry was louder.

Ace and I couldn't stop staring at her. She was the perfect mix of both of us.

She weighed in at almost nine pounds, with a head full of dark hair, a light brown complexion, and eyes that turned up at the corners.

Soon after, Aiden was allowed into the room to meet his little sister. He sat on the love seat across from me. When Ace placed Parker into his arms, Aiden vowed to protect and watch out for her always.

"Just like a big brother and man should." He looked up at Ace, as if asking if that was right.

I lost it again.

"Mama needs some more tissues," Aiden told Ace. "It's okay, Parker. Mama cries a lot. You get used to it."

"Hey," I griped. I'd been incredibly emotional throughout my pregnancy—even more than usual.

Aiden was able to stay for a few hours, but Micah and Jodi took him home with them after their visit, as Ace would remain with Parker and me in the hospital for the night.

"Knock, knock," Reese's voice sounded at the door, an hour before visiting hours were over. "I'm sorry to come by so late, but I had to pick up this beautiful bouquet for you."

In her arms was a huge arrangement of sunflowers.

"Her favorite," Ace said as he peered down at me with Parker in his arms.

"You can put them over there." I pointed at the windowsill. There were multiple bouquets from my job, Ace's job, family, and friends.

"She's beautiful," Reese said admiringly. "Congratulations, you two."

We thanked her and talked for a few minutes before Reese left us, telling us she was volunteering again that night.

"That's so sweet of her," I said when I opened the card she'd left. Inside was a gift card for a night of family dinners at one of our favorite restaurants.

"We'll have to send her a thank-you—"Ace broke off when there was a knock on the door.

Chael's large frame took up most of the doorway. Though I hadn't seen him in quite a few years, Ace's cousin, Chael, was a hard man to forget. Ace had told me Chael had something to do with Flores' deeds coming to light. But he didn't go into detail.

I stared over at Chael in gratitude, noting the angular planes of his face, long silky dark hair that hung loosely around his shoulders. His presence could stop a stampede.

Even Parker, who had been squirming in my arms, went still.

"Chael," Ace said, rising from the bed. He greeted his cousin with a hug.

Chael looked over at me and smiled. "Congratulations."

"Thank you."

He came into the room, took one look at Parker, and nodded as if approving. He patted Ace on the back and whispered something in his ear.

Ace smiled. "You were right."

"A gift." He held up a gift-wrapped box. "I will place it with the others."

I watched as Chael placed the box down and stood for a moment, admiring the assortment of flowers. He paused at the sunflowers that Reese brought. He stared at them before lowering to sniff them.

Something about the bouquet seemed to intrigue Ace's cousin.

He sniffed again then lifted his head to stare out of the window.

He said one word.

"Mate."

I looked up at Ace. "Did he just say what I think he did?"

Ace's face appeared just as astonished as I felt. "Yes, he did," he answered slowly.

Chael turned to us. "I must go. You both have done well."

He exited almost as quickly as he appeared. Chael had always been like that. Him and his brothers.

Ace came around and took a seat next to me on the bed, wrapping his arms around me as I held Parker.

"We made it, didn't we?" he asked.

"We sure did," I answered. "Don't quote me on this, but I'm even considering having sex with you again. Like, in the distant, distant, future."

He chuckled. "Sorry, Mrs. Townsend, but even the possibility of you not having sex with me won't scare me off. You're stuck with me forever."

"Doesn't sound too bad," I sighed and snuggled closer to him as we both watched our sleeping baby.

The End

More books by Tiffany Patterson

The Black Burles Series
Black Pearl
Black Dahlia
Black Butterfly

FOREVER SERIES

7 Degrees of Alpha (Collection)
Forever

SAFE SPACE SERIES

RESCUE FOUR SERIES

Eric's Inferno
Carter's Flame
Emanuel's Heat
Don's Blaze

NON-SERIES TITLES

This is Where I Sleep
My Storm
Miles & Mistletoe (Holiday Novella)
Just Say the Word
Jacob's Song
No Coincidence

THE TOWNSEND BROTHERS SERIES

Aaron's Patience
Meant to Be
For Keeps
Until My Last Breath

TIFFANY PATTERSON WEBSITE EXCLUSIVES

Locked Doors
Bella
Remember Me
Breaking the Rules
Broken Pieces

THE TOWNSENDS OF TEXAS SERIES

For You
<u>All of Me</u>

THE A**HOLE CLUB SERIES
(COLLABORATION)

Luke